The
SPECTACULAR
NOW

Also by Tim Tharp

Knights of the Hill Country

Badd

Mojo

The
SPECTACULAR NOW

TIM THARP

EMBER

Text copyright © 2008 by Tim Tharp
Cover art copyright © 2013 by A24 Films

All rights reserved. Published in the United States by Ember, an imprint of Random House Children's Books, a division of Random House, Inc., New York. Originally published in hardcover in the United States by Alfred A. Knopf, an imprint of Random House Children's Books, New York, in 2008.
Ember and the E colophon are registered trademarks of Random House, Inc.

Visit us on the Web! randomhouse.com/teens
Educators and librarians, for a variety of teaching tools, visit us at
RHTeachersLibrarians.com

The Library of Congress has cataloged the hardcover edition of this work as follows:
Tharp, Tim.
The spectacular now / Tim Tharp
p. cm.
Summary: In the last months of high school, charismatic eighteen-year-old Sutter Keely lives in the present, staying drunk or high most of the time, but that could change when he starts working to boost the self-confidence of a classmate, Aimee.
ISBN 978-0-375-85179-7 (trade) — ISBN 978-0-375-95179-4 (lib. bdg.)
[1. Self-destructive behavior—Fiction. 2. Dating (Social customs)—Fiction.
3. Substance abuse—Fiction. 4. High schools—Fiction. 5. Schools—Fiction.
6. Stepfamilies—Fiction. 7. Family life—Oklahoma—Fiction.
8. Oklahoma—Fiction.] I. Title.
PZ7.T32724Spe 2008 [Fic]—dc22 2008003544
ISBN 978-0-385-75430-9 (tr. pbk.)

Printed in the United States of America
20 19 18 17 16 15 14

Random House Children's Books supports the First Amendment
and celebrates the right to read.

Many thanks to: Lilli Bassett, Shari Spain, Emily, Michele, Katie, Clint, and Paden.

Also, special thanks to research assistants and consultants Rob, Dave, Brandon, Greg, Mark, Bill, Ricky, John, Perry, Jon, Danny, Don, Billy, Robert B., Goober, and Kal-Kak.

Chapter 1

So, it's a little before ten a.m. and I'm just starting to get a good buzz going. Theoretically, I should be in Algebra II, but in reality I'm cruising over to my beautiful fat girlfriend Cassidy's house. She ditched school to get her hair cut and needs a ride because her parents confiscated her car keys. Which I guess is a little ironic considering that they're punishing her for ditching school with me last week.

Anyway, I have this sweet February morning stretching out in front of me, and I'm like, Who needs algebra? So what if I'm supposed to be trying to boost the old grades up before I graduate in May? I'm not one of these kids who's had their college plans set in stone since they were about five. I don't even know when the application deadlines are. Besides, it's not like my education is some kind of priority with my parents. They quit keeping track of my future when they divorced, and that was back in the Precambrian Era. The way I figure it, the community college will always take me. And who says I need college anyway? What's the point?

Beauty's all around me right here. It's not in a textbook. It's not in an equation. I mean, take the sunlight—warm but not too brash. It's not like winter at all. Neither was January or December for that matter. It's amazing—we couldn't have had more than one cold week all winter. Listen, global warming's no lie. Take last summer. You want to talk about getting a beating from the heat. Last summer was a hardcore pugilist. I mean, burn-you-down-to-the-roots-of-your-hair hot. It's like Cassidy says—global warming's not for lightweights.

But with this February sun, see, the light's absolutely pure and makes the colors of the sky and the tree limbs and the bricks on these suburban houses so clean that just looking at them is like inhaling purified air. The colors flow into your lungs, into your bloodstream. You are the colors.

I prefer drinking my whisky mixed, so I pull into a convenience store for a big 7UP, and there's this kid standing out front by the pay phone. A very real-looking kid, probably only about six years old—just wearing a hoodie and jeans, his hair sticking out every which way. Not one of these styling little kids you see in their brand-name outfits and their TV show haircuts, like they're some kind of miniature cock daddy. Of course, they wouldn't know what to do with a girl if she came in a box with the instructions on the lid like Operation or Monopoly, but they have the act down.

Right away, I take to this kid, so I say, "Hey, dude, aren't you supposed to be in school or something?" and he's like, "Can I borrow a dollar?"

I go, "What do you need with a dollar, little man?"

And he's, "I'm going to buy a candy bar for breakfast."

Now that gets my attention. A candy bar for breakfast? My heart goes out to this kid. I offer to buy him a breakfast burrito, and he's okay with that as long as he gets his candy bar too. When we come back out, I look around to size up what kind of traffic the kid's going to have to negotiate in his travels. We live just south of Oklahoma City—technically it's a whole different city, but with the urban sprawl you can't tell where one leaves off and the other begins—so we have a lot of traffic zipping around here.

"Look," I tell him as he drips egg down the front of himself. "This is a pretty busy intersection. How about I give you a ride to wherever you're going so some big rig doesn't barrel down and flatten you like a squirrel."

He looks me over, sizing me up just like a squirrel might actually do right before deciding to scamper off into his lair. But I'm a trustworthy-looking guy. I have no style either—just a pair of reasonably old jeans, beat-up sneakers, and a green long-sleeve T-shirt that says *Ole!* on the front. My brown hair's too short to need much combing, and I have a little gap between my two front teeth, which gives me a friendly, good-hearted look, or so I'm told. The point is I'm a long way from scary.

So the kid takes a chance and hops into the passenger side of my Mitsubishi Lancer. I've had it for about a year—it's silver with a black interior, not new or anything but pretty awesome in a basic kind of way.

"My name's Sutter Keely," I say. "What's yours?"

"Walter," he says around a mouthful of burrito.

Walter. That's good. I've never known a little kid named Walter. It seems like an old man's name, but I guess you have to start somewhere.

"Now, Walter," I say, "the first thing I want you to know is you shouldn't really take rides from strangers."

"I know," he says. "Mrs. Peckinpaugh taught us all about that at Stranger Danger."

"That's good," I say. "You should keep that in mind in the future."

And he goes, "Yeah, but how do you know who's a stranger?"

That cracks me up. *How do you know who's a stranger?* That's a kid for you. He can't comprehend that people might be dangerous just because you haven't met them yet. He's probably got all sorts of sinister ideas about what a stranger is—a black, slouchy hat and raincoat, a scar on the cheek, long fingernails, shark teeth. But think about it—when you're six years old, you haven't met all that many people. It would be pretty mind-boggling to go around suspicious of ninety-nine percent of the populace.

I start to explain the stranger thing to him, but his attention span isn't all that long and he gets sidetracked watching me pour whisky into my big 7UP.

"What's that?" he asks.

I tell him it's Seagram's V.O., so then he wants to know why I'm pouring it in my drink.

I look at him and he has this authentic interest in his big, round eyes. He really wants to know. What am I going to do, lie to him?

So I go, "Well, I like it. It's smooth. It has kind of a smoky flavor. I used to drink the southern bourbons more—Jim Beam, Jack Daniel's—but if you're going for a nice, slow, all-day sort of buzz, those have a little too much bite. And to my way of thinking, people can smell them on your breath more. I tried Southern Comfort, but it's too sweet. No, it's the Canadian whiskies for me now. Although I've been known to mix a fine, fine martini too."

"What's a martinina?" he says, and I can see it's time to head off the questions before I end up spending the whole morning putting this kid through bartender school. I mean, he's a good kid, but my girlfriend *is* waiting on me and she's not the most patient person in the world.

"Look," I say, "I've got to be moving along, so where you headed?"

He finishes chewing the last of the burrito, swallows, and says, "Florida."

Now I can't give you mileage off the top of my head, but we're in Oklahoma, so Florida is a good five states away, at least. I explain that to him, and he tells me to just drop him off at the edge of town and he'll walk the rest of the way. He's serious.

"I'm running away from home," he says.

This kid is getting better all the time. Running away to Florida! I take a hit off my whisky and Seven and I can see it just like he does—a giant orange sun dripping down into the bluest ocean you ever saw with palm trees genuflecting at its glory.

"Look," I say, "Walter. May I be so bold as to ask why you're running away?"

He stares into the dashboard. "'Cause my mom made my dad move away and now he's in Florida."

I'm like, "Aw shit. I can sympathize, little dude. Same thing happened to me when I was a kid too."

"What'd you do?"

"I was pissed, I guess. My mom wouldn't tell me where my dad moved to. I didn't run away, but I think it was around that time that I set the tree in the backyard on fire. I'm not sure why. It was quite a sight, though."

That stokes his enthusiasm. "Really, you set a whole tree on fire?"

"Don't get any ideas," I tell him. "You can get into some deep dookie for that kind of thing. You don't want the firemen mad at you, do you?"

"No, I don't want that."

"So, about this running away deal—I can see your point. You'd get to visit your dad and you'd have adventures and shit. You could swim in the ocean. But to tell you the truth, I can't recommend it. Florida's too far. You try to walk and you're not going to find a convenience store on every corner. Where are you going to get your food then?"

"I could hunt it."

"Yeah, you could. Do you have a gun?"

"No."

"A knife or a rod and reel maybe?"

"I have a baseball bat, but it's at home."

"There you go. You're not prepared. We probably ought to go back and get your bat."

"But my mom's home. She thinks I'm in school."

"That's all right. I'll talk to her. I'll explain the whole situation."

"You will?"

"Sure."

Chapter 2

Now, I should've been at my girlfriend's five minutes ago, but this time I have a legitimate reason for running late. How can Cassidy—Ms. Activist herself—hold it against me for intervening in this kid's situation? I'm practically doing social work here. I might even get Walter's mom to vouch for me.

Unfortunately, Walter doesn't remember exactly where he lives. He's never had to walk there from the convenience store before. All he knows is there's a scary black van with no wheels parked in the driveway of a house on the corner of his street, so up and down the residential section I go, looking for that van.

For a six-year-old, Walter's a pretty good conversationalist. He has a theory that Wolverine from X-Men is the same guy who picks up the garbage on his street. Also, there was a big, redheaded kid at his school named Clayton who made a hobby out of going around and stepping on other kids' feet. Then one day, he got tired of hearing the littler kids squeal, so he stomped down on the teacher's foot for a change. The last time Walter saw Clayton, Mrs. Peckinpaugh was dragging him down the hall by the wrist while he slid along on his butt like a dog wiping itself.

"Yeah," I say. "School's weird, all right. But just remember this—weird's good. Embrace the weird, dude. Enjoy it because it's never going away."

Just to illustrate my point, I tell the story about Jeremy Holtz and the fire extinguisher. I knew Jeremy pretty well in grade school, and he was all right, always quick with a one-liner.

But in junior high, around the time his brother got killed in Iraq, he started hanging out with the "bad element." Not that I don't hang out with the bad element every once in a while myself, but that's just me—I hang out with everyone.

Jeremy changed, though. He got acne and started harassing teachers. One day after he let out a loud exaggerated fake yawn in history class, Mr. Cross told him he was only showing off his bad upbringing. That was too much for Jeremy. Without saying a word, he walked out of the class. About a minute later, he sauntered back in with a fire extinguisher, just blasting one direction and then the next, casual as could be. He was a walking blizzard-maker. Everyone in the back row took a hit along with most of the whole south side of the classroom. Mr. Cross made a charge for him, but Jeremy blasted him a good one, too, as if to say, "There you go, Mr. Cross. There's some motherfucking bad upbringing for you."

"Old Jeremy spared me, though," I tell Walter. "You know why?"

He shakes his head.

"Because I embrace the weird."

I don't know how many streets we've driven up and down, but finally there it is—the scary black van with no wheels. It's not that this is a run-down neighborhood or anything. It's just that you can't go too far on this side of town without coming across somebody's fixer-upper sitting on blocks in the driveway. In fact, Walter's house is a perfectly decent, little one-story suburban house with a perfectly decent Ford Explorer sitting out front.

I have to coax him to come up to the porch with me, and he looks a little scared as I ring the bell. There's a pretty long wait, but finally his mom comes to the door with this expression on her face like she expects me to try to sell her a vacuum cleaner or Mormonism. I'll say this for her, though—she's hot. She looks so young it's hard to even think of her as a MILF.

When she sees Walter, she opens the storm door and gives him the old "What are you doing out of school, young man" routine. He looks like he's about to bust out bawling, so I step up and go, "Pardon me, ma'am, but Walter's sort of upset. I found him at the convenience store, and he was talking about wanting to go to Florida."

Right then I notice her checking out my big 7UP. "Wait a minute," she says, squinting at me. "Have you been drinking?"

I glance down at the 7UP like it's some kind of co-conspirator that narced me out. "Uh, no. I haven't been drinking."

"Yes, you have too." She lets the storm door swing shut behind her and squares off right in front of me. "I can smell it on your breath. You've been drinking alcohol and driving my little boy around."

"That's not really the point." I'm backing off. "Let's keep the focus on Walter here."

"Don't come up here drinking and telling me what to do with my boy. Walter, get in the house."

He gazes up at me with a forlorn expression.

"Walter, now!"

So I'm, "Hey, you don't need to yell at him," and she's all, "I have a good mind to call the police."

I want to fire back something about how, if she had a good mind, her son wouldn't be trying to run away to Florida. But I know better. I haven't been in trouble with the police since the tree-burning incident and don't intend to let a mean, hot, twenty-five-year-old mother get me in any now.

Instead, I'm like, "Look at the time." I glance down at my wrist even though I'm not wearing a watch. "Wouldn't you know it? I'm late for Bible school."

She stands there watching me all the way to my car door, making it clear that she's ready to memorize my license tag number if I try to get smart. I can't let Walter down, though. It's just not in my nature.

"Your son's hurting," I say as I open the door. "He misses his dad."

She steps off the porch and twists her scowl a notch meaner.

I get in and start the car, but I can't drive off without rolling down the window and saying one last thing: "Hey, I'd watch Walter around the tree in your backyard if I was you."

Chapter 3

Okay, I am now officially late as hell to pick up Cassidy. Bad-boyfriend late. She's going to get that scrunched-up look on her face like she thinks I'm a spoiled toddler instead of her boyfriend. That's all right. I'm not one of these guys that cowers before his girlfriend's wrath. Sure she can hurl some serious, jagged quips when she gets mad, but I can deal with that. I welcome the challenge. It's like trying to dodge a fistful of razor-sharp kung fu throwing stars. Besides, she's worth it.

Cassidy is the best girlfriend ever. I've dated her for a full two months longer than anyone else. She's smart and witty and original and can chug a beer faster than most guys I know. On top of that, she is absolutely beautiful. I mean spanktacular. Talk about pure colors. She's high-definition. Scandinavian blond hair, eyes as blue as fiords, skin like vanilla ice cream or flower petals or sugar frosting—or really not like anything else but just her skin. It makes my hair ache. Of course, she does believe in astrology, but I don't even care about that. It's a girl thing. I think of it like she has constellations and fortunes whirling around inside her.

But what really sets Cassidy apart is that she's so damn beautifully fat. And believe me, I don't use the word *fat* in a negative way. The fashion magazine girls are dried-up skeletons next to her. She has immaculate proportions. It's like if you took Marilyn Monroe and pumped up her curves three sizes with an air hose. When I move my fingers along Cassidy's body, I feel like Admiral Byrd or Coronado, exploring uncharted territory.

But she won't answer the door. She's in there. I can hear her music—loud and pissed off. Just because I'm something like thirty minutes late, she's going to make me wait on the welcome mat punching the doorbell. After standing around for about three minutes, I go back to the car for my whisky bottle and take it around to the backyard. Sitting at the patio table, I freshen my drink and contemplate my next move. The big 7UP is a bit on the stout side now, but after a hearty swallow, an idea hits me. Her upstairs bedroom window is bound to be open a crack from her sitting up there with her cigarettes, blowing smoke out the window. She is crafty, but not as crafty as I am.

Let me tell you, the climb to her window is not an easy one, though. I've made it before, but not without nearly plummeting to my death wearing nothing but a swimsuit. Luckily, I have plenty of whisky to steady my balance.

Now the tree—being a magnolia with low branches—isn't hard to hoist myself into, but climbing to the tippy-top with a big plastic 7UP cup clenched in my teeth is another matter. It's tough. And then I have to creep out on this anorexic branch and let my weight bend it over to the rooftop. For a second there, I think I might just flop belly-first straight down onto the outdoor grill.

Even when I make it safely to the roof, I'm still not home free. Her roof tilts up at an outrageous angle. I'd give the degree of it, but I didn't do so well in geometry. I do have rubber soles on my shoes, so I spider-walk to the window without anything catastrophic going down. But sometimes I just can't seem to leave well enough alone. I always have to go for a little bit more.

I remove the cup from my teeth to take a good big victory drink, and wouldn't you know, I drop it and there it goes trundling along the gray shingles, whisky and 7UP splashing all over the place.

Of course, my natural reaction is to make a grab for it, which in turn causes me to lose my grip on the windowsill. Next thing I know I'm sliding down the roof face-first, trying to grab on to something, but there's nothing to grab on to. The only thing that stops me from following the big 7UP over the edge is the gutter. I'd feel relieved, but apparently the gutter isn't in real great shape. No sooner do I catch my breath, than it starts to groan. And groan. Until the groan turns into a shriek and the gutter pulls away from its mooring, and there's nothing left to keep me from nosediving over the edge.

Doom is imminent. My coffin flashes before my eyes. I wouldn't mind a red one. Or plaid. Maybe one with a crushed-velvet interior. But then at the last moment, the miraculous happens—I'm able to latch on to the gutter with my hands and sort of swing down onto the patio. Still, my butt-first landing rattles my tailbone good and hard and causes me to bite my tongue on top of that. When I look up, there's Cassidy, staring out the patio door, her eyes and mouth popped open in horror.

She's not horrified on my behalf, though. The sliding door shoots open and she's standing over me, hands on her hips, that familiar "you-are-such-an-idiot" scowl on her face, and I'm like, "Hey, it was an accident."

"Are you crazy?" she shrieks. "That is not cute, Sutter. I can't believe you. Look at that gutter."

"Aren't you the least bit worried about whether I fractured my spine or something?"

"I *wish*." She surveys the roof. "What am I supposed to tell my parents?"

"Tell them what you always do—that you don't know what happened. They can't bust you during the cross-examination that way."

"You always have an answer, don't you? What are you doing now?"

"I'm picking up the gutter. What does it look like?"

"Just leave it. Maybe my parents will think it blew off."

I drop the gutter and pick up my empty cup.

"Don't tell me," she says. "That was full of whisky."

"And a little 7UP."

"I should've known," she said, eyeing the whisky bottle on the patio table. "But really, isn't 10:30 a little early to be drunk again, even for you?"

"Hey, I'm not drunk. I'm just a little fortified. Besides, I didn't drink at all last night, so really, it's like I'm getting a late start. Did you ever think of that?"

"You know you made me miss my hair appointment." She starts back into the house.

I grab the bottle and chase after her. "I don't know why you want to get your hair cut anyway. Your hair's too beautiful to cut off. I like how it sways across your back when you walk. I like the way it hangs down on me when you're on top."

"Not everything's about you, Sutter. I want a change. I don't need your approval." She sits on a stool at the bar that separates the kitchen from the living room. Her arms are crossed and she won't look at me. "They don't like it when you miss your appointments, you know. It costs them money. But I'm sure you don't care about that. You don't think about anybody but yourself."

There it is—my cue to tell the story of Walter. By the time I'm done, I have drinks fixed for the both of us and her arms are uncrossed. She's softening but she's not ready to completely forgive me yet, so I set her drink on the bar instead of handing it to her. I don't want to give her the chance to reject me.

"Okay," she says. "I guess you did a nice thing there for once. But you still could've called me to let me know you'd be late."

"Hey, I would have, but I lost my cell phone."

"Again? That's the third one in a year."

"They're hard to hang on to. And besides, don't you think it's a little *1984* to go walking around with a device in your pocket that lets people locate you at all times? We should rebel against the cell phone. You can be Trotsky and I'll be Che."

"That's so you," she says. "Always trying to joke your way out of things. Have you ever sat down and really thought about what it means to be in a relationship? Do you understand anything about establishing trust and commitment?"

Here we go. Lecture time. And I'm sure what she's saying is right. It's well thought out and insightful and all those things that make for a good grade on a five-paragraph essay in English, but I just can't keep my mind focused on it when she's sitting there right next to me looking like she does.

Those colors of hers really begin their attack on me now, ripping through my skin, electrifying my bloodstream, sending sparks zapping around in my stomach. I take a long pull on my whisky but I can't keep a hard-on from starting. I only mention this because I have a theory that the hard-on is the number one reason for sexism down through history. I mean, it is seriously impossible to really soak in a girl's ideas, no matter how deep or true, when you have a stiffy coming on.

This is what makes guys think of women as cute, cuddly airheads. But it's not the women who are the airheads. The guys' brains have turned into oatmeal, so they sit there staring at the girl with no idea of what she's saying but assuming it must be cute. She could be explaining quantum physics, and the guy would hear nothing but some kind of cutesy-wootsy baby babble.

I know this because it's happened to me many a time, and now it's happening to me again. While she's delivering her perfect essay on relationships, all I want to do is lean over and kiss her neck and then take off her sweater and kiss along her breasts and down to her belly, leaving little red spots on her white skin like roses blooming in the snow.

"And if you can just do *that*," she says, "I think we can make it. We can really, really have a good relationship. But this is it, Sutter. This is the last time I'm going to say it. Do you think you can do it?"

Uh-oh. Big problem. How do I know if I can do it? For all I know, she could have been talking about making me wear a cocktail dress and high heels. This is no time to submit my theory on sexism and the hard-on, however, so I just go, "You know I'd do anything for you, Cassidy."

Her eyes narrow. "I know you'd *say* you'd do anything for me."

"Hey, didn't I just climb up on a two-story roof for you? I busted my ass for you. Look, I'll stand on my head and chug the rest of this whisky upside down for you."

"You don't have to do that." She laughs and takes a swig from her own drink and I know I've got her now. I go into the living room, set my glass on the carpet, and kick myself into a headstand against the end of the couch. This causes some dizziness, but still it's nothing for me to tip the glass and finish the whisky off in one upside-down swallow. Unfortunately, I can't quite maintain the headstand and topple over into a pile like one of those skyscrapers they dynamite to make room for something fancier.

Cassidy's really laughing now, though, and it's a beautiful sight to see. I shoot her my famous eyebrow tilt and big brown eyes, and she takes a drink and goes, "You really are an idiot, but you're my idiot."

"And you are a tremendous woman." I slip the glass from her hand, take a drink, and set the glass on the bar. She spreads her legs so that I can stand between them and brush her hair back from her face and slide my fingers along her shoulders.

"Your eyes are a blue universe, and I'm just falling into them. No parachute. I don't need one because I'm never going to hit the ground."

She grabs the front of my shirt and pulls me in closer. See, this is the other side of the coin. This is a girl's downfall. The guy goes soft in the head and starts talking to her like a moron, and she wants to take care of him. He's just her cuddly fool who can't make it without her. She melts and he melts and it's all over then.

The best way I can describe Cassidy in bed is *triumphant*. If sex were a sport in the Olympics she'd win a gold medal for sure. She'd stand there on the tallest platform with her hand over her heart, crying to the national anthem. Afterward, she'd sit in the TV studio with Bob Costas asking her questions about technique.

I know I'm lucky. I know being with her this way is like being a part of the deepest inner workings of the cosmos. But, for some reason, I feel a dark crack opening up way back in my chest. It's just a hairline fracture but definitely something you don't want to get bigger. Maybe it's the ultimatum she gave me a while ago. *This is it*, she said. *This is the last time I'm going to say it*. But what is it she wants me to do?

It's stupid to worry about it now, though. I'm lying here in my beautiful fat girlfriend's crisp, clean butterfly sheets. I have an extra-strength whisky sitting on the nightstand. Life is spectacular. Forget the dark things. Take a drink and let time wash them away to wherever time washes things away to.

Chapter 4

Okay, yes, maybe I do drink a little bit more than a little bit too much, but don't go getting the idea I'm an alcoholic. It's not some big addiction. It's just a hobby, a good, old-fashioned way to have fun. Once, I said that exact thing to this uptight church girl at school, Jennifer Jorgenson, and she goes, "I don't have to drink alcohol to have fun." So I'm like, "I don't have to ride a roller coaster to have fun either, but I do."

That's the number one problem with these anti-drug-and-alcohol programs they shoehorn you into starting in grade school. No one will admit any of that stuff is fun, so there goes all their credibility flying right out the window. Every kid in school—except the Jennifer Jorgensons of the world—recognizes the whole scam is faker than a televangelist's wife with a boob job.

I've taken those questionnaires on the Internet that are supposed to tell you if you're an alcoholic: Do you ever have a drink first thing in the morning to get your day going? Do people annoy you when they criticize how much you drink? Do you ever drink alone? That kind of thing.

First, sure, I drink in the mornings sometimes, but not because I *need* to. It's just a good change of pace. I'm celebrating a new day, and if you can't do that, then you might as well be laid out with your arms across your chest studying the pattern on your coffin lid. Second, who's not going to get annoyed when someone starts nitpicking at them? I mean, you could just have one beer and your mother smells it on your breath and she and your stupid stepfather start in with the good-cop/bad-cop interrogation routine, except there's no good cop. What, are you supposed to enjoy that?

And third, why is drinking alone so bad anyway? It's not like I'm some derelict drinking cheap aftershave alone behind the bus depot. Say you get grounded and you're watching TV or playing on the computer in your room—a couple of drinks can keep you from going stir-crazy. Or maybe your friends all have curfews on weeknights, so you go home and have three or four more beers sitting on your windowsill with your iPod before going to bed. What's wrong with that?

It's all in the attitude behind your drinking, see. If you're like, *Woe is me, my girlfriend left me and God hath forsaken me,* and guzzling down a fifth of Old Grand-dad until your neck turns to rubber and you can't lift your chin off your chest, then, yes, I'd say you're an alcoholic. But that's not me. I'm not drinking to forget anything or to cover up anything or to run away. What do I have to run away from?

No, everything I do when I'm drinking is about creativity, broadening my horizons. It's actually educational. When I'm drinking, it's like I see another dimension to the world. I understand my friends on a deeper level. Music reaches into me and opens me up from the inside out. Words and ideas that I never knew I had come flying out of me like exotic parakeets. When I watch TV, I make up the dialogue and it's better than anything the writers dreamed up. I'm compassionate and funny. I swell up with God's beauty and sense of humor.

The truth is I am God's own drunk.

In case you haven't heard it, that's a Jimmy Buffett song— "God's Own Drunk." It's about this dude who gets so wasted he falls in love with the world in its entirety. He's in harmony with nature. Nothing scares him, not even the most dangerous of things, like a gigantic, whisky-still-thieving Kodiak bear.

My father—my real father, not Geech, my stupid step-father—he loved Jimmy Buffett. LOVED him. "Margaritaville," "Livingston Saturday Night," "Defying Gravity," "The Wino and I Know," "Why Don't We Get Drunk and Screw"—my dad wore those songs out. I still feel good anytime I hear one.

In fact, the first time I ever had a drink of alcohol I was with my father. This was before the divorce, so I couldn't have been but six years old. We went to a minor-league baseball game at the old stadium by the fairgrounds, back before they built the new one in Bricktown. It was me and my dad and two of his buddies, Larry and Don. I still remember those guys perfectly. They were fun. Big and rowdy.

My dad was big too—he built houses. And handsome? He was George Clooney–handsome, only with the same gap between his front teeth that I have now. Even though I was little, I still felt manly being around these guys. They razzed the umpires and jeered the other team and called players on the Oklahoma City team their "boys." And they held tall, cold beers.

Man, did I want a drink of that beer. I wanted to drink beer and stand up on the seat and holler at the top of my lungs. It didn't matter what I hollered, I just wanted my voice to blend in with the men's. Finally, I pestered my dad enough that he let me have a drink. "Just a sip now," he said, and Larry and Don threw back their heads and laughed. But I showed them. I chugged down about half the cup before Dad pried it away from me.

They all laughed some more, and Don said, "You are a bad, bad badass, Sutter. You really are."

And Dad went, "That's right. That's damn right. You are my badass boy." And he squeezed my shoulder and I leaned into him. I can't say that I got drunk, but I sure did feel warm. I loved that ballpark and everyone in it, and I loved good old Oklahoma City off in the distance, the tall buildings growing soft and cozy in the twilight. I didn't throw up till the seventh inning.

It's not like I was ever some kind of Drew Barrymore, though, drinking my way through grade school and snorting cocaine at dance clubs before I even got pubes. I really didn't drink much at all till seventh grade, and then it wasn't like I was drinking every day.

What I'd do was fold a paper bag and stuff it down the front of my pants and then go in the grocery store, saunter very casually back to the beer aisle—they sell weak-ass 3.2 beer in grocery stores in Oklahoma—and when no one was looking, I'd pull out the sack and stick a six-pack inside, and then put on my most angelic Huckleberry Finn expression and walk out the front door as if I didn't have anything but a sack full of Count Chocula and Fig Newtons under my arm.

Me and my best friend, Ricky Mehlinger, made a regular routine out of this for about a month. We'd filch a sixer and drink it down in the concrete drainage ditch and let the Doberman chase us. The Doberman was one big, ugly, mean-eyed dog. He ruled three backyards. One day we were just finishing off our beer and looked up and there he sat on the corner of the brick wall looking down at us like an evil gargoyle. A split second before he leaped down, we took off running. Then here he came, snapping at our heels. I literally felt his teeth on the back of my shoe right before I scrambled up a stockade fence. It was a blast.

After that, we always made sure to walk by his domain after we finished our six-pack, and without fail, he'd spring out from nowhere, wild-eyed and slobbering. Then one day I bet Ricky five dollars he wouldn't try to make it all the way through the Doberman's backyard and touch the wrought-iron gate around the swimming pool. He chugged the rest of his beer and said, "You're on, dude."

It was hilarious. Ricky got about halfway through the

backyard before the Doberman came tearing around the corner of the house. Ricky's face went all Macaulay Culkin, and he took off at a sprint for the swimming pool gate, the dog chomping air right behind him. He tried to flop over the gate but got seriously hung up on the black, wrought-iron spikes. That's when I saw it. The Doberman kept barking and chomping at Ricky's ankles, but he never took a bite. He could've easily gnawed Ricky's leg off, but when it came down to it, he was just like us—out for a good time and nothing more.

That broke the spell. We knew the old Doberman wasn't really mean and he knew we knew. We'd still drink our beer down in the drainage ditch, but now the dog would sit there with us and let us stroke his head. It was September, the season of the dog. Our parents didn't know where we were and they didn't care. It was spectacular.

Chapter 5

I met Ricky in the fourth grade and we've been thick ever since. He's Germasian. His dad's folks were actual German immigrants and his mom's from Malaysia—Kuala Lumpur, I think. They met when Carl was in the navy. But it's not like you might expect—the big stern German dude bossing around the meek little Asian wife. Actually, his dad's a little dude like Ricky, and he seems kind of gay. I'm not saying anything Ricky hasn't said himself.

His mom's little too—I mean, she can't be five feet tall—but she is nowhere close to meek. She has this high-pitched, twangy voice, like an out-of-tune banjo, and you can't go over to their house without having to listen to her lay into poor little Carl over some nitpicky thing like leaving the water running while he's brushing his teeth. When she really gets going, you can't understand a word she says.

Ricky himself looks a lot more Asian than German, and girls think he's the cutest thing in the world. But he's talked himself into believing they don't see him as boyfriend material. Admittedly, they can be condescending sometimes, like when Kayla Putnam said she'd like to pick him up and carry him around in her purse, but Ricky's got a lot going for him.

For one thing, he's one of the funniest dudes you'd ever want to be around. And also he's smart. Maybe his grades don't exactly show it all the time, but that's just because he doesn't apply himself. If he actually studied, he'd have a 4.0. I make sure to learn at least one new word a day off the Internet just to keep up with his vocabulary.

I'm always reminding him of what all he has on the ball, but does he ever bother to assert himself and actually ask a girl out? No. He always has some excuse—either she's too tall or she's too into her looks or she's a racist. Okay, the racist one I can understand, but somewhere along the line, you have to tell yourself, Hey, this is just high school. All I need is a girl to go out with, like a practice girlfriend.

So considering his track record with girls, it's pretty ironic when he starts in giving me advice about Cassidy.

"Dude," he says, "you can't screw this up. I mean, really, it can't be that hard just to show up to take your girlfriend to get a haircut."

"Hey, there's nothing I can do about that now. It's like spilled milk under the bridge. I'm more worried that I didn't exactly hear what she wants me to do from now on to save our relationship."

"So, what, you weren't listening at all?"

"I had other things on my mind."

Ricky shakes his head. "Dude, if it was me, I'd be hanging on every word." He's very serious too. Sometimes I wonder if he doesn't have a little bit of a crush on Cassidy himself.

"You can't hang on every word," I say. "There's too much going on at any given moment. All you can do is absorb the general feel of it."

Ricky opens another beer. It's Friday night and we're sitting on the hood of my car in a parking lot on Twelfth Street. "If I had a girlfriend, it'd be like church when she talks. She'd be the pontificator and I'd be the pontificatee."

"You're high."

"No, really, dude. I'm the best listener in the world."

He has a point there. He's sure listened to a lot of my crap. "So why don't you ask out Alisa Norman, dude? You like her, don't you?"

He checks out a Mustang passing by, the really cool, old, fastback style from about thirty years ago. "I guess I like her all right, but she's like almost engaged to Denver Quigley."

"So? Ask her out anyway. Look, girls are transitional people. They don't just break up with a guy and then sit around and wait to get asked out. They keep their boyfriend hanging on till they know somebody else is interested in them. Then it's the ax for the old dude and hugs and kisses for the new guy. I'm telling you."

"Right. Have you seen Quigley lately? He's a caveman. All I'd have to do is say two words to Alisa and he'd pummel me into a thin paste. They'd have to take me to the hospital on a spatula."

"Excuses, excuses." I take a drink of beer and chase it with a shot of V.O. "But you know what? I'm tired of your excuses. This is it. Tonight's the night. You're getting a girlfriend."

"Screw you."

"No, really. You think you can third-wheel around with me and Cassidy forever? It's ridiculous. Come on, get in the car."

"Why? What do you have in mind?"

"Girls, that's what. They're everywhere." I wave my arm toward Twelfth Street. "It's Friday night, dude. The street is a cornucopia of girls. Every other car you see is full of them. Tall ones, skinny ones, fat ones, big tits, little tits, blondes, brunettes, redheads, wide asses, and asses you can fit in the palm of your hand. And you know what they want? They want a dude, dude. That's what they want. Now get in the car."

"Tits and asses, huh? You're a real romantic, Sutter. You really are."

He may be going all sarcastic on me, but he gets in the car anyway. He knows old Sutter's got his best interest at heart.

And the fact is I am a romantic. I am in love with the feminine species. It's a shame you only get to pick one, but since that's the rule, I'm very grateful for the one I have, and I want nothing more than for my best buddy to have the same thing.

Chapter 6

Twelfth Street's busy tonight. I wasn't exaggerating either—the girls are out in bold numbers. I'm being picky, though. This is a girl for Ricky after all, the dude I played Justice League with in fifth grade. He had my back then and I've got his now.

"You're not going to embarrass me, are you?" he asks.

"When did I ever embarrass you?"

"Do you really need me to list the times?" He pulls out a blaze and flicks his lighter.

"Dude, what are you doing?" I've got nothing against the weed—I just don't happen to see it as a good social lubricant.

"You don't have to smoke any if you don't want to," he says, taking a long drag.

"Just go easy on it, okay. I don't want to round up a carful of girls and have you go quiet on me, spiraling off into weird cosmos land and shit."

He exhales a rush of smoke. "Don't worry. I'll be entertaining."

"Yeah, sure. But I don't know how much girls like talking about the commercialization of God or whatever that was you were going on about last Saturday."

"It was, What would happen if they discovered the actual physical existence of God? I mean, there'd probably be this humongous battle over the patent rights. Like this whole competition over whether you should get God on cable or satellite. And then they'd have to launch a marketing plan too. They'd have these commercials: 'Call today and get God for $19.95 a month.

Get the Father, the Son, and the Holy Ghost bundle for only $24.95!'"

"Right," I say, chuckling. "And when you can't pay your bill they come in and cut off your God connection."

"See, dude," Ricky says. "That's some entertaining stuff."

I have to admit he's right. "But, still, what you and I find entertaining isn't necessarily going to cut it with the female kind."

"I know that. What do you think, I'm some kind of moron?"

There's no time to debate that question. Suddenly, a gigantic SUV loaded with girls draws up beside us. I don't recognize any of them, but the blonde in back rolls down her window, flashes her tits, and dies laughing.

Ricky goes, "Dude, did you see that?"

"Yeah, I saw it. I gave her the thumbs-up."

"Well, don't let them get away. Follow them."

"Relax, dude. Those girls aren't even from around here."

"So?"

"So, we could follow them all night long, but they aren't going to pull over. You know why a girl like that flashes her tits, don't you? Because she gets off on thinking guys are churning the chubby to her. Anyway, you need someone more natural."

"She looked pretty natural to me."

"She had *me-me-me* hair."

"I wasn't looking at her hair, dude."

Ricky's a little put out with me for not following them, but not really. I know him. The only reason he wants to chase after them in the first place is because he knows nothing will ever happen. It's just make-believe—no real chance of hooking up or getting shut down, either one. But I won't let him get away with that, not this time.

We make a couple trips up and down Twelfth Street with no luck until I see these headlights flashing at me from behind—Tara Thompson's little gold Camry. At the stoplight, she sticks her head out of the window and shouts for me to pull over in the Conoco parking lot. This looks promising. I know Tara pretty well—we have English together—and while she's not really right for Ricky, her friend Bethany Marks is.

Tara and Bethany are pretty much always together. They're mid-level girls—not hot hot or super popular but way above the dank outcast level. Softball players. Tara's a dyed-blonde and a little stocky but not in an unattractive way at all. Bethany's a brunette and more wiry with these spanktacular long legs and kind of a disproportionately short upper body. Nice tits. Her only drawback is that her nose always looks a little oily. But the way she is with Tara reminds me of Ricky. She's the quieter one next to Tara's outgoing personality. Guys don't notice her so much, but she's got a good laugh, and for jocks, she and Tara like to get a party on.

I pull up on Tara's side of the car and roll down my window.

"Sutter," she says, "you're just who I'm looking for. Know where we can get some beer?"

"Beer? Aren't you girls in training?"

"We're celebrating. My mom finally kicked my stepdad out of the house." They both laugh.

I tell them to park, and I'll see if I can help them out.

"Step around to my office, girls." I lead them to the back of my car and pop the trunk to reveal a treasure trove of beer. We've lined the whole trunk with plastic, covered that with ice, laid down row after row of beer, and poured more ice over that.

"You guys rule," Tara says.

"We were just getting ready to go cruise Bricktown," I say, which we weren't really planning to do, but we might as well now. "Why don't you come with us?"

Bethany goes, "We're on our way to Michelle's house."

So I'm like, "Hey, I'm ready to celebrate somebody's stepfather getting kicked out of the house since my mom won't kick mine out."

That's all Tara needs to hear. "Well, don't just stand there. Open me a beer."

I give her one and don't even need to figure out a way to finagle Bethany into the back with Ricky. Tara heads straight to the passenger seat so that there's nothing to do but for Ricky and Bethany to get in back. Now, you might think Cassidy would have a problem with this seating arrangement if she happened to get a look at it, but she's at the movies with her girlfriends tonight, and besides this is all about hooking Ricky up with Bethany.

"Full speed ahead," I say as I crank the ignition. "And damn the potatoes."

Chapter 7

Bricktown is the entertainment district in Oklahoma City. It gets its name from all the brick buildings and even brick streets. It used to be a warehouse district or something. Now they have bars and restaurants, concert halls and arenas, coffee shops, a multiplex, and a ballpark. You can also take boat rides on a canal that runs between two long rows of buildings like a river at the bottom of a canyon. The boat rides aren't real exciting, but girls think they're romantic. All I have to do is figure out a way to get Ricky and Bethany on a boat together while I steer Tara off somewhere else.

I make sure to keep the girls in beer while we drive over and then cruise up and down past the bars and restaurants. At first, Ricky's kind of quiet. He's one of those people that might seem shy at first, but once you get to know him, he's hilarious. He's absolutely kick-ass at doing impersonations—movie stars, teachers, other kids at school. Once I get him started on doing some, the girls eat it up. He does a dead-on Denver Quigley that gets Bethany laughing so hard it looks like her face might fall off.

"Hey, let's go on the boat rides," I say, like it just occurred to me. I don't have to say it twice either. The girls are all over it.

After finding a parking spot about a million miles away from the canal, we hike over, goofing on people and just in general laughing our way down the street. When we get to where the boat rides start, I tell Ricky to buy a couple of tickets, one for him and one for Bethany, but when I step up to the window, I'm like, "Wait a minute. I left my wallet in the car."

Stupid Ricky volunteers to lend me some money, but I'm, "No, dude. You two go ahead. I don't like the idea of my wallet sitting in the car in a dark parking lot. We'll meet back here in thirty minutes."

He gives me this suspicious look, but it's too late now. The boat's getting ready to shove off. Bethany wants Tara to come along, but I grab Tara's arm and say, "No you don't. I'm not walking all the way back over there by myself."

We give them the bon voyage as the boat starts off, and they do look good together, even though she's about three inches taller than he is. After they're gone, I volunteer to buy Tara some ice cream, and she's like, "I thought you forgot your wallet," and I go, "I just remembered I have it in my other pocket."

She looks at me and grins. "You're evil."

"I'm not evil. I'm Cupid. They make a cute couple, don't you think?"

"Yeah," she says. "I do."

On the way to get ice cream, we change our minds and decide to go to a bar instead. After trying about four places and getting rejected, I figure there's nothing to do but go back to the car, get a couple beers, and drink them over at the Botanical Gardens.

"Is it safe to go there after dark?" Tara asks.

"Hey," I say. "You're with me."

I load four beers into a plastic bag, and off to the gardens we go. It's beautiful out. Light-jacket weather. The city lights are shining down on us, and the weight of the beer feels very satisfying, like a promise of plenty.

The only thing about being down here in the evening is you're always likely to run into a panhandler, and of course we do. Tara grabs my arm and stands a little behind me, but there's nothing scary about this guy. He's got the typical faded ball cap, the thrift-store clothes that could stand a good washing, and a face that looks like it's made out of the leather from an old catcher's mitt.

I slip him a five and he's grateful as all hell, tipping his cap and giving me this look like I'm some kind of young lord or something. After he limps away, Tara says she doesn't think I should've given him any money. "He's just going to buy liquor with it," she says.

"Good for him."

"You might as well have just given him a beer."

"Are you kidding? We only have two apiece here. Let him go buy his own."

The Botanical Gardens consists of several walking paths that wind around through a bunch of different kinds of trees and plants and cross over little streams and ponds. At one end, you have the Crystal Bridge, which isn't just a bridge but a big cylindrical greenhouse for the more exotic plants. They even have one of those big stinky plants that only bloom like every three years or something and smell like a rotting corpse. I've actually never been in the gardens after dark, but when you're with a girl, it's always best to act like you're an old hand at everything—not to impress her, but just to make sure she feels safe.

So we're walking along, drinking beer and talking, and she starts in on the deal with her mom and her stepfather, Kerwin.

"Kerwin?" I say. "You mean his name is really Kerwin?"

She's like, "Can you believe it?"

At first the story's pretty funny. Kerwin is a real character. For one thing, he's a big slob, only shaves about twice a week, sits around watching the Food Network in his underwear, peels off his socks and tosses them in the general direction of the bedroom, and farts when her friends walk through the room. He has even been known to eat a TV dinner while taking a dump.

"I don't know," I say. "I think I kind of like him."

"You wouldn't if you had to live with him." She takes a drink.

"My stepdad's a fucking robot."

"Kerwin wasn't bad at first. I guess I did like him then. They got married when I was like nine so I thought it was fun that he was sloppy. My mom and him and my little sister would lie in bed and he'd tell us stories and then he'd go, 'Put your head under the covers. I'm going to spit in the air.' And when we'd stick our heads under the covers, he'd fart. It grossed my mom out, but my sister and I would just giggle like it was the funniest thing in the world. I guess when I was little I thought he was kind of a great guy. Other than the farting, he made my mom laugh. We were pretty happy."

There's a little amphitheater right next to the Crystal Bridge that looks down onto a stage in the middle of the pond. We walk down a few rows and sit there with our beers. "So what happened?" I ask. "One fart too many?"

She laughs. "More than one too many." She pauses and looks at the empty stage. "But it's really the painkillers."

"Painkillers? Like what, Vicodin or something?"

"Worse than that. OxyContin."

"Dude, that's hardcore."

"Tell me about it. At first, he just started out with Loritab. His neck used to kill him after he was in a car wreck. Now, he has this sock full of OxyContin in his dresser—like me and Mom don't know about it. It's not even about pain anymore."

"I don't know," I say. "There's more kinds of pain than just physical pain, you know."

"I guess. He doesn't have any self-restraint. He eats too much, drinks too much, farts too much. He takes too much OxyContin and goes stumbling around the house mumbling things you can't understand and trying to hug and kiss you."

"You mean really trying to kiss you, like with tongue and all?"

She makes a disgusted face. "Yuck, no. It's more like he thinks I'm still nine and he's trying to kiss me on the cheek and wrestle around with me like we used to do."

"Maybe he loves you."

"Please. He's just a mess. Can't hold on to a job. Passes out in the bathroom doorway. On my mom's birthday he got up and tried to cook breakfast for her and almost burned down the house. That was pretty much the last straw."

"That's a shame."

"Nothing lasts," she says, and there's a little crack in her voice. "You think it's going to. You think, 'Here's something I can hold on to,' but it always slips away."

Obviously, she's not as happy about this split-up as she was pretending to be. She may not want to admit it, but I can tell she has a soft spot for the old farter.

"That's why I'm never getting married," she says. "What's the use?"

A fat tear squeezes out of the corner of her eye. I didn't think she'd drunk enough to get to the crying stage, but maybe it doesn't take as many when your emotions are a little raw in the first place.

I want to comfort her. I want to say, "Sure things last. You'll find a great guy—someone who doesn't fart so much—and you'll get married and it'll last forever," but even I don't believe that fairy tale.

So I go, "You're right. Nothing does last. And there's nothing you can hold on to. Not one thing. But that's all right. It's actually good. It's like old people dying. They have to die so there's room for babies. You wouldn't want the world overflowing with old folks, would you? Think about how clogged up traffic would get—all these ancient, shriveled drivers with their enormous dark shades on, cruising around in their twenty-year-old, four-door Buick LeSabres at about three miles an hour, accidentally stepping on the gas instead of the brake and busting through the plate-glass window at the pharmacy."

She laughs at that, but it's a laugh with a sad crack in it.

"Really," I say, "you don't want things to last forever. Look at my parents. If they were still married, my dad—my real dad—would still be trapped in that little two-bedroom cracker box we lived in. He'd still be sweating away every day nailing houses together. Instead, he's like beyond successful. See the Chase building over there, the tallest one?"

She nods and takes a drink.

"My dad's office is near the top. See that one lit window up there right in the middle? That's him, burning the old midnight oil."

"Wow," she says. "Do you ever go up there?"

"Sure I go up there. All the time. You can see all the way to Norman from up there."

"Maybe we should go right now."

"No, not now. He's too busy. I have to make appointments to see him myself."

"What does he do?"

"High finance. One deal after the other."

We both sit and stare at that light on the top floor of the highest building in Oklahoma City. The night's getting colder, and something makes a sound out in the dark. Tara grabs on to my arm. "What was that?"

"Nothing," I tell her. But for some reason I'm feeling vulnerable now, like maybe something evil could really be creeping up on us, a horde of slobbering zombie panhandlers or maybe even something worse, something I don't have a name for.

"Maybe we ought to go back," she says.

"Yeah, it's probably about time."

Chapter 8

We're a bit late getting back to the canal, but Ricky's not pissed at all. He and Bethany are sitting shoulder to shoulder on a bench overlooking the water, grinning like a couple of grade school kids at a puppet show, and neither of them could care less if we ever came back.

On the drive home, Bethany talks more than I've ever heard her talk before. Really animated. She's going on and on about how Ricky did his own hilarious narration of the boat ride as if it were an attraction at Disneyland and how he made up stories for all the people passing by. It made her laugh so hard she thought she was going to throw up. Of course, making up stories for people is a regular routine for me and Ricky—and some of the stuff he told Bethany he stole from me—but that's all right. My plan's working to perfection. The Sutterman has done it again. I'm so proud of myself, at first I don't bother to pay much attention to the pair of headlights tailing us down Twelfth Street.

By the time we get back to Tara's car, Ricky and Bethany already feel like a couple. But it's not like Ricky's going to grab her and lay a big, wet kiss on her right there in the parking lot. He doesn't blow it, though. "That was fun," he says, "let's do it again sometime."

"That'd be great," she says, all sparkly.

"Next Friday would be a splendiferous time to do it," I add. The boy still needs a little help in sealing the deal.

"Friday would be perfect," she says. "I guess I'll talk to you at school."

"Oh, he'll call you before then," I say, and this time he's pretty quick on the uptake—"Yeah, I'll call you."

She gives him a sweet little shy smile and says, "Okay, good," and ducks into Tara's Camry.

A car's idling about fifteen yards behind us, the same one that was behind us coming down Twelfth, but I'm still not paying much attention to it. Instead, I plant a friendly hug around Tara's shoulder and tell her I hope everything works out all right for her mom. Next thing I know, she's wrapping both arms around me, squeezing me like a tube of toothpaste and pressing her cheek against my chest. "I'm glad we ran into each other tonight," she says. "Thanks for the beers and listening to me and my stupid problems and, you know, giving me advice and everything."

I pat her hair and say, "No problem."

That's when the car door slams behind me. I turn around, and wouldn't you know it but there's Cassidy. It was her friend Kendra's car behind us the whole time.

"Hi, Sutter," says Cassidy, and not in a friendly way.

"Hey," I say, prying myself out of Tara's arms. "Cassidy. Did you all have a good time at the movie?"

She stands there with her arms crossed. "Obviously not as good a time as you had."

"Uh, yeah. We just kind of lent the girls some beers." There's no way to explain my plan for hooking up Ricky and Bethany right now, not with Bethany sitting in the car right behind me.

Cassidy has THE LOOK on her face. "Uh-huh, right. I saw you crawling all over each other."

"No, really. Tara's mom's kicking her stepdad out of the house and they were celebrating and . . ."

Cassidy holds up a hand to stop me. "I don't want to hear it. All I asked you to do was one simple thing—to just consider my feelings when you're doing something. Just for once, put someone else's feelings before your own. That's all I asked, just that one thing. But you couldn't even come close."

Aha. So that's what she wanted me to do.

"Sure I can," I say. "I can do that." Really, I'm not so sure I can, but now that I actually know what it is she wants, I'm ready to give it a serious try.

She's not buying it, though. "It's too late, Sutter." She flings the car door open. "You're a lost cause."

"No, I'm not," I say. "I'm really not."

But she just climbs back into the car, slams the door, and rolls up the window.

"What's her problem?" Tara asks from behind me.

"High expectations," I say. "Misplaced high expectations."

Chapter 9

My job is okay. You know what an okay job is, don't you? It's a job you only hate some of the time instead of all of the time. I fold shirts at Mr. Leon's Fine Men's Clothing store over on Eastern. Actually, the shirt folding is just busywork. I'm supposed to be a salesman, but customers are pretty sparse. Who wants to come to Mr. Leon's when you can go to the mall? Last summer, we had four locations in the greater metro area, but now there's only two left. It's just a matter of time before Mr. Leon's completely dries up and blows away. Dead and gone. Like the Indian Taco place that used to be next door.

But the lack of customers isn't what I hate about the job. In fact, I dread hearing the bell above the door ring. Yes, we still have one of those bells above the door. Mr. Leon's gets two types of customers—old guys who want stuff that went out of style ten years ago and the young twenty-one- or twenty-two-year-old sales guys. Funny, it's the young guys that give me the creepy-crawlies the most.

Once I saw this documentary about some primitive tribe in the South American rain forest, and they were, like, so cool. They didn't wear anything but these little flaps that barely covered their downstairs business—the women included—and they walked around in the forest, free and wild, weaving baskets, shooting toucans with blowguns, and all sorts of cool stuff. Then civilization starts creeping in and the next thing you know, they're wearing these limp T-shirts and long-collared polyester shirts and looking like little winos. It was enough to break your heart.

Well, that's what these young dudes remind me of. You know, just a tick of the clock ago they were teenagers, free and wild, stunt-riding their bikes, slashing down sidewalks on skateboards, plunging from rocky cliffs into Lake Tenkiller. Now they come into Mr. Leon's wearing their salesman outfits and their bodies still haven't filled out enough to look right in them—the pants cuffs bunch up on top of their clunky shoes and their shirt collars hike about three inches away from their necks in the back. They have the hair mousse working, zits congregating around their noses and mouths from the stress of working their first *real* jobs and paying their own bills.

And you know what? It's even more heartbreaking than the rain-forest dudes because I know that's the world that's waiting for me out there too. I already have to put on the slacks, the stiff shirts, and the ties just to work at Mr. Leon's. The real world is coming, chugging straight at me like a bulldozer into the rain forest.

I can sell, though. If I wanted to, I could talk nine out of ten of these young dudes into buying one of those pastel-colored leisure suits from the seventies. They're coming back in style, I'd say. You look like Burt Reynolds. All you need is a mustache.

But that's not what I want to do. I don't want to spend my days nagging people to buy things they don't need. Maybe if I could find something to believe in—some radical new product that would save the ozone layer or something—I'd be a helluva salesman then.

But Mr. Leon's is what I have for right now. My stepfather, Geech, got the job for me. I wanted to work in a nuthouse, but those jobs are hard to come by, and Geech was so proud of himself for having connections in the business world that he couldn't hear anything I was saying. "I got into sales when I was fourteen," he boasts. "And I owned my own plumbing supply business before I was thirty-five."

Plumbing supplies. Big deal.

Anyway, folding shirts provides me with enough cash to make car payments and hold on to a decent chunk of partying funds in the process. Besides, the job's not all bad. You just have to look for the positive side, that's what I always say.

For example, my manager, Bob Lewis, is a great guy. I mean, I love this dude. He has dreams. He's always talking about how he's going to strike it rich. Depending on what day it is, he's all about starting up his own motivational seminars for babies or writing a screenplay about space dinosaurs or inventing a diet involving walnut ice cream and fish sticks.

He has all sorts of theme-restaurant ideas like places that revolve around the foods of different states—Alaskan Al's, Wisconsin Willie's, Idaho Ida's. I guess the Idaho one would serve nothing but potatoes. My favorite restaurant, though, had to be the miniature golf place. There'd be some different dish to sample at each hole and the price would depend on your score. I could see customers getting pretty full by the time they finished eighteen holes.

I never get tired of his stories. I egg him on to tell them. But I know he'll never do any of those things. You know why? Because he doesn't really care about getting rich. He just likes to dream. What he really, really cares about is his family—his lumpy little wife and two lumpy little children. That's where his commitment is. That's where all of his energy goes.

His wife isn't attractive in any official way, but she is beautiful. It's awesome when she shows up at the store—her face beams, his face beams, and I'm sure my face beams just from watching the two of them. Same thing with his kids, Kelsey and Jake. They're five and seven years old and can't wait for their dad to hoist them up in the air and toss them around. He calls Kelsey "butterbean" and Jake "spud." Every time they leave the store, I go, "Bob, why don't you adopt me?"

Anyway, since Bob's the world's greatest husband and family man, I figure he might have some decent advice to put forth on the whole Cassidy fiasco. It's late in the afternoon, and a customer hasn't walked through the door in two hours, so we're sitting around with our pop-machine pop, shooting the breeze. Bob's wearing his usual starched blue shirt that shows off his sweat stains royally about this time of day. He's got the look of a guy who probably had a pretty athletic build at one time— back before he started putting away his wife's chicken-fried steaks.

Of course, I've dosed my can of 7UP with just a dash of whisky but Bob doesn't know anything about that. Used to, he didn't mind if I doctored my drinks every once in a while, as long as it was late in the day. But I guess some old-man customer smelled it on my breath and complained. Now I go covert with it just to avoid putting Bob in an awkward position.

"I guess there's not a whole lot I can do about it now," I tell him about the Cassidy situation. "She's made up her mind— *c'est la vie.*"

"Don't give up so easy," he says.

"Why not? There's other girls out there. I've kind of got my eye on Whitney Stowe. Light brown hair, blue eyes, long porcelain legs. She's a little bit of an ice queen, drama-department diva, but that just means no one else ever asks her out—they're too intimidated. Not me, though. I'll just move on in that direction and never look back."

Bob shakes his head. "That's what you say, but I'll bet a hundred bucks that's not how you feel. Just admit it. You want Cassidy back. She's special. To tell you the truth, I thought she might be the one to yank your shifter out of neutral."

"What are you talking about? I'm not stuck in neutral. I'm in overdrive."

"Yeah, right. Did you at least try to talk to her?"

"Sure, I explained the whole thing. I mean, she didn't answer the phone or anything, but I left a long message that very night—completely detailed—and on top of that I e-mailed her. I got nothing back. Zero. The big platypus egg. I mean, at school she walks right past me like I'm the original invisible man."

"Did you follow after her?"

"No, I'm not a puppy dog."

"Did you apologize?"

"Not really. I just explained how I was only doing Ricky a favor—which has worked out splendidly, by the way, since he's going out with Bethany on Friday. The way I see it I don't really have anything to apologize for. It's just a misunderstanding."

Bob waggles his hand at me. "Doesn't matter. It never hurts to apologize. I don't care if she's the one who did something you didn't like—go ahead and apologize. It's the sacrifice of it. That's what shows you love her."

"Yeah," I say, "but then she's going to have a leash around my neck."

"You have to stop thinking that way. Don't worry about who has the power in the relationship all the time. If you make her happy, then that's the biggest power you can have."

"Hmm," I say. "I never thought of it that way."

Bob really does make a lot of good points. I don't know how effective he'd be at motivating babies, but he'd do a tremendous job with an advice-to-the-lovelorn column for teenagers.

"My advice," he says, "is to go over this evening. Don't call or text her. Don't e-mail. Just go over there in person. What's her favorite kind of flower?"

"I don't know."

He gives me the tsk-tsk headshake. "Just bring some roses,

then. Tell her you were wrong. But don't go into all sorts of promises about how you'll never do it again. Instead, tell her you've been thinking about how she must have *felt* when she saw that other girl hugging you. That way you can start her talking about her feelings. Then you've got to listen, hard. Let her know that her feelings are important to you. That's all she wanted from you in the first place."

"Damn, Bob," I say. "That is good. That is *really* good. You ought to be on *Oprah*. I'm not kidding."

"I've thought about writing a book about this kind of stuff," he says. "I might have to get a doctorate in human relations first."

Chapter 10

Good old Bob. For a guy with hair growing out of his ears, he sure seems to be in touch with how women feel. Too bad I can't get him to come along and do the Cyrano de Bergerac thing for me.

See, this is my problem with following Cassidy's rule about putting her feelings first. It's not that I don't want to do it, but I don't have the least grasp on what's going on inside a girl once she becomes my girlfriend. Just plain girls, now, I can read like a toaster-oven manual, but let me start dating one and it's like they reach up and slam that manual shut right in front of my nose. No more toast for me.

Take my girlfriend before Cassidy, Kimberly Kerns. Back in the flirty-flirty stage when we were first getting to know each other, she thought I was the funniest guy in the world. I'd do this gangsta-rapper routine that she loved:

> I'm grand and I'm glorious
> I'm semi-notorious
> I'm a real instigator
> And a mammary navigator
> Listen up, 'cause I'm serious
> I drive the girls delirious
> I'm the master fornicator
> I'm the king copulator
> Down below or up above

I'm the Sultan of Love
Yeah, the Sultan of Love
Yeah, the Sultan of Love.

She'd laugh till she got cramps. But after dating for a couple of months, I couldn't hardly get a sentence out of my mouth without her telling me I was gross or immature or some such routine. She used to tell me I wasn't like anyone else and then, all of a sudden, she's all about wanting to change me into her idea of what a guy should be. Why can't you talk about something serious? Why can't you wear nicer shirts? Why do you have to party with your buddies so much? She even mentioned something about how I ought to grow out my hair a little and put highlights in it. Can you believe that? Me, with fucking highlights?

Before Kimberly, there was Lisa Crespo and before her there was Angela Diaz and before her there was Shawnie Brown and before her—going back into junior high—there was Morgan McDonald and Mandy Stansberry and Caitlin Casey. They were all confident, heads-up-and-look-you-in-the-eye girls in their own ways, but I always seemed to let them down for one of two reasons:

Because I didn't quite stack up as impressive enough to their friends in some way that was beyond my comprehension.

Because—and this is more confusing yet—they expected me to shift into some gear that my love mobile just couldn't seem to reach.

When Lisa broke up with me, she said she felt like we never had a *real* relationship.

"What are you talking about?" I asked. "We do something together almost every Saturday night. Do you expect me to ask you to get married or something? We're sixteen, for God's sake."

"I'm not talking about marriage," she said, all pouty-faced.

"Then what is it?"

She crossed her arms. "If you don't know, I can't tell you."

Jesus. And she started out so fun.

Now, thinking back on my exes is like looking at a flowerbed on the other side of a window. They're beautiful, but you can't touch them.

I have no regrets, though, no bitterness. I just wonder what the hell was going on inside their brains, inside their hearts, back in those days when we should've been getting closer and closer. Why did they want a different Sutter than the one they started out with? Why is it that now I'm friends with every single one of them and it's always fun when we run into each other? Why is it that girls like me so much but never love me?

These are the thoughts flying through my head as I drive to Cassidy's after work. I have every intention of apologizing like Bob suggested, but even though I'm sure it works like a charm for him, I don't have a whole lot of faith in it working for me. And I'm already telling myself that's all right—nothing lasts. Besides, there's always Whitney Stowe, the drama star with the hot legs. Sure, she seems conceited, but I'll loosen her up. I've got a way about me, in the opening stages at least.

On the way, I stop by my favorite liquor store to make sure I have enough fortification for the task at hand. The guy behind the counter in there looks like he could've been the world's first Hell's Angel, but he's my buddy. Never asks for an ID, says I remind him of his long-lost son. Still, the closer I get to Cassidy's house the more the butterflies start spinning around in my stomach, even after two straight shots of whisky.

It's a little after 8:30 by the time I pull onto her street, and I'm still in my Mr. Leon's outfit. Her parents seem to like me better in a tie. I guess it fools them into thinking I'm going somewhere with my life, so maybe now it'll help convince them to let me inside—just in case Cassidy put the word out to banish me.

Her mom comes to the door, which is a good thing. I'm better with moms than dads. By that, I mean other people's moms, not my own.

She looks surprised to see me, so obviously Cassidy's broken the news to her about our split. That makes it pretty official, but still, I'm like, "Hi, Mrs. Roy, how's everything going?" Real casual, like nothing's happened, and I'm just over to see Cassidy like I've been doing this whole last six months.

She puts on a fake smile and goes, "Everything's just fine, Sutter. I didn't expect to see you."

"Really? That's okay. I just came over to chat with Cassidy for a little while, maybe go out and get a Coke."

"I'm sorry, Cassidy's not here." No mention of the breakup.

I'm sure she really wants to say, "You know what, necktie boy? Cassidy's in her room right now, but she never wants to see you again for all eternity, so why don't you and your stupid-looking Mr. Leon slacks vamoose on out of here." That's parents for you. They won't come right out and say something like that, even though everybody knows that's what they're thinking.

But I can play that game too. "Well, hmmm." I look over my shoulder at the driveway. "I see her car's here. Maybe she came back without you noticing."

"No, I'm sure she's not back yet. Kendra came and picked her up." Right away, her bottom lip tenses. Obviously, she wasn't supposed to divulge that top-secret information, but it's too late now. So I'm like, "Okay, tell her I came by, see you later. I've got to get home in a couple of minutes anyway."

But I'm sure—if Mrs. Roy is as smart as I think she is—she knows I'm not heading anywhere close to home right now.

Chapter 11

Kendra's car isn't parked in front of her house, but I go to the door anyway. Her mom's more helpful, telling me the girls went over to Morgan McDonald's house for the Christian jocks meeting. Morgan's my old junior high girlfriend, but that was so long ago now it's not like we were ever anything more than friends. The weird thing, though, is that Cassidy would even go to a meeting with a bunch of religious jocks. She's neither. In fact, she usually scorns them and their ilk.

Ilk. I love that word.

By the time I get to Morgan's neighborhood on the north side of town, I've had several more shots of whisky so I don't have the butterflies anymore. Instead, it's more like rusty bolts banging around in a tin can.

You should see all the cars parked up and down the block for this Christian jock thing. You'd think they must be handing out get-out-of-hell-free coupons. But don't go getting the idea that this is some kind of wholesome, clean-cut, vanilla-wafers-and-milk extravaganza. You don't even really have to be an athlete to come. No. Ninety-nine percent of the people who show up at these meetings are here for one simple reason—to hook up. And that accounts for the heft of those bolts rattling in my belly. Who is Cassidy planning on hooking up with?

I park at the end of the line of cars and start toward Morgan's house, mulling over what I'm going to say when I see Cassidy. I need something lighthearted to begin with, something fun and colorful like, "Imagine meeting you at a place like this. Did you ride over with Jesus or is he taking that donkey again?" Then, once I have her smiling, I'll launch right into the apology. "I was wrong," I'll say. "I wasn't thinking. But you know me, thinking isn't my specialty. I'm a moron at long-term romance. I need a special ed teacher to coach me. Someone like you."

Ahead, I see the silhouette of a couple against the street-light glow. By the height of the guy, I can tell it's Marcus West, the basketball stud, but the girl is leaning so close into him that I can't tell much more about her than that she has fairly short hair. "So," I say to myself, "Marcus has himself a new girl. That must mean LaShonda Williams is free. I always did like her." But as soon as that idea pops into my head, I shut it down. I'm not here looking for new girls.

Then, as I draw closer, Marcus turns so that he can lean against a car, moving the girl around with him and leaning down to lay a big kiss on her. Now I can see the silhouette of her ass perfectly, and there's no mistaking who it belongs to. It's Cassidy's big, splendid, beautiful booty. The bolts in my stomach turn into rusty hammers.

A lot of guys might look at Marcus West's size and turn right around, but not me. "So," I say, stopping about ten yards away. "I see the spirit of Jesus sure got into you two."

Cassidy spins around. "What are you doing here?"

"Hey, you got a haircut."

Her hand flits to her hair for a second. "It seemed like a good time for a change."

I nod and rub my chin like I'm some kind of connoisseur of style. "It is motherfucking stunning."

Now Marcus takes a step my way. "Are you drunk or something, Sutter?"

I smile as wide as I can. "If *drunk* equals A and *something* equals B, let's just say the answer absolutely is not B."

His brow crinkles, not from anger but, surprisingly, from sympathy. "Look, man, I know this isn't exactly the best time for you. Maybe you ought to let me drive you home."

"And behold! Marcus West spake even unto the lowly." I'm trying hard to pronounce all the words without a slur.

Cassidy's like, "Oh Gawd, Sutter." But I hold up a finger to let her know I'm not finished.

"And his blessing fell like a curse among the wicked. That, boys and girls, is the way the communion cracker crumbles."

Marcus walks over and reaches for my arm. "Come on, man, let's go over to my car."

I pull away. "Excellency, that will not be necessary. I am a fair-minded individual who thoroughly understands the meaning of the phrase 'kicked to the curb.' So now, I bid you a good night." I bow just far enough so that I don't lose my balance. "And I wish you a lifetime of marital bliss, for I am now free to begin my epic search for the perfect soul mate."

As I turn away, Marcus goes, "Sutter, look . . ." but Cassidy cuts in. "Let him go. He wouldn't even know how to drive if he wasn't halfway drunk."

"Thanks for the vote of confidence," I call to her without turning around. "You are a most understanding woman—in everything but love." And that would have been a perfect closing line if I hadn't tripped over a pile of trash bags and spilled my drink down the front of my pants.

Chapter 12

Another spectacular afternoon. This weather is unbelievable. Of course, that probably means summer is going to be vicious again, but I'm not worried about that now. I was never big on the future. I admire people who are, but it just never was my thing.

Me and Ricky are sitting on the hood of my car in a parking lot down by the riverfront in the middle of the city. I offer him a hit off the flask, but he turns me down, says it's too early in the day. Too early? It's two o'clock in the afternoon. On a Friday! But I'm not the kind of guy to put the pressure on someone to do anything they don't want to. Live and let live, I say.

I take a quick shot and go, "Look, you can see the Chase building from here. Right up there at the top . . ."

"Yeah, I know. Your dad's office is up there."

"I wonder what kind of deals he's making today."

"You know," Ricky says, "I'd go with you tonight if I could."

"I know you would. It's no big thing. I just can't stand going over to my sister's by myself. Her husband and his buddies make me want to puke sometimes. They're so full of themselves. They think anybody that's not them is riffraff. Actually, I don't mind being riffraff. I just get annoyed with people who think that's a bad thing."

"I can't break this date with Bethany. She's got everything planned."

"That's all right."

"Besides, I thought you were going to ask Whitney Stowe to go with you."

"I did."

"You did? Why didn't you tell me?"

"It didn't go so well. She said she doesn't go out with shallow party boys."

"She said that?"

"Yep."

"That's messed up."

"I don't know."

"Dude, you are not a shallow party boy. Anybody that'd say that doesn't know the first thing about you. They never sat in on any of our late-night conversations, that's for sure."

"But you know Whitney—she's an *artiste.*"

"I don't know why you don't ask Tara out. She wants to go out with you. Bethany said she does. Besides, I saw the way she looked at you when we were driving back from Bricktown."

"Dude, I can't date Tara."

"Sure you can. Think about it. She and Bethany are, like, tight. We could go out on double dates. We could have cookouts by the lake—hamburgers, drinks, a little weed. It'd be splendiferous."

"I'm sure it would be," I say, picturing the whole scene. "But it can't happen. I can never ask Tara out. Ever. If I did, that'd just make Cassidy think she was right. She'd go, 'Look at that little weasel. After he tried to tell me nothing was going on between him and Tara, now they're feeding each other French fries under the white oaks.'"

Ricky gets a chuckle out of that. "You know what?" he says. "I still can't believe she's already latched on to Marcus West. I mean, I can't see it. She's always making fun of jocks."

"Oh, I can see it." I take another hit off the flask. "You know Cassidy and her Greenpeace and Habitat for Humanity and Gay Pride parades, and all that. Then you have Marcus, who's practically a one-man Salvation Army. He's always up to something—serving Thanksgiving dinners for the homeless, working with the Special Olympics kids, mentoring delinquents. You got to hand it to him. He's a hard guy to make fun of."

"Yeah," says Ricky. "And then there's that whole enormous dick thing."

"What?"

"You know, they say black guys have these enormous, elephant-trunk dicks."

"That's bullshit. I don't believe in racial stereotypes like that."

"Me either," he says. "But it's kind of hard not to think about it."

I look at him and shake my head. "Well, it wasn't before you brought it up anyway."

"Sorry, dude."

I hit the flask a stout one. "That makes a real great picture. It was bad enough I have to go over to my sister's, now I'm going to have that snapshot in my head all evening."

"Here," Ricky says. He pulls a fat blaze out of his jacket pocket. "Take this with you. It's some hearty shit. It'll get you through the night."

Chapter 13

I have to work from three to eight, and for once, I don't want to leave. I'm completely ready to stay way after closing even. I'll do inventory till like ten o'clock or something, anything to postpone going over to my sister's soiree. Unfortunately, around seven, Bob pulls me aside and says he thinks I'd better go ahead and leave early.

I'm like, "No way. It might get busy, and you'll be stuck here by yourself," but he's, "Look, I know you've been drinking, and we can't afford to have a customer call into the front office about something like that again, you know?"

I start to deny the drinking thing, but I can't really lie to Bob, so I just say something about how I'll swig some mouthwash and chew some more gum. He's not buying it.

"I can handle the last hour by myself," he says. "Just go home and get to bed early. I won't hold this against you, Sutter. I know you're a good guy. But I also know you've had a rough week, what with the thing between you and Cassidy."

"Hey," I tell him, "I've forgotten all about her. Believe me, that is no big deal. I'm a free man. A new girl is just around the corner."

"Sure," he says. "Okay. But you're not going to find her at a men's clothing store. So go on home. I'll be fine. I'll talk to you tomorrow."

Going home is not an option, though. My mom will just tell me to get my ass straight over to Holly's. No, there's nothing to do but stop off for a big 7UP and cruise around for a while, then maybe take the long way over to Holly's so that I don't have to spend too much one-on-one time with her husband, Kevin, while she's mixing up the salad or whatever. You know, usually I'm a positive guy—I embrace the weird—but I can't help getting a little cynical about these two, and maybe I'm feeling a bit more than a little that way tonight.

Holly and Kevin live in that hoity-toit area just to the north of downtown Oklahoma City on a street full of really big, old homes for upscale professional types. Just for the record, Kevin doesn't pronounce his name *Kevin* the way an ordinary person would. He pronounces it *Keevin*. He's some kind of muckety-muck exec for an energy company. They do very well, especially considering Holly is only twenty-five. Kevin is like fifteen years older than she is, and has an ex-wife that Holly says should be on a poster for what can go wrong with plastic surgery. Holly used to be an administrative assistant at Kevin's company, but obviously she worked her way up.

I wouldn't be surprised if my mom doesn't actually love Kevin more than Holly does. In fact, Holly had to come up with some lame excuse about how his parents hadn't been invited to dinner, so she couldn't invite hers either. I'm sure he told his parents the same thing in reverse. Why they had to go and invite me, I don't know, but Mom actually seemed jealous about it.

Kevin's the golden boy where she's concerned. He can do no wrong. In a way, she probably feels responsible for the fact that Holly spelunked up a fifty-carat rock like him in the first place. After all, Mom did pretty much the same thing with Geech. She started out as his secretary, and I guess the picture of herself in his big, two-story house got the best of her, so the next thing you know, Geech is getting a divorce and Mom's riding around with him in his green Cadillac.

But even with all his money, Geech is still just a handful of rhinestones next to an upscale northsider with a sixty-dollar haircut like Kevin. You should see Mom sitting out by their pool with her shiny gold sandals. It's like she thinks she's royalty. She won't even stick her perfectly manicured big toe in that little pool Geech had built in our backyard anymore.

Being born eight years apart, Holly and I never were very close. She used to tell me that she was the reason our folks got married and I was the reason they got divorced. She said if they only had one kid, they never would've had all those money problems to battle over. Whatever. She was just trying to get back at me for always making fun of her little, walnut-size boobs. That was before the augmentation thing, of course.

So, what I'm saying is I suspect she has some kind of ulterior motive for getting me over tonight. She's like Mom. They both want me to have connections, see. "It's all in who you know," Holly likes to tell me. What she means by "it" she never does say and I don't ask. You might think she just wants to help me get ahead, but my theory is that she really wants to make me into a sort of accessory to her lifestyle. A golden little brother to show off to her golden friends.

The only car I recognize in front of her house is a little red sports car. It belongs to Kevin's buddy Jeff something who owns Boomer Imports down in Norman about a mile away from the University of Oklahoma. Everything's clear now. They want me to go to Kevin's alma mater while selling red convertibles to middle-aged divorced men who have delusions of becoming playboys.

Inside, my sister gives me an air kiss like I guess she thinks upper-crust types are supposed to do and leads me into the living room, where everyone else is already sitting around with their drinks in their hands. Of course, she doesn't offer me any booze, but that's why I hauled along the big 7UP.

Besides Jeff and his wife, there are five people I haven't met before, and I forget their names as soon as my sister introduces them to me. Except for this girl—Jeff's daughter as it turns out—who looks like she's about my age and has the most gorgeous red hair you'd ever want to see. Her name's Hannah and her sugar-cookie skin electrocharges my bloodstream on first sight.

Is it possible, I ask myself, that Holly's thinking about fixing me up with more than just a job?

If it hadn't been for Hannah, I would've been tempted to just wave at everybody and take a seat in the corner, but as it is, I work the whole assembly line, shaking hands till I get to her at the end of the couch. I hold on to her hand a little longer than the others.

"Where have I been all your life?" I say, flashing my irresistible space-between-my-two-front-teeth grin.

She doesn't say anything back. She only looks down shyly and then up again, and the green of her eyes just about cuts me in two.

Chapter 14

In a situation like this, you have to play it cool. You can't just squeeze yourself into a place on the couch and start drooling all over the girl. So, first, I go round up some of the fancy cheese Holly laid out and take a seat across the room on a stool at the bar. Maybe I take a quick glance or two at Hannah, but mainly I pretend to be interested in the conversation.

For the men, the talk is something like, "How was the golf out in Tahoe?"

"It was fantastic!"

And for the women it's "Have you checked out that new little antique shop on Havenhurst and Hursthaven?"

"No, how is it?"

"It's fantastic!"

I swear to myself on the spot that I will never have a party like this no matter how old I get. Is this what's supposed to pass for friendship when you get out of college? I don't see how you can hardly even call these people friends, at least not according to the definition of that word as I lived it growing up.

I guess it's different once you get out in the world and you don't have the same experiences every day like you do in school, but these folks don't have any inside jokes or old stories or theories about how the universe works or anything. There's no deep connection. They barely seem to know each other.

For a while, I test my psychic powers by trying to will Hannah over to the fancy cheese table so I can start a conversation with her, but I must not have been blessed in that department—she just continues sitting there, straight as a nail, with hands folded in her lap and her lips frozen into a polite smile. Now, with the way my mind works, I don't get bored too easily, but at this point in the party, I'm starting to feel like if something entertaining doesn't happen pretty soon I might just topple sideways off my bar stool and splat on the floor. Then I remember the blaze Ricky gave me this afternoon. That ought to spice things up a little bit.

The upstairs bathroom—the one connected to Holly and Kevin's bedroom—seems like the perfect place to fire it up, but what happens when I get up there? Right on this huge chest of drawers of theirs, I spy a tall bottle of thirty-year-old Macallan scotch. Thirty years old! That's Kevin for you. As much as he loves to impress people with swank brand names, he's not about to share his three-hundred-dollar bottle of scotch at a nothing little party like this. His boss isn't even here.

Me, I never was much of a scotch fan, but my big 7UP is starting to taste a little thin, and besides, how many chances am I going to get to slug down something like this? I mean, I read an article online about a sixty-year-old bottle of Macallan going for thirty-eight thousand dollars! And so what if it's not open yet? It's not like I'm going to drink half the bottle or something.

But I would prefer to open it somehow so that Kevin won't be able to tell. That's going to be a problem. Even if I crack the seal as carefully as possible, I'll have a hard time replacing it. I inspect it from every angle, chip at it a little with my thumb-nail, and twist back and forth, but no luck.

Finally, I decide to go ahead and light up my smoke, thinking maybe a little weed might help me figure something out. After taking a couple of drags and holding them in nice and deep each time, my mind starts to expand, and sure enough an idea hits me—I could break the neck of the bottle against the nightstand and start chugging away, gulping down liquor and glass both. And then when I threw up, it'd come out in perfect little airline bottles of scotch!

This is why I don't smoke pot as much as Ricky—my imagination is way too wired-up to handle more than a puff or two.

Anyway, the mental picture cracks me up, and I can hardly stifle my giggle when another picture pops into my head—Kevin stalking into the room and me waving the shattered bottle at him like a bar fighter in some old movie. I can't help but laugh out loud at that one.

Then the stairway creaks. Somebody's coming. Probably Kevin, worried about me getting into his three-hundred-dollar bottle of scotch. Talk about paranoid. You'd think he'd trust his wife's own brother.

"Sutter?" It's Kevin, all right. "Hey, are you up here? Why don't you come down and chat with Hannah for a while?"

He's heading my way. At the time—being all high and everything—I figure the natural thing to do is duck into the closet until he passes by. Anyone would do the same thing, I tell myself. Standing in there with all the suits and sport coats, I can see him through the crack between the sliding door and the door jamb, searching for me like I'm some kind of longtime cat burglar, and he just knows I must be up to my old tricks again.

He looks at the chest of drawers. Shit, I think, why didn't I put the scotch bottle back before running for cover?

"Sutter?" he calls, looking around. Did I mention that his hair looks like a toupee? It's not a toupee, but it sure looks like one. He starts toward the bathroom. "Have you seen my bottle of Macallan?"

I have to shake my head over that. Does he really think I'm in here burglarizing his scotch? I have a good mind to sneak downstairs, slip out the back door, and never come back to their fucking house again.

There's one problem with that, though—the blaze Ricky

gave me is still burning between my fingers. And what happens? It gets a little too close to the dry cleaner plastic on one of Kevin's thousand-dollar suits, and the whole thing bursts into flame right next to me. It's just like a ball of fire out of *War of the Worlds* or something. There's nothing for me to do but crash out of the closet and roll around on the carpet in case I'm on fire. That's what they tell you to do in grade school fire drills.

Now if you think Kevin cares whether I'm burning up, then you have no idea what he's like. No, all he can think about is putting out the fire on his precious suit by beating it with a pillow. Goddamn. That's Kevin for you, more worried about a pile of stitched-together cloth than a live human being.

It's only really the one suit that's altogether ruined. The others will probably smell a little funny, but a trip to the cleaner will fix that easy enough. He throws a complete fit all over me, though. And of course, when Holly comes in, she takes his side too. It's one of the worst things I've ever seen, the way he loses his temper and then her crying her head off like we're in some kind of cable movie on the women's channel. The whole episode's uglier than the time my mom and Geech overreacted about that dump truck thing when I snuck their car out without a license.

"Sutter, why do you have to act like that!" Holly bellows. "Why can't you be like normal people! Why don't you wake up!"

So much for their polite dinner party and all their high-class etiquette bullshit.

"Look," I say. "Did it ever cross either one of your minds that I came an inch away from burning to a crisp? I mean, I was almost the marshmallow in the middle of a tailor-made s'more."

"And whose fault is that?" says Holly, mascara tears tracking down her cheeks.

"Is that my bottle of Macallan you've got in your hand?" adds Kevin.

"Yeah," I say, handing it over. "Don't worry, I didn't open it. I was just looking at it."

He and Holly start in on me again, but I'm just like, "Hey, I'm sorry. That's all I can say. It was an accident. Why don't I just leave so you don't have to waste your lung power on having to bawl me out for the rest of the evening?"

On that, I'm out of there with them still jabbering behind me. Downstairs, everyone in the other room cranes their necks to catch a look at me passing by. For a second, I stop and stare at Hannah, trying to telepathically persuade her to leave with me, but she just gazes back, horrified, like I'm the Wolf Man or Leatherface or somebody.

"Good night, everyone," I say, tossing a jaunty salute Hannah's way. "Due to unforeseen circumstances, it is time for me to depart and get drunk off my ass."

Chapter 15

"Why don't nobody love me!" I scream out the window as I speed down the street. "I got a nice car. I got a big dick. Why don't nobody love me?"

Now, in case you're thinking that's pretty pathetic, let me explain that I'm being sarcastic. It's actually a quote from this dude I worked with one summer on the loading dock at Geech's plumbing supply business. His name was Darrel. We're sitting there on the dock, sweating in the sun, and little Darrel's wife has just dumped him, and that's what he says—"Why don't nobody love me? I got a nice car. I got a big dick. Why don't nobody love me?"

He was completely serious. It broke my heart and made me want to laugh at the same time. You ought to try yelling it sometime, though. It feels pretty good.

I'm no more than a couple blocks away when I realize the Chase building is staring me right in the face. I could get there in two minutes, but what's the use? Instead I pull over in a parking lot and sit there staring out the windshield at those black windows. After taking a slug of whisky, I say, "What's up, Dad? You making a killing up there? You making a million? You gonna show Mom how wrong she was? Make her beg you to come back after all these years?"

I take another slug. "Come on down, Dad!" I yell into the windshield. "Come the fuck on back down to earth!"

But there's no use dwelling on that. It's ridiculous to go

around getting all sloppy and morose. It's Friday. I'm magnificently free and wild. The whole night's stretching out in front of me. Forget my sister and Kevin's flame-broiled suit and Hannah's green eyes. Forget Cassidy and Mr. Leon's and algebra and tomorrow. I'm going to grab hold of this night and crack it open, eat the fruit right out of the middle, and throw away the rind.

Down in Bricktown, I park in the tower by the ballpark and then carouse around up and down the sidewalks with what's left in my flask, giving the eye to all the pretty girls. For a while, I stop and talk to this dude who always plays this weird Chinese guitar on the corner. I try to drum up some extra business by challenging passersby to throw out some extra coins. I've got a pretty good spiel too, like what they use along the midway at the state fair, but the dude doesn't seem to appreciate it much, so I move on.

I try the bars, getting turned away from one after the other till finally I find one where there's no bouncer at the door. The place is packed with young up-and-comer types, so I squeeze into the back to size up my next move. It's great. I can't wait till I turn twenty-one. I'll be out at the bars every night.

At a table next to the wall, there's a group of girls, probably college students, two blondes and three brunettes, all pretty but in different ways, like a variety pack of your favorite kinds of cookies. Yes, God is taking care of me, I tell myself. God will not let me sink.

At first, the girls are suspicious of me, but I grin and launch right into the story of falling off of Cassidy's roof. They laugh and invite me to sit down. We trade names and they say they're all students at OU. I could try to lie and say I'm in college too, but I'm too free in myself to lie, and besides they couldn't be more delighted to find out I'm a high school boy out at the bars by myself in the wake of getting dumped by my girlfriend.

They let me in on their beer and giggle at all my stories. Their eyes dance and their hair shakes. I'm in love with every one of them simultaneously. Two of them kiss me on the cheeks at the same time and one runs her fingers through my hair. For a second I entertain the idea that I'll go back to their sorority house with them, and we'll get naked and frolic together on a round bed with red silk sheets. It'll be like a *Girls Gone Wild* video, only with me right in the middle.

That doesn't happen, of course. They have other bars to hit tonight, and I'm not invited to go along. One by one, they hug me goodbye. They pinch my cheeks and even my ass, but it's just done in that big-sister-little-brotherly kind of way. This, I realize, must be how Ricky always felt with girls before I hooked him up with Bethany.

My night's not over, though. I wander down by the canal and then over to the cineplex to see who might be hanging around outside. Nothing much is going on, so I head back to the parking garage but can't remember what level I left my car on. I don't really care—it just gives me a chance to meet more people while searching, and I know God will lead me to my car eventually because I am God's own drunk. The only problem is my flask is starting to get a little light.

Sure enough, God has not forsaken me. Miraculously, my car appears, and just five minutes to the east, right next to the interstate, stretches a string of convenience stores and truck stops fully stocked with 3.2 beer. All I have to do is find one that doesn't care too much about checking IDs or else persuade someone to go in and buy the beer for me.

At the second truck stop I go to, a girl in a microscopically short denim skirt is hanging around outside. She gives me the eye and a flirty smile. She's probably about twenty-five or so and kind of pretty except her teeth are bad. It dawns on me she's a meth-head hooker.

That's okay with me. I don't look down on anyone, except maybe for the pretentious, and you can even feel sorry for them if you think about it. We joke around a little bit, and she's got a good, quick wit. Her name turns out to be Aqua—at least that's the name she gives me—and although she wants to "party-party" with me, she's not too let down to make ten bucks just for going in and buying a twelve-pack.

"You come back sometime, Sutter," she says as she hands over the beer. "I'll give you my special discount."

I kiss the tips of my fingers and touch them to her cheek. "You let me know when you want to go on a real date, and I'll be at your door in a second."

So, maybe it's a little late to start on a twelve-pack, but I'm in no hurry to get anywhere—especially home. No doubt Holly's already called to tell Mom what an enormous screwup I am. But I'll worry about that tomorrow. Right now, there are new sights to see and loud music to listen to.

Who knows how long I've been cruising around, but the next thing I know I'm in the middle of some neighborhood I don't recognize, side windows down, the cool wind flapping in my clothes. At first the houses aren't bad, but then they get scuzzier and scuzzier, until I'm surrounded by these little lopsided houses that look like they're made out of shingles. Swaybacked roofs, stark concrete porches, scabby trees, bald lawns. Here and there, tricycles or something like a faded plastic pony with wheels leaning sideways in weedy, flowerless flowerbeds. There are families pinched into these flimsy boxes—just like me and my family used to be back in the day.

These are people I understand. These are people I love.

"You are beautiful!" I holler into the wind. "You are holy!"

Suddenly, I'm moved to jump the curb and drive across the

barren lawns. "Down with the king!" I scream. "Down with the motherfucking king!"

And that's the last thing I remember before waking up under a dead tree with a blond-haired, blue-eyed girl looking down at me.

Chapter 16

She jerks back, startled to see me move. "You're alive," she says. "I thought maybe you were dead."

I'm like, "I don't think I'm dead." But right now I can't exactly be sure of anything. "Where the hell am I?"

"You're in the middle of the yard," she says. "Do you know someone who lives here?"

I sit up and look at the house—an ugly little pink brick one with a window air-conditioner unit. "No, I never saw it before."

"Were you in a wreck or something?"

"Not that I know of. Why? Where's my car?"

"Is it one of those?" She points toward the street, where two cars are parked along the curb on our side and a junky white pickup is parked on the other side. The pickup's engine is idling so I guess it must be hers.

"No, I drive a Mitsubishi," I say. "Jesus, I must have gone to sleep." I look around, trying to gather my wits a little. A scraggly elm tree hangs over us and you can just see the moon through the branches. There's a rickety lawn chair stationed in the middle of the yard, and two beer cans lie in the grass a couple of feet away. I vaguely remember sitting in that lawn chair at some point, but I don't remember how I got there.

"So," she asks. "You don't know where you left your car?"

"Let me think for a second," I say, but my head's not really up for thinking. "No, it's no good. I don't remember where it is. Maybe I parked it at home and just went out for a walk."

She shakes her head. "No, I don't think you live in this neighborhood, Sutter."

That surprises the hell out of me right there. "How did you know my name? Were we talking a while ago or something?"

"We go to the same high school," she says, but she doesn't say it like I'm an idiot. She has a kind voice, kind eyes. She looks at me like I'm a bird she found with a broken wing.

"Do we have a class together at school?" I ask.

"Not this year. We did when we were sophomores. You wouldn't remember me."

Her name turns out to be Aimee Finecky, and she's right, I don't remember her, even though I pretend to. According to her, it's five a.m. and the reason she happens to be out at this time is because she's throwing her paper route.

"It's really me and my mom's paper route," she explains, "but Mom and her boyfriend went to the Indian casino over by Shawnee last night, and I guess it got so late they decided to stay in a motel or something. That happens sometimes."

The paper route gives me an idea. Since she's driving around anyway, maybe she could haul me along with her. Surely my car is somewhere close by. In the condition I was in, I probably didn't walk too far before sitting down for a rest.

This sounds el fabuloso to her. After all, usually her mother drives the truck and she heaves the papers out the window. If I can get the right throwing motion down, she figures I'll be a real ace paperboy.

The back of the junky white pickup contains three bundles of unfolded newspapers and the cab is piled high with folded ones, crisp as new ears of corn. "How big is this paper route of yours?" I ask as we pull away from the curb.

"Practically this whole side of town," she says, and I'm like, "Jesus Christ, I didn't know newspaper throwing was such big business. You must reel in a lot of cash."

"My mom does. She gives me an allowance out of it."

"That doesn't sound fair."

"It doesn't?"

"Of course not. If you do half the work, you ought to be fifty-fifty partners. Maybe more, since you have to do all the work when she goes out blowing her money at the Indian casino."

"That's all right," she says. "She pays most of the bills."

"Most of them?"

"Sometimes I have to chip in."

"She sure saw you coming."

Down the street we drive, moving at senior-citizen speed since she has to tell me which houses to deliver to. I take to the throwing part right away, though—it's a sideways motion from the chest out, kind of like throwing a Frisbee. Before we make a whole block, I'm already pitching way into the yards, almost to the porches. I'm a natural.

My head's still a little woozy, but gradually, it's clearing up, which isn't necessarily a good thing. Thoughts of what Mom and Geech will have to say about me staying out all night start to trickle in. It's not hard to predict—Geech is bound to come with the good old military school threat. He must have that recorded on a chip and installed in his robot head.

Mom, she'll go into her routine about what the neighbors would think if they saw me traipsing in at such-and-such time in the morning. What I want to know is why should she care? She doesn't even like the neighbors. But that doesn't matter. She worries more about what people think than anyone else in the universe. I'm always embarrassing her somehow. I guess I must have inherited that trait from Dad.

But I don't know why I should have to explain anything to anybody. Why shouldn't I be doing exactly what I'm doing? It's superb to be out in the early, early morning before the sun comes up. There's this sense of being super-alive. You're in on a secret that all the dull, sleeping people don't know about. Unlike them, you're alert and aware of existing right here in this precise moment between what happened and what's going to happen. I'm sure my dad's been here. Mom might have been once. But Geech? Robots don't have any idea of what it's like to be really alive, and they never will.

Chapter 17

After finishing up three streets, we're out of rolled newspapers and still haven't run across my car. Aimee pulls over and brings a bundle from the back around to the cab so we can get some more ready to throw. She shows me her method of folding, then rolling, then slapping on the rubber band, but there's no way I can keep up with her once we get started. Her hands are magic. I swear the girl gets three done for every one I finish.

"How many of these things have you folded in your life?" I ask as she pitches another finished product onto the floorboard by my feet.

"I don't know." Her hands keep working. "It feels like about a hundred million."

I ask if her mom has a day job too, but she says no, the paper route is her only job. Her mom's boyfriend is on disability with a bad back. He collects his disability check and buys and sells things on eBay. That's when he's not sitting around watching TV in his sweatpants. A lot of kids might have sounded bitter about that, but not Aimee. Her voice is gentle, like she's talking about someone with a terminal disease.

We trade a few stories about our parents. Her mom's a real gamble-oholic it sounds like to me—the Indian casinos, the lottery, bingo, anything to try to make a quick buck. Only she hardly ever wins. She has the luck of an armadillo trying to cross a six-lane highway. Still, Aimee doesn't judge her. Losing the gas bill money is just a fact of life for her. She probably thinks it happens to everybody.

I mention a few things about Mom and Geech and my real dad's office at the top of the Chase building. Nothing too deep, although I have the feeling that I could say anything to Aimee and she wouldn't judge me. Her voice would remain cool and soft, like a pillow to lay your head on after a hard day.

She's cute, too, in a nerdy sort of way. You know the look—glasses that ride down on the nose, pale skin from staying inside too much, mouth hanging slightly open in that classic nerd mouth-breather style. But she has full lips and sweet, little blond eyebrows and a nice, slender neck. Her hair isn't pure Scandinavian blond like Cassidy's—it's more dirty blond and sort of lank. And she doesn't have the fjord-blue eyes either—hers are paler, more like a public swimming pool. Still, she has a way about her that makes me want to do something for her. Not *to* her. *For* her.

"You know what?" I say. "If we find my car, I'm still going to help you finish off your route."

"You don't have to do that," she says, but her eyes tell me she'd like nothing better.

"I know I don't have to," I tell her. "I want to."

Once we get a good-size batch of papers folded, we're on the road again. Still no sign of my car, but the further we go the better we work together. I start calling her Captain and tell her to call me Special Agent Danger. Instead of having her point out which house to throw to by saying something boring like "here" or "this one," I coax her into yelling, "Fire the torpedo, Special Agent Danger, fire the torpedo!" After a while, we're zipping down the road at almost the speed limit and I never miss a yard.

"You know what?" she says. "I think this is the first time I've ever actually had fun doing this."

"We make a good team."

"You think so?" There's a hopeful look in her eyes.

"Absolutely."

Then all of a sudden, there it is—my car, sitting sideways in the middle of a lawn. One of Aimee's customer's lawns yet.

"Jesus," I say. "I can't believe I walked all that way from here. It must be a mile and a half."

"What's it doing in the yard?" she asks.

For a second the vision of me cutting across lawns yelling at the top of my lungs shoots through my mind. "I don't know," I say. "I guess it's a pretty safe place to leave a car if you have to. But I'd probably better get it off before these people wake up or the cops come by."

Turns out, the car's out of gas, which is a relief. I'd hate to think I didn't have a good reason for leaving it there. Getting it off the lawn is simple in concept but not so simple to actually do. Aimee gets behind the wheel to steer and I push from behind. The problem is that the yard is real spongy, so it takes all the effort I have. By the time we finally get it parked decently by the curb, I feel like I'm about ready to pass out.

"I guess I'll have to go get some gas," I say as Aimee steps out of the car.

She's like, "I guess so," and looks back at my car like it's some annoying person that broke up our good time. "There's a convenience store just a couple of blocks over. I'll drive you."

"What about the rest of your route?"

"That's all right. I can finish it by myself. I'm sure you probably need to get home."

But I'm like, "No way, Captain. I said I'd help you finish and whatever Special Agent Danger says he'll do, he does. Do you roger that?"

The light flips back on in her eyes. "Yes."

"No, you have to say *ten-four*. Say, 'Ten-four, I roger that.'"

She looks down, her pale eyelashes hiding her eyes. "Ten-four," she says. "I roger that."

It takes about another hour to finish throwing her papers, and I keep her spirits high most of the time, but both of us lose a little enthusiasm toward the end, mostly because we know time is running out. She'll have to go back to her empty house, and I'll have to go back to meet the wrath of Mom and Geech.

We go by the convenience store for a couple of gallons of gas, and I buy us both donuts and strawberry-guava drinks. After getting my car gassed up, we're standing there in the middle of the street, and she has this sort of shy look on her face like we've just been on a first date and she's wondering if I'm going to kiss her.

"You know what, Aimee Finecky?" I say. "I had a pretty rotten night last night until you came along and found me."

She looks like she wants to say something back but can't find the right words.

So I'm like, "Where do you eat lunch Mondays?"

And she's, "In the cafeteria." Which, of course, is where any red-blooded nerd would eat.

So I'm, "Aw, dude, that's lame."

And she's like, "It is?"

I can tell she feels like she said something stupid, so I go, "I don't mean you eating there's lame. I mean the food's lame. No, are you kidding? I'd eat in the cafeteria every day if the food was better."

"They have pizza on Mondays," she says.

"Oh, yeah?" I say, like that's the greatest news I've heard all year. "I am the man when it comes to pizza. Why don't I meet you outside the south door, and we'll eat pizza and relive our greatest triumphs of newspaper delivery?"

"Really?" She looks at me like I might just be planning a practical joke of some kind.

"I'll be there right after Algebra."

"Me too," she says. "I mean, not after Algebra but after Calculus, or I mean after French. I got mixed up."

I give her hand a squeeze. "Wish me luck for when I get back home. I'll need it."

"Good luck," she says, and she's so earnest I'm tempted to believe it just might help.

Chapter 18

So why do I call my stepdad Geech? That's simple. His actual name is Garth Easley, so of course, I started calling him Geasley and then it was the Geast and then it was Geechy and now it's just Geech. Which is perfect because it sounds like how he makes you feel if you're around him for more than fifteen seconds. Geeeech. Kind of like *retch*.

He came along when I was eight, and believe me, I wasn't happy when we loaded up and moved in with him. Holly thought it was the most fandangulous thing that ever happened. It was like she didn't miss Dad at all. She was just happy to have a pool in the backyard so she could invite over all the high school hotshots who never really liked her before.

Mom changed when she and Geech got married. She started spending all sorts of money on her hair and makeup. She traded in her long hair and jeans and started dressing like something out of a hoity-toit magazine all the time. I don't think she really even likes him all that much, though. You'll never see her leaning in close to him on the sofa, running her fingers through what's left of his hair or sneaking up behind him and grabbing his bony ass or dancing to Jimmy Buffett songs on the patio in the moonlight. All that disappeared when she kicked Dad to the curb.

She'll be on Geech's side this morning, though. They'll present a united front against me. Luckily, I still have a couple of beers left from the twelve-pack I bought last night. They're pretty warm, but that's all right. I'm not exactly drinking them for refreshment purposes this morning.

The sun's been up for a while when I get home. This has been one hell of a long day or two days or whatever. Time for a swig of the mouthwash I keep in the glove compartment. There's not much chance I can sneak in, but I try it anyway. Quiet as a second-story man, I get the front door open and shut with barely a sound and creep upstairs without a single creak. The safety of my room is at the end of the long hall, but I make it there fine and am just starting to take my shoes off when the door flies open.

Mom starts in first. "Where have you been, Mister? And don't even try saying you spent the night with a friend. We called everywhere, including all the hospitals between here and your sister's house."

For someone in pink pajamas, she can sure pull off an angry pit-bull look, but actually it's nice of her to warn me about having called my friends because that's exactly the defense I've been planning to present. That's all right. Something close to the truth will work better anyway.

"I went driving around," I say. "It got to be pretty late and I ran out of gas, so . . ."

"Your sister called." Mom pauses to let the horror of that information sink in. But I figure it'll be better to keep quiet until I find out exactly what the charges against me are.

So she's like, "I'm at a loss, Sutter. What am I supposed to do with a boy who tries to steal an expensive bottle of liquor from his brother-in-law and then nearly burns his own sister's house down after she worked so hard to get it?"

Worked hard? I don't know where Mom gets that—unless she considers getting a boob job hard work, because that's pretty much what got Holly married to Kevin and living in the big house. Of course, this isn't the time to point that out, so all I can say is that I never tried to steal the bottle.

Nobody listens to that, though. Instead, Geech is all, "I'll tell you what you do with a boy like that—military school."

It sure didn't take him long to throw out that old line. Usually, I have to spar a few rounds with him before he goes military school on me.

"He needs to understand the meaning of discipline," he says, using the third person like I'm not sitting right there in front of him. "He needs to understand the value of other people's property. A good, tough drill sergeant will pound that into him."

"When did drill sergeants start caring about people's personal property?" I say. "I thought they were just concerned with destroying your individuality."

That gets the vein in his forehead pumping overtime. "Don't get cute with me, young man. I won't take it in my own house." He turns back to Mom. "That's another thing military school needs to pound into him—respect for authority."

It's not all that easy to take a short, balding, red-faced guy with glasses for much of an authority figure, but I don't need to point that out right now either. His military-school threats are stale—nothing but bluster. Mom's never thrown her support behind that proposition. I mean, after all, there's a war going on. She's not about to pack her only son off on the road to Baghdad.

Or so I used to think.

"Is that what you need, Sutter?" she asks, but she doesn't bother waiting for an answer. "Because I'm starting to think it is. You can just finish out the semester in the military academy over by Tulsa and then go straight into basic training. Let's see how you handle a tour overseas. That ought to shape you up."

She sounds like she means it one hundred percent too. She's pissed off enough to actually throw me to the crazy suicide bombers. But I guess I can't be surprised after the way she ditched my father.

I'll tell you who *is* surprised, though—Geech. He absolutely wasn't expecting such strong backup from Mom. "Uh, well," he says. "Right. The military academy. That'll get you straightened out. I'll check into the cost first thing Monday morning."

And right then, I know nothing will ever come of it. Anytime Geech starts talking about checking into the cost of something, that's the end. For all his plumbing-supply money, he's the original Mr. Cheap.

For now, though, I'm stripped of my car keys and grounded indefinitely. Plus, I have to give Kevin fifty dollars a month till I pay off his suit. That equals out to about two years of indentured servitude. Okay, I can understand the part about the suit, but I try to make the argument that they can't take away my keys since I'm the one paying for the car.

Do they care about that? No. They're paying for the insurance, they say. I'll have to find someone to take me to school—or else ride the dreaded bus—but they admit that they have to let me drive to work and back after school. Which means, since they both work in the afternoons, they'll actually have to let me keep my keys after all.

"You know, Sutter," Mom says. "It's going to take a long time to rebuild our trust in you."

"I'm sorry," I say. "I'll try to make it up to you." And I am sorry about making her call my friends and the hospitals and all, but I know my mom. Trust in me isn't real high on her list of priorities. A good trip to the beauty shop next week and she'll forget all about it.

Chapter 19

Okay, so I had a bad day. I'm not going to let that keep me down for long. I'm not even going to think about it. I mean, having to ride to school with Ricky is not exactly the harshest punishment in the world anyway. And how grounded can I actually be in the afternoons when Mom and Geech aren't anywhere around? Of course, they say they'll call and check in with me, but I'll believe that when it happens.

"Hey, it's the firebug," says Ricky when I get into his car on Monday morning. "Burned up any more thousand-dollar suits lately?"

"Very funny, Mr. Goodweed. You know, that never would've happened if you hadn't pawned off that blaze on me."

He laughs. "Right. That was my master plan, and you fell right into it."

But like I say, I don't even want to think about that night, so I change the subject to Ricky's date with Bethany. Of course, we've already hashed it over on the phone once, but I figure he won't mind doing it again.

"Dude," he says. "I'm telling you—this is *the* girl. Everything went perfectly. Except when I had to borrow a couple of dollars off her, but she was even cool about that. I mean, who would've thought dinner and a movie would cost so much?"

"Oh, just about anyone who's gone out on a real date before, that's all."

He brushes that off. "The best part was that we could talk

about anything. Not just shallow stuff either. We had a pretty deep conversation about religion."

"Good kisser?"

"Amazing."

"Tongue action?"

"Oh, dude, she could win state with that tongue."

It's tempting to take credit for fixing him up with this Wonder Woman, but I didn't do it for credit. So instead I move on to the next subject—where we're going for lunch today.

He pauses.

"What's the matter?"

"Dude, I can't make it for lunch today. Bethany and I are going together."

"You can't take me along?"

"It's a little early in the relationship to be dragging a buddy along."

"I guess." That's what I say, but I'm thinking about all the times he third-wheeled it with me and Cassidy.

"Besides," he says. "Didn't you say you were having lunch with what's-her-name, the paper route girl?"

"Oh, yeah. Aimee. I completely forgot about her. Thanks for reminding me, dude. I'd hate to screw her over. She's too—I don't know—naive or sweet or whatever."

Ricky takes his eyes off the road and studies me for a second. "You know what you're doing, don't you?"

"What?"

"You're on the rebound, dude. From what you told me, it sounds like you and this girl don't have anything in common. You're just bouncing off Cassidy to the first easy thing that comes along. And I really can't see you dating this girl. She's the exact opposite of Cassidy."

"Dude," I say. "You couldn't be more wrong. For one thing, she's not the exact opposite of Cassidy. The exact opposite of

Cassidy would have black hair and brown eyes. And for another thing, I don't have any interest at all in *dating* Aimee. None."

"Then what are you having lunch with her for?"

"Moral support. This girl needs it. She lets her family run all over her. You can see it in her eyes. It's like she doesn't think she's important enough to even stand up for herself."

"So what are you gonna do, give her a makeover like in the movies where they turn the nerd girl into a raging hottie?"

"No. It's not about trying to turn her into a hottie. She could never be a hottie. She doesn't have the attitude—that inner positive charge. You can tell by just looking at her slouchy little duck-footed walk. A real authentic hottie has a completely different way of standing and walking—shoulders back, tits out, ass swaggering. She has to know she's hot to be hot.

"There's, like, this whole training process. First off, the other girls fall all over themselves trying to hang out with her. Then she has dudes straggling after her like puppy dogs everywhere she goes, and on top of that, at probably about the age of twelve, she realizes even grown men can't keep their eyes in their sockets every time she walks by.

"I'm telling you—you could take Aimee's glasses off, put some bounce in her hair, and stick her in a short red skirt that shows everything but her bo-bo and she's still going to walk around with her shoulders slouched and a look in her eyes like the world's getting ready to punch her in the mouth."

"So what are you going to do, save her soul?"

"Maybe. You never know."

Chapter 20

A lot of people might consider Algebra II with Mr. Aster—a.k.a. Mr. Asterhole—the most boring place on earth, but my theory is that boredom is only for boring people with no imagination. Sure, if I actually paid attention to Mr. Asterhole's monotone drone, then I'd be bored too, but there's not much chance of that.

One of my favorite diversions is Motojet. The motojet is like this sleek silver dirt bike, only it can fly and has these cool machine guns and rocket launchers. When you need some speed, you just kick in the jets and *vrooooom!* You're gone.

It's like I have a whole video game in my head, and instead of sitting in algebra class, I'm out saving the universe, or at least my high school. I don't know how many times I've rescued Cassidy from terrorists and gangsters and evil warlords. Of course, every once in a while, I wreck in some spectacular way, the motojet swooping down out of the evening sky, clipping the top of a water tower, and then smashing out the football stadium lights right before I go flipping end over end across the field in front of the whole student body.

And when I finally roll to a stop against the goal post, you should see the girls running over, bawling their eyes out, to where I lie in an awesome, crumpled, smoldering heap. Even my mom is there. "Don't worry," I tell them as the dust settles around my fractured body. "I'm all right. Everything's fabuloso!"

Today, my motojet mission keeps getting interrupted by thoughts of Aimee. I can't believe I almost forgot about meeting her for lunch. Now, instead of Motojet, I play a movie in my head of Aimee standing alone outside the cafeteria door, checking her watch, looking at all the people who aren't me pass her by.

Sutter, I say to myself, you cannot disappoint this girl.

Finally, class ends. I gather up my backpack and start for the door, planning to get to the cafeteria pronto so that Aimee doesn't even have to wait a second. It's not that easy, though. Before I can escape, Mr. Asterhole calls me to his desk.

"Have a seat," he says, pointing at the desk directly in front of his desk. "Mr. Keely, I seem to have noticed that once again you didn't turn in your Monday homework."

"It was a bad weekend," I tell him, and he's like, "Yes, well, you seem to have a lot of those." With Mr. Asterhole, everything *seems* to be some way. It never just *is*.

Unfortunately, instead of yelling at me or something, he decides it seems like a good time to quiz me about what he talked about in class today. Needless to say, I don't do very well, so he starts in on how it seems that I didn't listen adequately in class. I check the clock, thinking maybe I can still get to the cafeteria at the same time Aimee does.

But Mr. Asterhole isn't finished. Now he's going on about how he has my best interests at heart and how if I fail that means he fails. It seems to him that, to have any hope at all of succeeding in college, I need to have at least a basic understanding of what he's trying to teach me in this class.

I agree with him wholeheartedly. I've been meaning to get my act together, I explain. I'm really going to put the nose to the old grindstone for the rest of the semester. You'd think that would be good enough for Mr. Asterhole, but no, he's got to go and lay out a problem for me to try my hand at, just to see how bad I am. Which, as it turns out, is pretty bad.

He looks at me over the tops of his glasses. It's a tsk-tsk look only without the sound effects. "Let me show you how it's done, Mr. Keely," he says. "Watch closely."

And I'm like, Errrrrrrrrg! I can't believe this. My earlier vision of Aimee alone by the door is turning out to be real. I can just hear her saying to herself, "I should've known he wouldn't come. That's how everybody treats me."

"And that's how it's done, Mr. Keely," says Mr. Asterhole, finally. "Does that seem to make sense to you?"

"Yes, sir," I say. "It sure does. It seems to make a lot of sense."

By the time I finally get out of there, I'm fifteen minutes late and counting, so I break into a jog. Ms. Giraffe-neckowsky sticks her head out of her history classroom, but I'm too far gone to yell at. A couple of friends—or quasi friends, actually—call out, "What's the rush, Sutter?" and "Yeah, is there a fire or a party?" But I don't have time to trade jokes right now.

When I get to the cafeteria, I can't believe my eyes. There's Aimee standing by the door alone. She waited. She actually waited. This girl is steadfast. She has faith in the Sutterman.

I slow down to a saunter. "Hey, you're here," I say, catching my breath. "Sorry I'm late."

"That's all right," she says, and I have to wonder how many times she's said that to the people in her life who screwed her over somehow.

"No," I say. "It's not all right. But I couldn't help it."

Chapter 21

As we walk in to get our pizza, I explain the situation with Mr. Asterhole. It turns out she also had him for Algebra II, but that was about a millennium ago or something since she's now in AP Calc.

"You probably thought algebra was a breeze," I say.

And she's like, "Kind of." Her voice is so soft. If it were a food item, it'd be a marshmallow.

"Maybe I could get you to tutor me."

"Okay," she says, and she has this little near-smile on her face like she thinks something good might actually happen to her but she can't quite trust it.

Of course, the cafeteria is not the popular hot spot for lunch—I mean, I never go there—so we don't have any difficulty finding a table. In fact, it's kind of weird, like an alternate universe where there's all these students who I never knew existed.

You might think that Aimee and I wouldn't have much to talk about, but hey, I can talk to anybody. I start off with a story just to relieve her of the load of trying to come up with something to say. It's one of my favorites, the time Ricky and I took a float trip down the Tuskogee River last summer.

We weren't exactly bona fide canoeing experts and paid more attention to cracking jokes than navigating, so the occasional rollover was unavoidable. Once, we both ended up in the river with a semi-raging current around us. The canoe started spiraling away downstream, but what did Ricky and I do? We both swam straight for the ice chest. Save the beer at all costs! That was our attitude. Luckily the canoe got hung up on the bank and everything turned out fine.

Aimee's like, "You guys are crazy," but you can tell she kind of wishes she could be a little crazy herself sometimes.

"That's not the craziest part of it," I say. "The craziest part was when we decided to jump off the bridge."

"You jumped off a bridge?"

"Of course. And not some puny little bridge either. It was one of those big iron bridges with the framework that arches way up. I mean, it must be about a mile from the top of that framework down to the water. It's so high you have to watch out for low-flying aircraft up there. Some other dudes were jumping off of it, so we thought, What the hell? Might as well give it a try. We'd had quite a few beers by this time."

She's staring at me wide-eyed and rapt as all twelve apostles rolled into one.

"So up we climbed." I gaze toward the ceiling to hint at just how high we had to go. "But the thing is the farther you climb the more you start to wonder if this is such a good idea. Somehow it looks higher when you're actually on the bridge compared to when you're just standing around on the ground staring up. But what can you do? Once you're on your way, there's no crawling back down without looking like a complete pussy."

She nods her understanding, although I'm not so sure girls fully get the whole *looking-like-a-pussy* dilemma.

"So, anyway, I do the Spider-Man all the way to the very top and take a seat up there in the breeze. And let me tell you, the view's stupendous as long as you don't look straight down, which of course, I happen to do. But like I say—there's no turning back. So I take a humongous breath"—I demonstrate—"and down I go."

"Did you dive headfirst?"

"Are you kidding? I'm not that crazy. No, I went feet first. And you know what? On the way down I discovered that you have an amazing amount of time to think while you're in the air. So, there I am, and this idea hits me—what if a canoe comes floating under the bridge? I might plummet straight down and break someone's neck. You know, it's like I could take it if I just killed me, but I'd never forgive myself if I killed someone else while I was at it."

"That'd be awful," she says.

I gaze back toward the ceiling. "There I am in midair, looking down between my toes, and it's like the water's rushing up toward me, and then—*whooom!* I hit the surface." I clap my hands and she jerks back.

"Now," I say, "let me stipulate one thing right here. When jumping off anything high into a body of water, a dude should always remember to keep his legs together at impact. It will be very painful otherwise. I know from experience."

Pain shoots across her face. She is the absolute best audience ever.

"On top of that, I also didn't take into account that if you jump from a very high place you are going to shoot very far down into the water. I mean, deep. And I didn't think to take an extra breath before going under either. So there I am, underwater for what feels like ten minutes. My eyes are bulging. I'm kicking and flailing, nothing but a gray ceiling of water above me. A newspaper headline flashes before my eyes—IMBECILIC YOUTH PLUNGES TO DEATH FROM TUSKOGEE BRIDGE.

"Then I see it—a pale circle of light shining through the water—and I know I can make it. My head breaks through the water, and sweet, sweet oxygen fills my lungs. Saved!"

I settle back in my chair. "By the time I got to the bank, I was almost sober, and here comes Ricky shooting down from the bridge like an arrow. 'Hold your legs together,' I yelled. But he couldn't hear me, and splat." I clap my hands again and she jerks back again.

"Anyway, obviously we both lived to tell the story, but I'm not sure we can have children now."

Aimee smiles the biggest I've seen yet. "Wow," she says. "That's about the most amazing thing I ever heard."

Chapter 22

"So," I say, picking up a slice of pizza. "How about you? Do you have any good stories?"

She thinks for a moment. "Well, I remember that time we had English together sophomore year, and Mrs. Camp got called out of the room, so you stood up in front of the class and delivered this whole lecture about symbolism in that old movie *Dumb and Dumber*. You had the whole class cracking up, but Mrs. Camp wasn't too happy when she came back in."

"Yeah," I say. "*Dumb and Dumber*, that's like one of my all-time favorite movies."

"And then there was the time I saw you surfing on the hood of a car and it ran over a curb and you went flying off into a hedge. I thought, Oh my God, he's dead! But you just jumped right up and got back on the car. Do you remember that?"

"Yeah, vaguely." It's kind of flattering that she remembers these things, but I wasn't looking for more stories about me. "What about you?" I ask. "Don't you have some stories about yourself?"

She scrunches up her nose. "I'm boring."

"No, you're not. Think about it. You're probably the only person in here who's out roaming the neighborhoods at five o'clock every morning, even during the school week. I think that's pretty amazing."

She smiles. "Well, I guess some things have happened on the paper route that are kind of interesting. There was this one time—I don't know whether I should tell you this or not."

"You can tell me anything."

"It's kind of gross," she says. "It happened back when I was twelve."

And I'm, like, shaking my head over the notion that her mother's had her slaving away in the paper route mines since she was prepubescent.

"Back then," she goes on, "my big sister was still helping with the route, so Mom would drop me off with a bag and I'd deliver my houses walking while she and Ambith delivered another section. It wasn't till I was fourteen that she let me drive sometimes. So I was walking along kind of daydreaming—or actually, I guess you'd call it early-in-the-morning dreaming—and all of a sudden this man walks out from behind a hedge, totally naked!"

"Jesus. What'd you do?"

"I dropped my bag and took off running. I must've run four blocks before I saw our truck, and I stood in the middle of the street waving for Mom to come down and get me."

"Did she call the cops on the dude?"

"Uh, actually, no." She looks down at her limp pizza. "She made me go back and get the bag and throw the rest of my houses."

I can't believe it. What a mom! "I'll bet you were pretty scared walking around there with some naked maniac in the bushes."

"I was," she says. "I kept thinking I heard something sneaking up from behind me. Later, I saw him walking around from the back of another house, but this time he got in his car and drove off. It was a Lexus. I always thought that was odd."

"Next time that happens, don't let your mom make you go back."

"Next time? Do you think it'll actually happen again?"

"Well, no, maybe not that exact thing."

I'm getting ready to explain some of my theories on the prevalence of the weird in daily life, but I'm interrupted when some girl I don't remember ever seeing before barges up and says to Aimee, "So, he finally got here, did he?"

Aimee's head sinks toward her shoulders. "Hi, Krystal."

I stand up the way a gentleman should and put out my hand. "My name's Sutter Keely. Glad to meet you."

She doesn't take my hand. "I know who you are."

Aimee goes, "This is Krystal Krittenbrink."

And Krystal's like, "We've been friends since second grade." Somehow she makes it sound snotty, like I'm an insignificant insect in the scheme of their glorious friendship. I know her type—all her life her parents spoiled her and told her she was "the most specialest little honey-bunny snookems in the world" and she never figured out that the rest of the universe doesn't necessarily share that opinion.

The fact is she's very much a non-beautiful fat girl. Whereas Cassidy's voluptuous with grand monumental curves, Krystal Krittenbrink is what you'd call amorphous—a blob. She has a very little face in the middle of a big pink head. Her mouth alone is about the size of a dime. But the real clincher is she has her dull brown hair done up in this weird ponytail that starts at about the crown of her head. You have to know she looks in the mirror every morning and thinks that is the height of style.

She's Aimee's friend, though, so I invite her to have a seat, but she just turns to Aimee and says, "Hurry up. The meeting starts in like five minutes."

"Oh, what kind of meeting is it?" I ask, trying to show some polite interest.

But Krystal's like, "French club. You wouldn't know anything about it."

So Aimee goes, "Why don't you go ahead, Krystal? I can be a little late."

"Don't be stupid," says Krystal. "The whole meeting won't last but like five or ten minutes."

Aimee looks a little stung, but you can tell she's used to Krystal calling her stupid. "I guess that's right," she says and turns to me. "Actually, I guess I'm going to have to go. I forgot about the meeting. I'm sorry."

"But you haven't finished your pizza."

"She can take it with her," says Krystal.

"Yeah, I guess I can just take it with me."

"Don't forget about tutoring me for Algebra."

A smile pops back onto Aimee's face, but Krystal goes, "That'll be a waste of time."

I just ignore her and keep my gaze fixed on Aimee. "Why don't you give me your number?"

"My number?"

"Yeah, your phone number."

"Like my home phone number?"

"Yeah. Or your cell phone number." She seems to be having a hard time comprehending the concept. Maybe no guy ever asked for her phone number before.

"It'll have to be my home number. I don't have a cell phone." She starts digging through her backpack for a piece of paper and a pen, and Krystal's right at her shoulder going, "Come on, let's go."

Aimee gets the number dashed off and hands it to me. There's a smiley face at the end.

"I'll call you and we'll set up a time," I say. "When are you home?"

"Who knows?" says Krystal as she practically drags Aimee away. "You think all she has to do is wait around the house for you to call?"

Chapter 23

Surprisingly, my mother really does phone me at home around two o'clock to see if I'm living up to the rules of my magnificent groundation. She's all stern and everything, giving me the *Mister this* and the *Mister that*. I don't know why calling someone *Mister* is supposed to underline the seriousness of a situation, but it seems to be a pretty common tactic among adults.

I've got to hand it to my mom this time. She really has stuck to her guns. Again, she comes with the line about the military academy. To be honest, though, it was kind of shitty of me to set Kevin's suit on fire. But it's not like I did it on purpose or anything.

Ricky's cocked back in the recliner about five feet away during the whole conversation. When I hang up, he's like, "Dude, do your folks really think you're buying this military academy yarn? I mean, you're graduating in like three months. Even if they did stick you in there, what good would it do for three months?"

"Yeah, I know. It doesn't make sense. I think it's just their way of letting me know how much they think I suck." I head for the bar. I don't have to work today, so it seems like a good time to mix up a pitcher of stout martinis.

"I'll tell you what," Ricky says. "They wouldn't think it was too fucking fortuitous if you got spit out into the real military and they sent you over to Iraq to get blown up like Jeremy Holtz's brother."

"I don't know. They like to pretend they're all patriotic. It'd be the best thing that ever happened to them if I got blown up over there. They'd be bragging about it for years. Might even get their pictures in the paper pretending to cry over my flag-draped coffin."

And Ricky's like, "Oh right. As if that's real patriotic. People like that go around acting like if you want peace, then you're some kind of anti-American, anti-military traitor scum. Seems more pro-military to me if you want to stop getting Americans killed. I've grown up around military people all my life—my dad, my uncles. I don't want them even leaving town if there's not a damn good reason for it. This fucking war pisses me off. You know what it is?"

"A quagmire?"

"Oh, it's quaggish to the extreme, dude. It's a sewer swamp. With turds the size of ottomans. I mean, is that what the politicians think of us, that the youth of today are nothing but roadside-bomb magnets for their trumped-up invasion? My dad was in the navy, and I wouldn't mind joining it myself, but I'm not about to now. The whole thing's run by vampires, dude. Virulent atomic vampires. And their leader is, like, this ancient, bulbous-headed bloodsucker named Generalissimo Hal E. Burton. Jesus. You think I'm fighting in an atomic vampire war? Give me a break. Sign me up for the protest movement instead. But where is it? There isn't one. It's like everyone's lazy. Or brainwashed."

"Look out," I say. "You better stop that kind of talk, you damn hippie. Generalissimo Hal might have this room bugged right now. Next thing you know we'll be over in some Cuban prison chained to the floor without a lawyer in sight."

"Dude, that'd be funny if it wasn't so real."

When I get my pitcher of martinis just right, I offer Ricky one, but he declines it. "I'm watching my waistline," he says sarcastically.

98

I wave the glass in front of his face. "Come on. You know you want it."

"No, really, dude. I'm cutting back."

"That's okay. More for me." I sit down and flick on the TV.

"It's my new resolution," says Ricky. "No more partying during the week."

"What about the herb?"

"I'm cutting back on that too."

I study him for a moment. "Listen to you," I say. "The king of weed. One date, a weekend full of phone calls, a Monday lunch, and already Bethany has you remodeled."

"That has nothing to do with it, dude. I'm just worn out with it. It's old. I need a change."

I hold up my glass to the light. "The perfect martini never gets old."

"I'm serious," Ricky says. "It's not working for me anymore, not doing it all the time. Back when it was new, that's when it was fabulous. Everything's fabulous when it's new. Like when you're a little kid. Everything is a sparkling wonder."

"Oh yeah." I take a long pull on the martini. "Childhood was a fantastic country to live in."

"No doubt," says Ricky. "I remember going to a bank with my dad when I was like four or something. And, you know, nowadays a bank lobby is the most boring place in the world next to the post office, but back then it was magic. They had this little pool of water in there with a fountain in the middle of it. I couldn't believe my eyes. A pool of water—indoors! I'm calling my dad over, telling him to look at this, and he's like, 'Yeah, it's a fountain.' Like it's nothing special at all.

"But then I see that it's not just a pool of water—it has coins in it. So I'm like, 'Dad, look, there's money in there!' And he goes, 'Yeah, people throw coins in fountains and make wishes.' Wishes! Dude! This is getting better all the time. It's a *magic* fountain. I'm in total awe. But there my dad is, writing out a deposit slip with no idea of how completely amazing the world is."

"Yeah," I say, "I had a moment like that with my mother and a dead cow along the side of the road."

"So then what happens?" Ricky asks. "You get to be about eleven or twelve and everything's old hat. They've drummed the miraculous out of you, but you don't want it to be like that. You want the miraculous. You want everything to still be new. So when you take that drink or you smoke that blaze, it's like you're getting that back."

"Gotta love the miraculous," I say. "Does all this mean you want a drink after all?"

"No, dude. I'm saying that stuff gets old too. It has its own built-in obsolescence like everything else. That's how our system works. It's a giant con game. One thing gets old, then you have to buy the next thing that gets old, then the next thing. Our whole society's a training ground for addicts."

"You think so, Professor?" I love to get him rolling with his theories.

"Of course, dude. I'll bet a million bucks someone's already invented a perpetual motion machine, but the atomic vampires squelched it. Same thing with fabrics that never wear out."

I'm like, "Yeah, I bet they have golf tees that never break and corndog trees too."

"You may be joking," Ricky says, "but you're probably right."

"I'll miss it when you stop smoking weed and don't have any more theories like this."

He scoffs at that. "I don't need the weed to fuel my theories, dude. It's all right in front of your face. I mean, look at MTV." He points to the TV. The screen's filled with hard-bodied college girls and guys in swimsuits flailing around to some schlock song.

"They've even turned our own bodies into products, dude. Abs and mamms and glutes and pecs. You have to buy the next workout equipment or diet book or whatever. Or you have to go into the plastic doc and have him tuck your tummy or suck the fat out of your ass."

I'm like, "Yeah, it's weird, dude. Embrace it."

But he's all, "I'm not embracing this bullshit. Don't you see what I'm talking about? They're turning us into products, dude. The same atomic vampires are behind it. They send out their minions to hypnotize you with the latest pop-singer-slash-stripper, or the newest video game or cell phone or the latest *blam-blam-kablooie!* movie at the cineplex. And then, once they have you hypnotized, they lure you into their huge mega-electric castle."

"A mega-electric castle? Cool."

"No, it's not cool. Because once they get you in there they run you through this CAT-scan-looking machine called the de-soul-inator, and when you come out on the other side, you're nothing but a product."

"And what's this product called?"

"*Emptiness*, dude, that's what it's called. And for the rest of your life, they sell you over and over, right to the end when they package you one last time and plant you in the ground."

"Wow," I say. "Are you sure you haven't partaken of the weed today?"

"Not a puff." He gives his head a weary shake. "I'm telling you, dude. I need a change. I'm fed up with the atomic vampires. I don't want to be their product. I don't want to be the sacrament for their Holy Trinity. You know what their Holy Trinity is?"

"Beer, wine, and whisky?"

He waves that off. "No, dude, the great Holy Trinity of the atomic vampires consists of the sex god, the money god, and the power god. The sex god pays tribute to the money god, and the money god pays tribute to the power god. The power god is what ruins it. The others would be okay on their own, but he's an asshole. He's the one that sends out his minions to hypnotize us with the Next New Thing. But it's not the miraculous. It's just a substitute for the miraculous. It sucks. Now, I'm not saying I don't want to have fun anymore. I just want to find something that sticks for a change."

I pause to make sure he's finished and then hold up my drink. "Amen, Brother Ricky! That was one helluva sermon."

"Is it true or not?"

"Absolutely. We all want something that sticks." I don't mention that *wanting* it is a whole different thing from actually believing you can get it.

"Well." He raises an imaginary glass in the air. "Give me another amen, Brother Sutter!"

"Amen, Brother Ricky, amen!"

"Hallelujah, brother, Hallelujah!"

We're both laughing pretty hard now. I take a nice slug off my martini and say, "I'll tell you what, after today, I'll join in with you—no more drinking till the weekend. Then we'll throw an extra big drunk."

"I thought you were grounded."

"That never stopped me before. I've got a window in my bedroom, you know."

He doesn't come back with anything right away, but finally he lets it out that he's going to some concert with Bethany on Friday and having dinner with her and her parents on Saturday.

I'm like, "Dinner with her parents? Jesus, dude. You are getting the makeover treatment."

He shrugs. "I just want to be with her, like you wanted to be with Cassidy."

"Yeah, but I didn't want to be with her the whole weekend every week."

"Why don't you ask out your paper route girl for Friday or Saturday? Aren't you supposed to call her up sometime this afternoon anyway?"

"Hey, I told you—I'm not going to ask her out for a date. Let me repeat, she is not a girl I'm interested in having sex with. Not now or any time in the future. I will not have sex with her in a car. I will not have sex with her in a bar. I will not have sex with her in a tree. I will not have sex with her in a lavator-ee. I will not have sex with her in a chair. I will not have sex with her anywhere."

"Oh right, I forgot. You're out to save her soul. Give me a hallelujah for Brother Sutter and his messianic complex."

"My what?"

"Messianic complex. That means you think you have to go around trying to save everybody."

"Not everybody. Just this one girl."

"Hallelujah, brother!"

Chapter 24

Sometimes I have trouble sleeping. It's weird—I can feel exhausted but still, I just lie there wide awake, staring up into the dark with all sorts of ideas bombarding me like dead pelicans. Tonight, for example, I get to thinking about Geech's stale military school proposition, wondering if maybe it's not such a terrible idea after all.

Maybe I should've joined up when I was about fourteen or fifteen, worked hard for a year—marching ten miles a day, hustling through obstacle courses, scuttling under barbed wire with a wooden rifle cradled in my arms. Then come back home muscled up and spit-shined and tight as a snare drum on the inside. How else are you supposed to know when you're not a kid anymore in this society?

I remember reading about these primitive initiation rituals in school. They had one where they take the kid way out into the wilderness and drop him off and he has to get back by himself without any weapons or tools. He's just out there with his bare hands, digging up roots to eat, making fires with rocks and sticks or whatever. I mean, he could starve or a mountain lion could eat him or something, but that's all part of the test. When he gets back, he's a man. And not only that, he finds his Spirit Guide. Talk about embracing the weird.

But nowadays they don't do anything but leave you at home by yourself with a kitchen full of potato chips and soft drinks. Then, in your bedroom, you've got your TV, video games, and the Internet. What do they expect you to get from that? A big fat case of *I don't give a shit?*

These days, a kid has to go looking for his own initiation or make his own personal war to fight since the wars the atomic vampires throw are so hard to believe in. It's like Ricky says—every time they trump one up, it gets worse.

If I was in charge, it'd be different. You wouldn't have to go to military school or get dropped off in the wilderness or fight in a war. Instead, you'd head off for what I'd call the Teen Corps. It'd be like the Peace Corps, only for teenagers. You'd have to go around and, like, pile up sandbags for people when hurricanes blow in and replant trees in deforested areas and help get medical attention to hillbillies and so forth. You'd do it for a whole year, and then, when you got back, you'd get the right to vote and buy alcohol and everything else. You'd be grown.

I have most of the details of the plan worked out when sleep finally takes me.

Unfortunately, the next morning the excitement wears off. It's too late for me anyway. If I were a dreamer like Bob Lewis, I'd wax on about becoming a politician and establishing the Teen Corps for the next generation or whatever, but like I say, I'm more of a right-now kind of guy. And right now I have my own miniature aid plan to work on—going to Aimee's to get tutored.

See, by letting her help me, I'll be helping her. She gets confidence and I get the satisfaction of bringing confidence to someone who needs it worse than a pop singer needs rehab. Hey, it may not change the world, but for the two of us, it's a win-win situation.

The problem is, since officially I'm grounded, I have to pass the idea by Mom over breakfast. Usually, in the mornings, she tries to avoid talking to me—except maybe to say, "Get it yourself"—but when I hit her with the Aimee proposition, she hits back with a barrage of questions that are supposed to sound like she's trying to get a read on Aimee's character.

I know better. What she really wants to know is whether Aimee has any uppity-up social connections. If that was the case, I'm sure Mom wouldn't have any problem with me going over there. But, of course, since Aimee's mother is nothing more than the queen of the paper route and the Indian casino, Mom suspects I must have some sneaky ulterior motive.

"So," she says, "how do I know you're not just trying to get out of being grounded all afternoon?"

I go, "Hey, if you don't believe me, why don't you call her up and ask her?"

And she's like, "Because, for all I know, this is just some little thing you want to date, and she'll say anything you tell her to."

"Believe me," I say. "I do not want to date this girl."

Why does everyone have to automatically assume it's a sex thing?

Mom's still not convinced, so I tell her to call Mr. Aster and ask him whether I need a tutor. That does the trick. She'll never call him. I know all too well that she doesn't like to get involved with my actual schooling if she can help it. Something must have happened in her childhood to make her afraid of teachers.

So we work out a deal. I still can't drive to school, but I can drive to Aimee's in the afternoons. And Geech will check my gas level every evening to make sure I don't go driving around all over everywhere. Like I can't just put more gas in the tank if I want to. Jesus.

Chapter 25

Driving over to Aimee's that afternoon, my intentions are good, but I have to admit this girl's going to be a challenge. Judging from how her parents and her best friend treat her, she may be the biggest pushover I've seen since Kenny Hoyle.

Poor little Kenny. He reminded me of a character out of a fairy tale. He lived down the street with his stepfather and three stepbrothers. His mom committed suicide. The stepbrothers were enormous thugs. While they were out vandalizing road signs or inhaling spray paint or whatever, scrawny little eight-year-old Kenny was outside cleaning the windows or pulling weeds or pushing their giant lawnmower up and down the steep front yard in the hundred-degree heat. But you knew there wasn't any fairy godmother waiting out there to zap Kenny into some shining prince. All I could do was go over and help him mow the lawn now and then before he got sucked underneath the mower and spit out the side like a batch of hamburger meat.

Anyway, I'm expecting Aimee's house to be a real shack, but it's actually a lot like the house I lived in before the era of Geech—basically a small brick cube with a gray roof that needs new shingles and a scruffy little bare yard with no trees or shrubs or flowers or anything else. At least my old house had an overgrown hedge and a cool redbud tree to climb in, but this house doesn't have even a shot glass's worth of character to it.

After taking a hit of whisky with a mouthwash chaser, I head up to the cramped porch and give the doorframe a jazzy little knock. Inside, a whiny voice calls out, "Aimee! Your boyfriend's here!" Which is followed by Aimee going, "Please, Shane, don't embarrass me, okay?"

A second later, the lock clicks and the door opens.

"Sutter," she says with a cautious smile. "You're here."

"Right on time."

Something's different about her. It takes me a moment, but then I realize she's wearing lipstick. Usually, she doesn't wear any makeup at all, and let me tell you—this isn't better.

As for the inside of the house, it's an absolute sty—clothes piled on the backs of the faded sofa and recliner, fast-food sacks gaping open on the coffee table, obsolete VHS tapes littering the floor. And in the middle of all this, her little brother's sprawled out, his legs flinching and twitching as he proceeds to blow up bug-eyed, saw-toothed video game aliens on their ancient PlayStation.

"Um, this is my little brother, Shane," Aimee says. "He's eleven."

"Hi there, Shane."

He doesn't bother to look at me. "Mom says you're supposed to go to the store and get a big bottle of Dr Pepper," he says, his hands still twisting and popping at the game.

"I'll get it later," she tells him, but he's like, "You better get it now. Randy might want some pretty soon."

"That's okay," she says. "There's a little bit left in the fridge."

"I'm just saying what Mom said."

"You know, Shane." I step up next to the sofa. "You could go get it yourself. There's a convenience store right down at the end of the block."

Shane responds by splurting out a raspberry.

Aimee laughs nervously and gives me a sheepish *boys-will-be-boys* look.

Usually, I'd hit the kid with a scalding putdown—which

I'm all too capable of doing—but that's not going to help Aimee any, so I'm just like, "That's no way to act toward a guest, little man."

.And he's like, "You're my stinky sister's guest, not mine."

Aimee's face flushes crimson all the way to the tips of her ears. It looks good on her, better than the lipstick. "Why don't we go back to my room to study," she says, waving her hand in the direction of the hall.

"Ladies first," I say. She seems like she could use the gentlemanly treatment for a change.

"You all better be quiet," calls Shane. "Randy's trying to sleep."

Randy turns out to be their mother's disability-collecting boyfriend. "Don't worry," Aimee says. "One time Shane set off a bottle rocket in the bathroom and Randy never woke up."

After wading through the debris in the living room and hall, I'm awestruck when Aimee opens the door to her room. It's like that moment in *The Wizard of Oz* when Dorothy opens the door and sees the land of Oz for the first time, only instead of going from black-and-white to color, this goes from an absolute dump to an awesome, almost geometric neatness.

Welcome to Aimee's world.

The giant map on the wall stretches out so smooth you'd think maybe Aimee ironed it, and the same goes for the big picture of the Milky Way and the pencil drawings that hang on the other walls. The desk looks thrift-store cheap and the computer is practically twentieth-century like their VCR, but everything—the pens and notebooks and ceramic cats—is arranged to perfection. Her chest of drawers is similarly cheap and neat, but the thing that really strikes me is her books.

A plastic snap-together set of bookshelves stands against one wall, row after tidy row of paperback books lining each shelf. And even though she ran out of shelf space and had to stack probably a hundred more paperbacks against the wall, those rows are just as spruce as the others.

"You must really like to read," I say, admiring the stacks.

"They're mostly science fiction." She gazes at the books with supreme fondness. "Some are mysteries and I have quite a few old classics like *Wuthering Heights* and *Jane Eyre*."

I pick up a book titled something like *The Androids of NGC 3031*. On the cover, a woman android with one hell of a bod dashes away from low-flying spaceships as they shoot pink laser bursts at her. "This looks interesting," I say, but what I'm really thinking is, Wow, Aimee, science fiction? Really, could you try any harder to brand yourself with the mark of the nerd herd? What's next, anime?

"I like to think about space," she says apologetically.

"Space is cool."

"I want to work for NASA someday." She sounds kind of tentative, like she's afraid I'll think that's a stupid ambition or something.

"That'd be spectacular," I say. "I really think you ought to."

"Yeah," she says, a new enthusiasm sparking in her eyes. "And after I've worked there for about five years and get some money saved up, I'm going to buy a horse ranch to live on."

"I don't see what could be better than that. I guess that's why you have all these drawings of horses on the walls." I walk over and have a closer look at the drawings. Actually, her horses look more like dogs, but there's no need to mention that. I'm pretty sure, for her, drawing them is a lot more important than what they end up looking like.

"I guess this is you riding the horses, huh?"

"Um, no. That's Commander Amanda Gallico from the *Bright Planets* books."

She's standing right next to me now, and I know she sees a lot more in the pictures than I do.

"What's her story?"

"She commands the Neexo Ark 451. They're escaping from the Dark Galaxy and trying to find their way to the Bright Planets system."

In the drawings, Commander Amanda Gallico looks a little too big for the horses, at least her body does. It's all athletic and superheroey, but her head's kind of small and I'm still of the opinion that she looks like Aimee in the face, without glasses.

"You must really like her," I say.

"Yeah," she says with that drawn-out, half-committed way she has of saying anything positive. "I guess she's kind of like my hero and everything."

This is all too heartbreaking. I mean, I quit on heroes by the time I got to fifth grade. This girl needs some help and she needs it now.

So I'm like, "You know what? You'll be my own personal hero if you can straighten me out on this algebra business. Where should we do it?"

I realize my wording might have sounded a touch on the sexual side as we both look at her neat little bed with its plaid comforter. It's the only furniture in the room big enough for two people. She says, "Um," but that's as much as she can get out.

So I go, "Me, I always do my homework on the floor where I can spread everything out."

That sounds good to her, so we get down to it. As soon as we start, she clicks into a more confident mode. But it's a sort of soft confidence. A kind confidence. She could easily start coming off all superior or even ridicule me for my mathematical idiocy, but she doesn't even come close to that. She doesn't need to. Here in the realm of books she's self-assured. She has some of the control she doesn't have anywhere else. And you know what? If I was a better listener, I'll bet she could get me to understand some things that Mr. Asterhole never came close to.

Chapter 26

After we get my homework done—or I guess I should say after *she* gets my homework done—she starts explaining some more basics that I need to get me through the rest of the semester. It's a nice thought, but my attention span isn't really up to it, so I decide to steer her onto another topic.

"You know," I say, leaning back against the side of her bed and looking at her bookshelves. "With as much reading as you do, you should try writing your own book."

She studies me for a second as if she's not sure whether I'm making fun of her.

"I'm serious," I tell her. "I'll bet you could write a science-fiction novel that'd sell a million copies."

She sets her pen down and says real soft, "I don't know about a million copies, but I am writing one. I've got about two hundred pages done, and it'll probably end up being about six hundred pages long."

I'm like, "Jesus. Six hundred pages?"

"Yeah," she says. I'm beginning to see that her "yeahs" are almost always two syllables, one for "yes" and the other for "but I don't know if anything will ever come of it."

"That's cool. What's it about?" I ask, though I suspect I may be opening a can full of boring.

She's like, "Do you really want to hear about it?"

And I'm, "Yeah." One syllable.

She starts off telling me that this is just going to be the summary version, but it ends up getting pretty involved. And surprisingly it's not boring at all. The basic idea is that there's this teenage girl who gets beamed aboard a spaceship while she's out throwing her paper route, and the crew—which consists of a race of genius horses—recruit her to help fly the ship back to its home planet. The twist is that it turns out the home planet is really Earth of the future, where genius horses and humans coexist on an equal level, and the girl—who is somehow really of Earthling descent—has been living among aliens on the planet Gracknack all along.

As she's telling the story, it hits me—this is how she escapes. She runs away to her perfectly tidy room and disappears into faraway galaxies. I'll bet it's the same with her schoolwork because, from what I can tell, she gets no encouragement in that direction from her family.

Her brother and mother and Randy, the unemployed boyfriend, are Gracknackians. They'll never understand her. And her best friend, Krystal Krittenbrink, is a big, type-A nerd who treats her like an employee in a Gracknackian geek factory. But this room is Aimee's space capsule and she's a long-distance galactic traveler, winning every battle along the way.

Or almost every battle. Right as she's getting to the end of her story, a scratchy voice calls out from the next room, "Aimee! Hey, Aimee! Bring me a Dr Pepper, why don't you?"

It's Randy. He woke up and now he wants room service. Aimee's shoulders slump. "I'll be right back."

After a couple of minutes, Randy's voice booms out again. "What's this supposed to be? You know I like my tall blue glass. This is like a thimble or something."

If Aimee says anything back, I can't hear her, but Randy's loud and clear. "Well, go down and get some more. What have you been doing all afternoon?"

So Aimee slinks back and tells me she's sorry but she has to go to the 7-Eleven. It doesn't seem to have crossed her mind that

I might drive her. When I volunteer, she's like, "You don't have to do that. It's my fault. I should have gone right after school."

And I'm, "What are you talking about? It'll take like a minute and a half. Of course I'm going to drive you."

That perks her up a little, but any trace of the confidence she showed earlier has shriveled up about to the size of plankton. It's even worse after we pick up the Dr Pepper. Looking through the windshield at her front porch, she has this expression on her face like her spaceship just crashed and she's found herself back on Gracknack.

So the next thing I know my mouth's open and these words are spilling out: "You know what? There's a party this Saturday. I think you should go with me."

It was like a reflex action. I had to do it. What else was I going to do, let her traipse back into that house with nothing?

True to form, her response is a surprised "Me?"

And I'm, "Yeah. You and me."

And she's, "A party?" Like I've been speaking Mongolian or Gracknackian maybe.

"Yeah, a party. Saturday night. You and me. I'll come by and get you around 8:30. What do you say?"

"Um, okay?"

"Is that an answer or a question?"

"No," she says. "I mean, yes, I'll go." And this time it's a one syllable *yes*.

"All right, then. Fabulous. We'll have fun."

And as she walks back to her house with her head held high and the liter of Dr Pepper dangling casually from one hand, I feel pretty damn good about myself. It was a drastic measure, but it needed to be done. And it's not like I asked her out for a date or anything. I just figured a party would be good for her. I know it'll be good for me.

Chapter 27

Friday night and I'm grounded. Of course, I could easily sneak out. The climb down from my second-story window is much easier than the climb up to Cassidy's window, and I can't remember the last time either Mom or Geech paid a visit to my room in the evening. They're probably afraid they'll catch me spankificating the mighty Cyclops to online porn. Which I'm sure Geech got caught at many a time during his stupendously boring teen years when porn was something you could hide under your mattress.

But the thing is I'll have to sneak out tomorrow night for the party, so I decide a Friday night in the privacy of my room won't be a bad change of pace. After all, I have my TV, my computer, my phone, and my tunes, not to mention my little blue ice chest for my 7UP and whiskies. Basically, I'm all set.

The first order of business is to punch up a little Dean Martin for mood music. There is no better introduction to a session with the brown bottle. Dino is the Man. I have the essential collection—"Everybody Loves Somebody Sometime," "You're Nobody 'Til Somebody Loves You," "Love Me, Love Me," "Little Ole Wine Drinker, Me," and my theme song, "Ain't Love a Kick in the Head." Smooth, smooth stuff.

Now, I'm on record about how I hate the clothes I have to wear and sell at Mr. Leon's, but if I could wear a tuxedo all the time like Dino, I'd do it. That'd be the only fashion statement worth making. And out of all the Rat Pack dudes, Dino was by far the coolest. The Rat Pack consisted of these ultra-suave playboy singers from back in the days before the hippie bands changed everything—Dean, Frank Sinatra, Sammy Davis, Jr. These guys knew how to party. They tore Las Vegas to pieces.

I watched a biography of Dino on TV, and there was this woman who said, "Frank Sinatra thought he was God. Dean knew he was." How about that? I mean, the dude had panache. They also said the whisky glass he waved around while he sang was actually filled with apple juice, but I never did believe that.

So here I am—Friday night—waving my own whisky (no apple juice) glass around, crooning along with Dino while Jennifer Love Hewitt's spanktacular breasts cruise majestically across the TV screen. I could be thinking about a million things but for some reason Commander Amanda Gallico pops into my head.

Since she's Aimee's big hero, I figure I ought to go online and study up on the intrepid commander a bit so we'll have something to talk about Saturday night. See, this is part of my grand master plan for Aimee's inner makeover. She needs to know that her dreams are important. And I'm not being fake about this either. Space travel, super-intelligent horses, working for NASA, owning a vast ranch—you really have to admire dreams like that.

I had big dreams once myself. I wasn't much into science fiction, but when I was a kid and still heavily into baseball, I used to pretend I was Rocky Ramirez, all-time major-league MVP. The Rockinator wasn't a real baseball player. He was my own concoction—a center fielder with superpowers. For example, he could run a hundred miles an hour and even fly if he had to. Plus, he wielded a nine-hundred-pound bat. It never crossed my mind that the major leagues would probably ban him, even though he didn't take steroids like everyone else.

But my number one biggest fantasy was that my parents would get back together. I dreamed that one so hard that sometimes I'd have to go look in the closet to see if Dad's stuff was there. Then we moved in with Geech, and damn, my heart went splat on the carpet when I saw his stupid striped shirts and cheap slacks hanging up where my dad's jeans jacket and Levi's should have been.

That type of dream just kind of wears out with time like a favorite old T-shirt. One day, it's nothing but tatters and all you can do is throw it over on the rag pile with the others. Still, I can't help looking back every now and then at how it used to be.

Summer evenings in the backyard, all of us together. I must've been three or four and my dad would grab my wrists and swing me around and around in circles. When he finally set me down, I couldn't do anything but stagger from the dizziness. I loved it.

And one time, we made a fort out of lawn chairs and blankets and sat inside while Dad told werewolf stories and Mom leaned into his side, looking at him like he was the original Mr. Wonderful. It seems like it's always summer in my memories of those days. The cold memories—the fighting memories—when those start to creep in, it's time to move on.

Chapter 28

Commander Amanda Gallico is no challenge for Google. You'd be amazed at how many sites there are for her. I never heard of her before, but someone sure has. Before hitting the fan sites, I browse the more official sites—the bookstores, the author's page, sci-fi magazines, even a Wikipedia entry. The more I read the more I like this space chick.

Sure, she's brave and has a big rack and all, but she's also a philosopher. According to Wikipedia, she believes that humanity has wasted too much energy chasing after power. They've made the mistake of thinking that power over others and leadership are the same thing.

As I read, I can practically hear Aimee explaining it in her soft marshmallow voice. We're riding together through cyberspace and she's going on about how, according to Commander Amanda, the drive for power is not as super-evolved as the drive for well-being. Deep down, women know this, see. Nurturing is their natural gig. They've seen how ultimate power has pushed dickhead dictators—like this Hitler-type dude, Rolio Blue, of the Dark Galaxy—into some kind of raging, slobbering paranoid freak while any sense of well-being flies completely out the old spaceship porthole.

On the other hand, a true leader, like Commander Amanda, doesn't seek power over others. Instead, she's out to lead them into greater and greater prosperity, both inside and out. So instead of going all crazoid and unraveling like Rolio Blue the evil douche, she gains more and more inner strength.

Book after book, she becomes more amazing as she searches for the Bright Planets system where she's going to build a whole new super-evolved society that's like one big, blooming family.

Now, if you ask me, that's some pretty deep stuff. I wish I had a blaze to smoke to go along with it. Maybe then I could almost believe Amanda Gallico was out there, coming to save me and Earth from its own Rolio Blues.

Who knows how many whiskies I've put away or how long I've been surfing through fan sites, message boards, blogs, and so forth. That's how it is online—there's no time in cyberspace. It's almost like everything physical evaporates, and it's just your mind and the different sites floating in a void. For some reason, this makes me feel really close to Aimee. I know her mind's floated in and out of these same sites tons of times. She knows everything about the Dark Galaxy and the Bright Planets system up and down and back and forth. I can feel her here—this real gentle presence—just like Commander Amanda Gallico, searching for a place to flourish.

Suddenly, I'm startled back into myself by a booming voice: "You've got mail!" For a second, I feel like I've been invaded right in the middle of something intimate. But then I'm like, Wouldn't it be weird if it's from Aimee? It's not, though. It's from Cassidy.

I'm almost scared to read it. I really don't need to get bawled out by a girlfriend who's not even my girlfriend anymore. After a long pause, I open it, and what do you know—it's the opposite of a bawling out. She's actually waxing sentimental all over the place, going on about how she misses the fun we used to have, the wild times, the spontaneity. She wants us to be friends again.

Yeah, right. *Friends*.

It doesn't take *CSI Oklahoma* to see what's going on here. Marcus West—Mr. Perfection—is starting to petrify her brain cells with boredom. We all know what a snooze perfection can be. I'll guarantee he never ditches school. Never does one damn thing he hasn't planned out a week in advance. You won't see Marcus West falling off her roof in the middle of a school day. The guy doesn't even drink. How fun could he be?

No, I'm pretty sure it's more than friendship Cassidy's itching for right about now. But you won't catch the Sutterman playing it any way but cool. With perfect Dean Martin nonchalance, I dash off a quick note about how being friends would be fine by me. Yes, I can always use another good buddy. But at the end, I can't help myself. I have to add on a tempting little note about how there's going to be a party at the lake tomorrow night. I'll be there. It'll be fun. Cheap beer.

My finger hovers for a moment above the mouse, probably about a microsecond, before I click *send*.

Chapter 29

Lakeside on Saturday night, it's more than a little nippy. That's Oklahoma for you. Warm February and then here comes March and a cold spell has to move in. Still it's not nearly cold enough for the kind of jacket Aimee's sporting. It's this huge, down-filled purple monster that makes her look like a giant billiard ball. She might be the only girl I've ever met who still hasn't learned to sacrifice bodily comfort for fashion's sake. She did paint on the lipstick again, but putting lipstick on a billiard ball still doesn't give it sex appeal.

The girl is definitely making it tough. How am I supposed to pair her off with any of these party-hound dudes when she won't do her part?

And that is the plan. She needs a social life beyond Krystal Krittenbrink. She needs a dude, someone kind of like me, only not me. Cody Dennis, for instance. Cody's a lot of fun, but he's not what you might call advanced in the sex department. The last thing Aimee needs is some letch dude drooling on her.

One problem—Cody is actually less skilled even than Ricky when it comes to talking to the ladies. But I figure I'll take care of the conversation part until they warm up to each other. Then I'll wander off about the time Cassidy makes her fashionably late entrance, and *boom*, all will be right with the universe again.

There's a good crew out, just like I knew there would be. Someone lit an old mattress on fire—who knows where that came from—and now everyone's stoking it with dead branches.

The flames reflect on the lake along with the stars. The wood smoke smells good.

Probably about twenty kids have already shown up. Someone hoisted a keg onto one of the concrete picnic tables, and Gerald the dancing maniac's going full speed right next to it. I swear, the way this guy moves, he must have no bones.

"See anyone you know?" I ask Aimee.

She looks around. "Uh, I know who a lot of people are, but I don't really know them."

"You will." I reach up to give the back of her neck a little squeeze, but her giant puffy collar gets in the way.

First things first, we head over to the keg. I have to admit that on the way several people slap me on the back and shake my hand. From left and right, it's "Hey, Sutter, what's going on? Ready to party hearty?" Someone asks if I plan on chugging a beer while standing on my head, but I play it off like I've never heard of such a thing. The next guy calls out, "Sutter, my man, let's see you run through the bonfire tonight."

I wave him off. "Been there, done that."

At the keg, the three dudes in line turn and give me a salute. I'm just the kind of guy people like to see at a party, I guess.

Not too surprisingly, once I take charge of the spigot, Aimee mentions she doesn't exactly drink alcohol. I tell her that's okay, all she has to do is hold on to a beer and at least give off the impression that she might be having fun. That said, I chug my beer and immediately pour another one just to get started off on the right foot.

The bad news is Cody Dennis is nowhere around to introduce her to. The worse news is here comes Jason Doyle.

"Hello there, Sutterman," he says in that way he has of pretending to be smarmy while all the while he really *is* being smarmy. "I guess it's officially a party now that you're here."

"Must be."

He looks Aimee over, sizing up the down-filled coat. "You know what, Sutter? You better hang on to this balloon before she sails off over the treetops."

Luckily, Aimee doesn't seem to get the joke. "Well," I say. "Thanks for stopping by, Jason. You take care now. Don't let the bedbugs bite."

He clamps his hand on my arm. "Whoa, there, buddy. What's your hurry? Aren't you gonna introduce me?"

Now let me explain right here that Jason Doyle is the last person I had in mind to introduce Aimee to. The dude is a full-on letch. Anything in a bra and panties is fair game in his book. Check that. Anything in a *training bra* and panties. Just last fall, one of his best friends—Ike Tucker—found him fooling around with Ike's thirteen-year-old sister. Okay, so maybe she did have a bit of a body on her, but still, *thirteen?* Needless to say, Ike kicked his ass. Actually, Ike cracked his head open with an alarm clock. Took about a million stitches to sew him up. They're friends again now, though.

The point is—I can tell from the look on his face, Jason is already wondering what's going on under the giant purple coat. Is there a plump set of boobies wrapped up in there, a sweet ass? It's all a mystery, but he's more than ready to do the detective work necessary to solve it.

"Hey, check it out," I say, looking over his shoulder, "Alisa Norman is sure looking fine tonight. That red sweater is a scorcher."

Jason looks across the party grounds to where Alisa is laughing with some of her friends. She is not wearing a giant puffy coat.

"Spicy," says Jason. "But what the hell? Wherever she is, Denver Quigley is bound to be close by."

"Not this time," I say. "Didn't you hear? They're over. She

jettisoned him like a lump of frozen turds out of a 747. She's on the prowl."

"No shit?"

"I shit you not."

He stands there sizing up the situation. The red sweater is impossible to resist. "I'll catch up with you two later on. I think I'm gonna amble over and congratulate her on her good judgment."

"Go for it," I tell him.

Of course, Alisa didn't actually break up with Quigley at all, and in fact, he should be turning up any second now, but do I feel guilty? Not a chance. A guy like Jason Doyle can always use a black eye.

Chapter 30

Aimee must be a little nervous. I catch her taking a sip of beer after all. She makes a face like she just downed a pint of bleach, but at least it's a start. I try to soothe her a little by giving her the background on all the characters at the party, but I can't make much headway, what with person after person dropping by to shoot the shit with me, including three ex-girlfriends. The problem is I'm just not really a benchwarmer when it comes to parties. No sidelines for the Sutterman. I like to get right in the middle of the action.

Aimee, though, she doesn't even know what the game is, much less how to play. I try to drag her into conversations, but I'm not having much success, even when Shawnie Brown, my girlfriend from sophomore year, comes over. Shawnie's very touchy-feely and loud. She makes these great exaggerated facial expressions to go along with her stories and loves to do this deal where we talk to each other like Italian mobsters. It's hilarious. But I swear, with each second, Aimee seems to shrink further and further into the giant purple coat.

Then, finally, there he is—Cody Dennis in all his puppy dog–eyed glory.

Immediately, I wrangle him over and introduce him to Aimee. He eyes the coat but doesn't make any wisecracks. In fact, he hardly says anything. It's up to me to keep the stories cranking so that the conversation doesn't freeze into a long, hard stretch of tundra. On and on I go—about the party at Paxton's house, the one at the La Quinta Inn, and the really, really kickass one at Lake Tenkiller last summer—until finally I run out of party stories and, out of sheer luck, hit on the perfect topic—my online research into Commander Amanda Gallico and the *Bright Planets* books.

At that, the light in Aimee's eyes supercharges. She knows all the Web sites I visited and starts in quizzing me about what I thought. Surprisingly, I remember quite a bit and impress her with my take on the philosophy behind Commander Amanda's journey. "Inner prosperity," I say. "That's the thing. I mean, take me up to the Bright Planets right now. Screw a bunch of power. Screw enslaving the world. We don't need that. No way. We just need to grow wild, like alfalfa or something."

She's all over that. "You've got to read the books. You remind me of Zoster, kind of. He's the only one that really understands Commander Gallico. In the third book they get trapped in a Shuxushian cave prison together and escape into the underland of Marmoth, which is where I got my idea for the kind of ranch I want to have someday. I'll lend you the book. It's a pretty good one to start out with."

"Great," I say. And it does something to me to see her little white face beaming with so much enthusiasm against the background of purple coat. It's like my beer buzz just cranked up to a whole new level. I almost forget about Cody standing next to us, not to mention the whole reason for rounding him up in the first place.

"Sorry, Cody." I slap him on the back. "Didn't mean to leave you stranded here in a different galaxy."

But he doesn't look bored in the least. "No, man," he says. "That's cool. I'm into sci-fi. Have you guys ever read this graphic novel series, *Solar Bull* by Lawrence Black?"

I'm like, "Can't say that I have," but of course, Aimee's all, "*Solar Bull*, yes, I love *Solar Bull*."

Then there they go, leaving me behind this time. And I

know I should be happy. This is exactly why I carted Aimee out to the party. But the truth is it's a little cold here in my own little non–*Solar Bull* galaxy.

She laughs at something Cody says about a rocket-powered llama, and he reaches over and touches the sleeve of the giant purple coat. She leans a little toward him, her face still beaming. It's stupid, but I want to step in between them, maybe even lead her away somewhere. But just then, Cassidy appears in the clearing on the far side of the keg, looking like a beautiful fat goddess, and I'm transported to a new sparkling warm galaxy, far, far from Solar Bulls and llamas.

Chapter 31

I tell Aimee and Cody I'll be right back, but they barely notice. Across the way, Cassidy stands beneath the bare branch of an oak. She still hasn't seen me, but I can tell she's searching. Then Marcus West steps out of the shadows and puts his arm around her. Have you ever started to wave at someone and then realized they weren't really waving at you, so you abort and go for a head scratch instead? That's how I felt. Only instead of scratching my head, I break off my beeline for Cassidy and abruptly turn toward the keg.

My cup needs a refill anyway. It always needs a refill at a party like this. Cheap 3.2 beer. In fact, I chug one down and go for another. Cassidy and Marcus are now talking to another one of the basketball players and his girlfriend. That's all right, I tell myself. There's no reason I shouldn't go over there. Of course, Cassidy was bound to show up with Marcus. This isn't the night we hook up again. This is just the night when she realizes how inevitable it is for us to hook up again.

"So, what's up, people?" I say, approaching Cassidy's little group. "What's the deal, no one has a beer yet?"

"I'm not drinking," says Marcus. "But I see you have two beers yourself."

"I just brought an extra in case anyone else wants one." I'm looking straight at Cassidy.

"Sure," she says. "Thanks." Not even one sarcastic remark about me and beer to go along with it. Now the friends they're talking to—Derrick and Shannon—that's a different story.

They're both staring at me like I'm some kind of notorious strangler who just showed up with a bouquet of dead roses at his latest victim's funeral.

I'm not here to make any trouble, though. At least nothing blatant. I'm just going to hang around and let my natural positivity vibrate, maybe drop a code word here and there that only Cassidy and I know the meaning of. I don't need to make any big declarations. I don't need to pick fights or show off or come riding in on a gleaming white steed. Just letting the good old inner Sutterman radiate out in waves will be more than enough to remind Cassidy of what she's missing.

We haven't been talking for more than ten minutes before I have everybody laughing, even Derrick and Shannon. They're rolling over this story about the time in grade school when I staged a footrace between a schnauzer and a poodle and sold tickets. Listen, it's hard not to have a good time around me. I know what I'm doing. I'm a fun guy. I spread the prosperity to each and all.

I've just reached the end of the story when I hear a voice over my shoulder. "What's so funny?"

It's Denver Quigley. He's tall with wiry blond hair and a big, heavy, Neanderthal forehead. I never could understand what Alisa Norman sees in him, not so much because of his looks but because he's about as entertaining as ten pounds of asphalt.

So I look him in the eye and go, "Schnauzers."

And he's like, "What?"

"Schnauzers. That's what's funny. It's just a hilarious word, don't you think?"

A dull, annoyed look falls across his eyes. "Whatever, Sutter. Has anyone seen Alisa?"

"Sure," I say. "I saw her a while ago walking down by the lake with Jason Doyle."

His eyes flare. "Doyle?" He spits the name out like a mouthful of spoiled milk.

"They were just having a little friendly conversation," I say, and Quigley goes, "Well, maybe I'll just have to give him a little friendly ass-kicking."

He starts away into the crowd and Marcus is right behind him going, "Hey, Denver, now, I'm sure it's nothing. Slow down." Derrick and Shannon are tagging along too, and Marcus looks back over his shoulder and tells Cassidy to wait there, he'll be right back.

After they disappear into the crowd, she shoots me this withering gaze. "What are you up to now?"

"Me? I'm not up to anything."

"Is Jason Doyle even with Alisa?"

"He might be. He seemed to have the idea that she dumped Quigley like a lump of frozen shit out of a 747."

"And you didn't have anything to do with that?"

"Would it piss you off if I did?"

She smiles. "Not really. Jason deserves it."

"I do what I can in the name of justice. Ready for another beer?"

"Sure."

So now it's just me and Cassidy, the way it should be. We hit the keg, and I give her the lowdown on how well Ricky's making out with Bethany. She's happy for Ricky and has to admit I did a good thing helping them get together.

"So, do you believe me now that I was just hanging around with Tara Thompson to help Ricky out?" It's a bold question considering the touchiness of the subject, but sometimes you just have to open the hatch and make the leap.

She stares at me for a moment, then nods. "Yeah," she says.

"I guess I do. But I don't think you were making all that much of a sacrifice. I mean, Tara's pretty cute."

"Well, let me see, who would I really prefer?" I hold my hands out like scales. Cassidy's my beer hand. "Over here I have cute Tara." I lower my non-beer hand a little with the weight of Tara's cuteness. "And over here, I have spanktaculiciously beautiful you." I drop the beer hand way down. "I think it's pretty obvious, don't you?"

She scrunches her nose and shakes her head. "Don't smile at me like that. You know what that smile does to me."

"Oh, I'm irresistible, all right." I turn the smile up a notch to high beam. "There's nothing I can do about that."

Just then, a shout rises up on the other side of the crowd. Somebody's pissed off.

"Uh-oh," I say. "Quigley must've found Jason."

Sure enough, sounds of a scuffle follow another angry shout, and the crowd surges back. Cassidy and I circle around to get a better view, and it's Quigley, all right, but it's not Jason he's pounding. I don't even recognize the guy. Must be some dude from another school who doesn't know the dangers of flirting with Alisa Norman.

But if it's not Jason at the end of Quigley's fist, I ask myself, where is he? There's Alisa in her dangerous red sweater, and there's Derrick trying to pull Quigley back and Marcus wedging himself between Quigley and the poor dude from another school. And all around there's kids laughing or gasping or yelling encouragement, but no Jason. And no Aimee.

Cassidy yells, "Marcus, look out," as Quigley breaks away from Derrick's grip. But it's too late—he slings a punch that misses its target and smacks Marcus square in the ear.

Cassidy goes, "Pull him back, Derrick, pull him back," and takes off running through the crowd. It's okay now, though—

Derrick and Marcus both have a hold on Quigley, and the other kid's buddies are pulling him away. Cassidy's right behind Marcus now, touching his back gently, I guess just to let him know she's there to support him.

This is a development I didn't foresee. I mean, a punch in the ear while performing an act of heroism is bound to draw Cassidy's attention away from fun with me for at least thirty minutes. Talk about a plan backfiring.

Then, suddenly there's a voice in my ear. "Guess you were wrong about Jason Doyle." It's Shannon, standing next to me. "Looks like he found someone else to flirt with."

I'm like, "Where?" and she points to a dark corner of the clearing, far away from the fight. There's Jason standing under a big oak, whispering something, his lips not even an inch from Aimee Finecky's ear.

Chapter 32

Okay, so maybe what I have to go break up isn't as perilous as Marcus wading into the middle of a Denver Quigley beating, but does that mean it's any less noble? I don't think so. The stakes are probably even higher. I know what Jason has in mind. He's thinking, I'm getting ready to peel me a giant grape and taste some sweet, sweet nerd nectar. It's just too bad that Cassidy doesn't know what I'm up against here.

"So, where's Cody?" I say just as Jason leans his head over Aimee's, sniffing her hair.

"Oh, he left." Jason holds his ground. "Guess he couldn't take the competition."

Aimee has a look on her face like she just stepped off the Tilt-A-Whirl and is about to puke.

"What happened?" I ask her. "Did you drink some more beer or something?"

Before she can answer, Jason goes, "I may have got her a cup." He grins slyly. "She just needed to loosen up some. Socially, I mean."

I touch my fingertips to her chin to get her to look at me. "Are you all right?"

She tries a weak smile. "Yeah," she says in that two-syllable no/yes way of hers. "I'm just really not used to drinking."

"You were wrong about Alisa and Quigley," Jason says. "They're not broken up after all. I guess some poor dude over there found that out." He's sneering now. I'm sure he suspects I played him.

So I'm like, "That's why I came over here. That fight's over. But Quigley's not satisfied. He's asking who all was talking to Alisa before he got here. He's taking names, dude."

The sneer evaporates from Jason's mouth. "Wait a minute. All I did was ask her if it was true that they were broken up. When she said no, I was outta there."

"That's cool," I say, all sympathetic. "I'm sure Quigley'll understand. You know how he is."

Now, it's Jason that's looking a little sick. "Yeah, I know how he is. Shit." He glances at Aimee, the little pale face, the lipstick, the giant purple coat. "You know what? I've gotta go. I'll talk to you at school."

"Hey, Jason," I call as he starts away. "You might oughta take the long way around to your car."

He waves me off, but you can be sure he puts plenty of distance between himself and Denver Quigley.

Aimee tries an awkward version of the old *now-it's-just-you-and-me* smile, but to tell the truth, I'm not sure what I'm going to do with her. I've saved her from Jason Doyle's sex-maniac clutches, and Cody Dennis was a washout—what's left?

The rest of the party has returned to normal after the Quigley dustup, and there's Cassidy across the way, standing apart from a group of jocks. She's looking right at me. What's going on in that female mind of hers, I can't tell, but when Marcus walks over and wraps his arm around her waist, she returns the favor. Still, she's staring straight at me, so I do the only thing I can think of at the moment—squeeze my arm around Aimee's puffy purple shoulder.

"Let's take a walk down by the lake," I say, still gazing at Cassidy. "This party's getting lame."

"Really? Are the other parties usually different?"

"No, they're all the same."

———

There's a dirt road that runs along the side of the lake, and on the way over I bum a strawberry wine cooler from Shawnie, not for me, of course, but for Aimee. She looks like she could use it.

"Oh, I like this," she says after a sip. She takes a bigger drink. "This is good."

As we walk along under a big, fat, almost-full moon, we talk some more about Commander Amanda Gallico and Zoster, the underland of Marmoth, and Adininda, the beautiful Siren of the second moon of the planet Kosh. I'm starting to think I'd actually like to read some of those books. I mean, I am a big reader, but mostly just stuff on the Internet, blogs, MySpace, zines, all sorts of crazy things.

I'm always reading biographies online—Dean Martin, Socrates, Joan of Arc, Rasputin, Hank Aaron, Albert Schweitzer. And of course, you have to love the three-namers—Edgar Allan Poe, Lee Harvey Oswald, Jennifer Love Hewitt. People's lives are interesting. Books seem a little old-fashioned, but hey, I can do old-fashioned if it's good.

After finishing the last of my beer, I pull the flask out of my jacket pocket. "So, if you could go on any adventure here on this planet—I mean, like a real-life adventure—what would it be?"

She sips at her wine cooler. "I guess it'd be something with horses. Someday, I'm going to take a trail ride into the mountains, maybe like the Sangre de Cristo Mountains in New Mexico."

"I've never been there."

"Me either. I've just seen them in books."

"That'd be cool," I say, though it's a little hard to picture a pale bookworm riding the high country in a pair of chaps and a Stetson hat. "So, you'd just ride up there alone?"

"No, I'd have someone with me."

"Who? Someone like that Zoster guy?"

"Maybe." She looks off down the road. "How about you? What kind of adventure would you go on?"

"Hey, every day's an adventure for me. I'm not much of a long-range plan maker. But I've thought some about going to the Amazon. I'd go down there and, like, fight against these rain forest–bulldozing corporations that run the natives out of their Garden of Eden and stick them in little wino outfits. That's what I'd do."

"That'd be great," she says, but I get the feeling she was hoping I'd jump on board with the horse idea, so I go, "Have you ever thought about riding horses in the rain forest? I mean you wouldn't want to just hike around down there and get your foot eaten off by an exotic tarantula. No. What you'd do is take horses in by boat and then ride them around on these ancient Incan trails and everything."

That perks her up. "I bet you could. I bet they have mountains down there with views that nobody's ever seen before."

"Oh, it'd be panoramic, for sure. You never know—they might even have some hidden valley with pterodactyls flying around and stuff."

"Yeah," she says. "I bet that'd be an amazing trip."

Our shoulders touch as we walk, and she looks up and smiles.

A ways down the road, there's a covered pier that people fish from, so we walk out there and sit on the railing facing the water. The stars are bright and make crosses of light on the little black lake waves. Aimee's about to the bottom of her wine cooler. I wish I'd got her a couple more. When she finishes it off, I take the bottle and toss it, end over end, at the trash barrel about twenty feet away. Real loud, it clangs against the inside, and I'm like, "He scores from three-point range!"

As a reward, I take a swig from the flask, and surprisingly, she asks if she can try a little.

"You sure? It's pretty stout stuff."

"I'll just take a sip to see what it's like."

She turns it up and more than a sip goes down, and the next thing, she's coughing and gagging all over the place with her eyes bugged out. I slap her on the back but there's too much coat back there for that to do much good. Finally, she calms down and goes, "Wow, I guess some went down the wrong pipe."

"I told you it was stout."

"I'll be careful next time."

"Next time? That's what I like to hear. You fall off the giraffe, you gotta get right back on."

"Give me a couple of minutes." Her eyes are watering but she's smiling and not a sickly little smile like before either. She's enjoying the shit out of herself.

We stare off at the lake for a moment. "You know what?" she says. "There's something else I'd like to do too. It's not like a big grand adventure or anything, but it would be a big deal to me."

"What's that?"

She looks at my flask. "Can I have another drink?"

"Already?"

She nods. This time she just takes a little sip. When that doesn't throw her into a fit, she takes a bigger one. "That's not bad," she says. "It kinda burns going down, but it's not bad."

"Yeah, it's good stuff." I take a shot myself. "Anyway, what's this big deal thing?"

"Well, this isn't something I've told anyone else, not even my friend Krystal. But what I really, really want to do is go live with my sister in St. Louis and go to college where she goes— Washington University. It's a great school."

I'm wondering what the big secret is. Seems like a perfectly normal thing to want to do. "No reason why you can't. I'm sure your grades are plenty good enough."

"It's not my grades I'm worried about. It's my family. My mom says I have to stay here and help with the paper route and the bills and everything. She's not as healthy as she used to be with her heart and all. In a couple of years my brother can help out more, but until then, I'll just go to the community college."

"You're kidding, aren't you?" I'm staring at her, all amazed at what she's saying, but she just gazes down into the black water. "I mean, you're like this extraordinary genius chick, and your mom's making you go to the community college? No way. You need to get yourself to St. Louis with your sister *tout de suite*."

She explains how it is, though. Her sister, Ambith, had this humongous blowup with their mother about moving off to college and now they hardly talk. Ambith got a scholarship but she still has to work a full-time job to get by. So, like, about every other day their mother gives Aimee the spiel about how the family will collapse if she quits the paper route.

And then there's Krystal Krittenbrink who's planning on going to OU, which is only about twenty minutes away, so she's counting on having Aimee around to keep being her best—and probably only—friend. It's ridiculous.

I'm like, "Wow, these people have really done a job on you."

"Why's that?"

"Look, they've got you thinking you're like Atlas, you know, carrying the whole world on your shoulders. You're not. You're just you. You have your own problems to worry about. Here's what you need to do. First, take another swig of whisky, nothing big, just a little one."

"Why?"

"Trust me."

"Okay." She takes the flask and tilts it up. "Whoa, that one really burned."

"All right now, I want you to repeat after me: Get off my goddamn back, Krystal fucking Krittenbrink."

"What?"

"Just say it."

She gives it a try, only way too soft and without the *fucking* and *goddamn*, but I'm not about to let her get away with that.

"No," I tell her. "You've got to say it like you mean it, and you have to say *fucking* and *goddamn*. Curse words are absolutely one hundred percent necessary for something like this."

"Maybe I better take another drink."

I pass her the flask, she hits a good one, and then tries again. This time she really puts some heart into it, except you can tell her curse words need some work. So I tell her to go again, only louder, and I demonstrate by yelling across the lake, "Get off my goddamn back, Krystal fucking Krittenbrink!"

And then she goes for it, and I tell her, "Louder," and she really belts it out. I know it has to feel good because she lets go with another one without any prodding at all, and this one flies out of her like a big, jagged hunk of igneous rock and goes flaming across the lake.

Next, I get her to let loose on her mother and then Randy, her mother's lazy, good-for-nothing, Dr Pepper–swilling boyfriend. It's great. We're both belting them out, one after the next.

"Get off my goddamn back, Krystal fucking Krittenbrink!"

"Get off my goddamn back, motherfucking Randy!"

"Get off my goddamn motherfucking, sonofabitching back, Mom!"

You can practically see all the dank creepy-crawlies that have been weighing down her stomach go spewing out in the wake of every volcanic shriek. Louder and louder we scream until, finally, we're laughing so hard we can barely get a word out. I've never seen her laugh like this before. It's a sight to behold, a wonder, like the Eiffel Tower or the World's Largest Prairie Dog.

"Feels good, doesn't it?"

"No," she says. "It feels *great*!"

"And now we just have one more to do. One more person to shout down."

"Who?"

"The guy that broke your heart."

"What guy?"

"Now, you're not going to tell me no one's ever broken your heart, are you?"

She stares across the water and fiddles with her fingers.

"Come on," I say. "You can't get to be seventeen without at least one rotten, brain-curdling relationship."

It takes a while before she says anything. "The truth is I've never been in a relationship."

"Well, it doesn't have to be, like, some huge, heavy thing. I just mean some dude that you kinda went out with some."

She looks down at her hands. "Guys don't think of me like that."

"What are you talking about?"

"Guys don't look at me like a girlfriend, you know? They don't think I'm pretty and all that kind of thing."

This is brutal. I mean, sure, she's no super-hot spank machine, but she's no gargoyle either.

"You're crazy," I tell her. "Didn't you notice Cody Dennis and Jason Doyle were both hitting on you a while ago?"

"No, they weren't."

"Yes, they were. You're a sweetheart. I mean, look at your soft little eyebrows, look at your cute, pouty mouth. You're sexy."

140

"Oh, sure." The girl can absolutely not look me in the eye. "You're just saying that because you're a nice guy."

"Me, a nice guy? Are you kidding? I'm not a nice guy. I'm completely serious. I mean, if I wasn't serious would I do this?"

I tilt up her chin and lay a big fat kiss right on her. And I don't mean some polite, brotherly, nice-guy kiss either. I'm talking a long, deep, molar-swabbing French kiss with all the toppings.

"Whew," she says when I pull back.

"You're damn right, *whew*." Just to make sure she gets the point, I go back for another one. What else am I going to do, let the girl sit there on a railing in the moonlight thinking she's damned to go dudeless for the rest of her life?

Chapter 33

Hangovers are tricky. They're kind of like practical jokers. You never know quite how they're going to hit you. I used to enjoy them. They didn't give me a headache or a sick stomach or anything like that. Instead, I'd feel cleansed. Redeemed. If it was a really serious party the night before, I'd get this survivor-like sensation, like Robinson Crusoe after a shipwreck, washed up on the shore of a new day, ready for the next adventure.

Lately, though, my hangovers have started to take on a mean streak. It's the opposite of that fine redemption feeling— a vague, weird guilt instead. Maybe it's just a chemical thing, the old brain misfiring, the wiring short-circuiting. Or maybe it comes from not exactly being able to remember everything you did the night before.

For example, I'm not exactly sure how I got back in the house without Mom and Geech finding out I was ever gone. Normally, you'd just chalk something like that up to being God's own drunk—he's looking out for you in your beautiful intoxication—but then you start wondering what else you might've got up to the night before, what you said, what you did, who you did it with. Then, the next thing you know, you end up spending half the day feeling like the Antichrist when the fact is you didn't do a thing to hurt a soul.

That's the kind of hangover that hits me the morning after the party. I say *morning*, but really it's after twelve when I wake up. For some reason, as soon as my eyes open, I start in worrying about Aimee. It's ridiculous. I didn't do anything but try to build the girl up. She liked the kissing. There's no doubt about that. And to tell the truth, I didn't mind it myself. I would've laid another one on her when I took her home, but I ended up having to hold her hair while she puked off the side of the porch instead.

But what happened between the time we left the pier and when we said good night is a little sketchy. I keep trying to remember what all we talked about on the drive home, but my memory is like a broken watch that you can't find all the pieces to. I know we talked about doing something else together, but I'm not sure what it was. There's a gnawing feeling that I might have told her I'd take her to the prom, but that might just be a trick the hangover's playing on me. I mean, why would I do that? The prom is still a good way off, and I'll probably be back with Cassidy by that time.

Then another memory slinks back in, and this time I'm pretty sure I really did it. I told her I'd help with the paper route this morning. I meant it too. I sincerely did intend to get up at three a.m. and drive to her house with a big thermos of instant coffee. Apparently, I never did actually set the alarm, though. It was an honest mistake. Could've happened to anyone. Still, the idea of her sitting and waiting on that cold front porch is enough to smack the Antichrist heebie-jeebies right up the side of the pope's head.

The best thing to do for a hangover like this is take a shower, consume some hearty protein, take a shot of whisky, and go over to Ricky's. Nothing makes you feel more regular than just being around your best buddy. With Mom and Geech out hobnobbing all afternoon, I shouldn't have any problem getting away, except for one extraordinary development. When I call Ricky's house, his mother says he isn't back from going to church with Bethany. This is astounding. Ricky at church? What's the world coming to?

Luckily, he calls back about an hour later, and I talk him into heading over to the mall for our usual people-watching deal. I don't mention a thing about church. Not yet. On the way over to the mall, I do take note that he's not firing up a fat blaze, though. When I ask him about it, he says he's out of weed completely.

"You're out? Since when do you ever run out?"

"I told you, dude, I'm cutting back. I mean, what's the use of getting high all the time? It's not special anymore. There's no celebration to it."

"I guess that's one way of looking at it." I'm really starting to wish I'd never hooked him up with Bethany.

"Besides, it gets a little tiresome when you're so high you go to the movies and look up at the marquee and think the starting times are the ticket prices. I mean, I remember standing there going, 'Ten-fifteen? What kind of price is ten dollars and fifteen cents?' It's a hassle."

"Yeah, one time I was putting gas in my car and thought the number of gallons was the price. I even got into an argument with the cashier. It was hilarious."

"I mean, it's not like I can't go pick some up if you're wanting to get high."

"That's all right. You know me—I only smoke the stuff if I've had a few drinks first. Besides, my head's already hungover-weird enough."

"Wasted last night?"

"I wouldn't say wasted. Just heavily fortified."

Chapter 34

At the mall, we snag a couple of lattes and park by the escalator for prime people-viewing. The only thing is, I keep feeling like everyone's staring at me instead of the other way around. They're not, but it's just this creepy paranoia that I don't quite fit in, kind of like how it is sometimes if you don't drink enough before hitting the killer weed. Like everyone else is something normal—beagles or dachshunds—and I'm this big hairy cross between a Newfoundland and a Shetland pony. I can practically hear them thinking, What's that damn Shetfoundland pony doing with that latte over there?

Ricky goes, "Kind of a boring crowd out today," and I'm like, "That's because you're not high. I could use a drink myself."

"I thought you were cutting back."

"Where'd you get that idea?"

"From you. We were talking about it. I said I was cutting back to just partying on weekends."

"It's Sunday, dude. It still is the weekend, officially."

"You know what I mean. Quit overdoing it. All things in moderation."

"All things in moderation? What's happening to you? No weed, going to church on Sundays. Listen, dude, we were born to be jungle children. We were born to roam the wild in loincloths bearing blow guns and knives. Now look at you. Next thing I know I'll be calling you Deacon Ricky. You'll be preaching me the fire and brimstone. And I'll say, 'I used to know that dude when he thought religion was out to turn us all into zombies.'"

He shakes his head. "Dude, what do I need a blowgun for? What am I going to do, fell myself a burger at Mickey D's? Anyway, I'm just going to church because that's what she does."

"Can we say *hypocrite*, boys and girls?"

"Screw you, Sutter. I'm not a hypocrite."

I'm not letting him off the hook that easy, though. "Yeah, it's *Dawn of the Dead* all over again, starring Ricky the zombie, stumbling through the mall. That guy getting off the escalator over there is going to be you, wearing sandals and socks and a fanny pack, leading his kid around on a leash."

Ricky gets a chuckle out of that even though it's aimed at him. "Dude," he says. "You don't know what you're talking about. For one thing, I don't have anything against religion. It's not like I don't believe in some kind of God. It's just the holier-than-thou crap that rankles me. Besides, I'm not looking to get saved. I'm only going with her because it's what you do when you're in a relationship. You know? You slide into the third pew from the front and sit there thinking about how desperate all these people are to feel like something loves them. They'll believe all kinds of hocus-pocus. But your girlfriend likes it, and you like her, so you do it. It's called compromise. The only way you're going to get something to last in this world is to work at it."

"Right. And then it'll last for ever and ever." I'm all sarcastic and everything. "But aren't you the dude with the theory on built-in obsolescence?"

"That doesn't mean I have to just give up. That's not how relationships work."

"Listen to you. You've had one girlfriend for two weeks, and all of a sudden you're the Guru of Love."

"Well, at least I've got a girlfriend."

I sink back in my seat. "That was a low blow."

"Sorry, but, you know, if you want Cassidy back, you need to change some things, dude."

"A lot you know." I tell him about Cassidy's e-mail and our little chat at the party last night. "It's obvious, isn't it? She's jonesing for the Sutterman."

"Is that right? Well, how come we just happened to see Shannon Williams at church and she said Cassidy left with Marcus, and she saw you walking off into the woods with some girl in a giant purple coat, who I assume was Aimee Finecky?"

"Hey, it doesn't matter who Cassidy left with last night. All that matters is who she winds up with, and by the end of next week, you can bet it'll be me."

"And you're using Aimee Finecky just to make her jealous, is that it?"

"No, that's not it. I explained the whole Aimee thing to you already."

"Oh, right, you're rescuing her from the abyss. But, dude, let me ask you this—what happens when she falls in love with you?"

"Love?" I take a hit off my latte. It's a little bitter. "Believe me, dude, no way is that girl going to fall in love with a guy like me."

Chapter 35

At school the next couple of days, it's not like I'm dodging Aimee. I'm just not going out of my way to run into her. After all, we don't have any of the same classes or anything. Cassidy, on the other hand, I just happen to run into a bunch—in the parking lot, on the front steps, outside the girls' bathroom. Only a couple of times is she with Marcus, so we're able to get some good conversation in, a few laughs, a little touchy-touchy on the arm, the back, that kind of thing.

By Thursday, we're completely comfortable in each other's space again. We're practically intimate. "So," she says, "do you have to work this afternoon?"

"No, Bob cut me back to three days a week."

"Are you still grounded?"

"I guess not. Mom and Geech really don't have the interest to keep track of something like that for very long."

"Good, because I need to go shopping and could use some company. You want to come with?"

"Maybe if you twist my arm."

She grabs hold of my wrist—tight—and I'm like, "Uncle, uncle, okay, I give."

"Pick me up at two," she says. "Don't be late."

All right, so I'm going to follow Ricky's advice, at least a little bit. He says I have to make some changes to get Cassidy back, so I will. I pledge to myself that I'll be on time to pick her up, and what do you know? I am.

She's looking very hot. White cable-knit sweater, blue jeans, boots, gold hoop earrings. The girl knows how to put herself together without seeming like she went to any effort at all. We hit several stores—Old Navy, the Gap, a local place called Lola Wong's—but they don't have the certain kind of pants she wants for her friend Kendra's birthday present.

I have to admit, in the past, when I went to stores with Cassidy, about half the time I'd end up waiting in the car. I mean, I don't understand the female fascination with shopping. For me, I just want to go in, buy what I want, and get out. This isn't how girls operate at all. It's like a police investigation with them. No piece of evidence can go without thorough inspection. They might as well pack along a forensics kit.

But I'm the new, patient Sutter. I go into every store and look at every item and nod and make listening sounds— hmmm, oh, uh-huh. I even let her hold up pants to my waist to see how they're going to look. As if Kendra and I had anywhere close to the same build! The pants all look the same to me, but none of them are quite what Cassidy's looking for. Luckily, I brought along my flask.

Actually, it's good that we have to hit so many stores. I want the afternoon to last. It gives us both plenty of time to take nips off the whisky and start getting past that awkward balancing act of the ex-boyfriend and ex-girlfriend trying to pretend they're just friends now. By the time we leave Lola Wong's, we're having a great time, walking along doing the playful shoulder-bump thing, laughing at whatever, everything but holding hands.

She says screw the shopping, she can always find Kendra's pants later, so I fill up the gas tank to go cruising. It doesn't matter where to. We don't have anyplace we have to be. The afternoon is ours.

I steer the conversation to the good times we used to have together, the parties, the concerts, the haunted house at Halloween. There are funny stories to go along with all of them. One memory really gets her going—last August when we sat on my roof in the rain and watched the lightning going crazy off to the west. It was charging straight our way, but we didn't care.

"That was amazing," she says, her eyes lighting up. "The rain felt so good on my skin. And the lightning cracking across the whole sky—it was better than any fireworks show ever. I mean, that must have been so dangerous, but I don't know—I could just feel the electrical power like it was running through my veins or something."

"It wasn't dangerous," I say. "We were immune to lightning that night. We had a spell on us."

"We did. We did have a spell on us." She pauses for a second. "I don't know how many times I felt like that, just a handful. And every time was with you."

I give her the old Sutter grin. "Well, you know me—the Amazing Sutter, master of prestidigitation."

"You are." She smiles and gazes through the windshield. "You bring the magic. I feel it right now. It's like nothing can touch us, like everything else in the world—the problems, the responsibilities—have just disappeared. We're in our own universe. I'd really miss it if we lost that."

I give her neck a squeeze. "You don't have to miss it. It's right here. No worries, no fears, just a big fat Thursday afternoon wrapping us up in its arms."

She leans over and nuzzles her head against my shoulder. "That's right," she says. "There's nothing but right now. I don't want to think about anything but that. Is that okay? Can we just do that?"

I rub my cheek across her hair and go, "Hey, it's me, Sutter. Of course, we can do that."

By the time we get back to my house, we've polished off the flask and started on beer, but we don't even put a dent in that. I don't know how many times we've made out on the living room couch, but kissing Cassidy was never sweeter than it is this time. Her hands swirl under my shirt like wild minks and mine do the same under her sweater. Every time I start to say something, her mouth clamps back on mine.

It's a challenge to keep kissing while walking up stairs, not to mention peeling off clothes at the same time, but you know what they say—you gotta do what you gotta do. As we lie down on my bed, this feeling swells up in me like my whole chest could burst open and a bunch of new undiscovered colors would come flying out. Her body has never looked so beautiful, except for maybe the first time I saw it.

"You know how I feel about you," I tell her, and she says, "Don't talk."

Then a weird thing happens. Her hands stop skittering and her body stiffens. I'm still kissing her heavy and firm but she's not kissing back. It's like yelling across a beautiful canyon and waiting for an echo that never comes.

I'm like, "What's wrong?"

"Nothing. Just go ahead."

"What do you mean, 'just go ahead'?"

"Just go ahead and do it." She's lying perfectly still now. Her eyes are closed, and all the electricity has drained out of her.

I prop myself up on one elbow and look down at her. "I can't do it if that's how you're going to be."

Of course, part of me is thinking I really could *physically* do it, but that wouldn't be any good. The whole magnetic thing about sex is you want the other person to want *you*. I mean, that's what separates us from the animals. That and haircuts.

"Are you thinking about Marcus or something?" I hate to

mention another guy's name when I'm in bed with a naked girl, but it's a question that has to be asked.

Her eyes clench tighter.

"Are you, like, in love with him?"

"I don't want to talk about him right now." Her bottom lip's trembling.

"It's just a yes or no thing. I'm not asking for a whole essay."

"I don't know." The tears start to track down. "Maybe. I'm, like, really confused right now."

"What about me? What about this afternoon?"

"That's what's got me so confused." She pauses and sniffs. This is looking like it's going to be one of those real red-faced, high-snot-content kind of cries. "This afternoon has been wonderful. It really has."

"But?"

"But, you know, it's just one afternoon."

"There'll be other afternoons."

"I know. And believe me, I don't have fun with anyone like I do with you, but I can't go around having fun all the time. I have my serious side too."

"Hey, I'm serious. I'm one hundred percent serious about not being serious. Now, that's a commitment."

"I know you are." There's just the slightest upward curve at the corners of her mouth. "But you know how it is with Marcus—he has a plan. He doesn't just talk about making a difference in the world, he does something about it. It's just that sometimes it's too much. I mean, he already has this whole plan for where our relationship is going and how I can go to New Mexico to college with him, and after a year we'll start living together and then get married right after we get our degrees."

"Married? He's already talking about getting married? After

what, two weeks? Does this guy not know the definition of *creepy?*"

"And sometimes he makes me feel like we're responsible for fixing every homeless, poor, starving, downtrodden person in the whole city. And you know me. I do care about those things too. I do. You've heard me talk about them a million times. But I can't think about it all the time. Sometimes I have to let loose, forget about everything else, and just live in the *right now.*"

"Of course, you do. Everyone does. You go around worrying about that stuff all the time and next thing you know you're giving yourself an aneurysm. You have blood spurting out of your ears. Doctors are wheeling you into the emergency room, yelling 'stat' and 'code blue' and everything. You don't want that, do you?"

"No, I don't want that. But I don't want just Thursday afternoons either. I don't want just moments. I want a whole life."

"Cassidy, don't you know—life is made out of Thursday afternoons. You just keep having them one after the other and let everything else take care of itself."

She opens her eyes and gives me a warm smile. There's love in it, but not the kind that sticks. "I wish it could be like that," she says. "You don't know how much I wish it could be like that."

"It can be. You just have to believe."

"I guess that's my problem," she says. "I'm too realistic."

I can see where this is going—and it doesn't end up in Happily-Ever-Afterland either. The best thing for me to do is head her off and get there first.

"That's all right." I kiss her on the forehead and pat her shoulder. "You and I'll just be friends, then. You come to me when you need a laugh. You can have your *real* life with Marcus."

She reaches up and strokes my cheek. Tears stream into the

corners of her smile. "You really are magic, Sutter. And I wish that was enough. I really do."

I want to tell her it is. I want to swear to the king of the king of the kings it's enough. But this afternoon the magic has all run out.

Chapter 36

Friday night I get drunk with Jeremy Holtz and Jay Pratt and break stuff. Nothing big. Lawn ornaments, bird baths, flower pots. Mainly, they do the breaking, but I kick the shit out of a couple of shrubs. It feels pretty good.

Saturday night there's a motel party. About once a month you can count on someone renting a couple of adjoining rooms at some local motel for a birthday bash. This Saturday it's for Bethany's friend Courtney Lane. They play softball together. I don't know her all that well, but Ricky invited me to tag along with him and Bethany. Finally. I was beginning to wonder if he didn't really want me around her. Of course, maybe he just felt sorry for me after I told him what happened with Cassidy on Thursday.

Personally, I always thought Courtney was kind of boring, but the party's at one of the nicer motels by the airport, so there is an outside chance it could still be fun. At least it's interesting to finally get a chance to really study Ricky and Bethany as a couple.

On the drive out to the motel, they try to make me feel included at first, but that only lasts about five minutes. Then Bethany starts in on the subject of how her parents are adding on an extra room to their house and how they're planning to decorate it in an early French style or something like that. You know—the kind of boring topic that girls like to talk about but that makes a dude's eyes glaze over.

Funny thing, though, Ricky jumps right into the conversation. He's all about how he'd design his own house and what kind of furniture he'd put in it, and Bethany comes back with her own ideas. I can't believe it. It's like they're practicing for the day they buy a home together.

To me, this seems like a big rookie mistake on Ricky's part. Any time a girl starts to talk about the FUTURE I try to change the subject pronto. I don't do conversations about homes, weddings, careers, or kids anymore. Topics like those are quicksand. They'll pull you under before you know what happened.

One time, when I was dating Kimberly Kerns, she dragged out the what-kind-of-house-do-you-want topic, and I said I'd like to live in a tree house. For some reason, that made her mad, like I was being disrespectful or something. It was ridiculous. I mean, have you ever seen some of those cool tree-house condos they're building in Costa Rica?

Anyway, it's like Ricky and Bethany have completely forgotten that I'm even in the backseat. They're going through each room of their imaginary house, describing everything from wall hangings to coasters. As Ricky's best friend, I figure I better head them off before they get to the nursery.

"So what's this package you have back here?" I cut in, referring to the brightly wrapped box on the seat next to me.

Ricky says it's the present they got for Courtney, and I'm like, "Were we supposed to bring presents?"

Bethany goes, "It is a birthday party, you know."

"Yeah," I say, "but usually a motel birthday party's just about getting blasted."

"Well," says Bethany. "This one's just about having fun."

I'm like, "What's the difference?"

"Don't worry," says Ricky. "I'm sure everyone isn't bringing a present. You can just think of paying the cover charge as your gift."

"What? A cover charge? Presents? What are these people, a bunch of capitalists?"

Ricky gets a chuckle out of that, but not Bethany. It is weird, though. Why should I pay a cover charge? I'm bringing my own whisky.

I have to admit this motel is a cut above the usual for these kinds of parties. There's a downstairs club, an indoor pool, a workout room, and an atrium with pool tables, Ping-Pong, and arcade games. The adjoining suites are pretty plush. Much bigger than the usual.

Unfortunately, there is almost no electrical charge to the party atmosphere. When we first arrive, there are only six people sitting around talking. A microscopic boom box leaks out some lukewarm tune so softly that you can barely hear it. Presents are piled in the corner and there's a fat white Wal-Mart cake on the bureau. They have two ice chests, one with beer and the other with Cokes.

That's right—*Cokes!*

Good thing I have the trusty flask.

Right from the first, it's clear that I won't get in much socializing with Ricky. He and Bethany are lost in each other. They stand there talking, staring into each other's eyes, with no more than a couple of inches of space between them. They're even doing the double handhold. Next thing you know, they'll be calling each other honey-bunny.

Here's my problem with the public display of affection—it's undemocratic. It's like here's this couple and they're reigning over their own little universe and no one else is invited. My universe is way too vast for that. Once I get a girl alone, it's different, but until then I'm like, Come one, come all! Bring your cousins, bring your dogs. No one's excluded. But here's my best friend, practically building a border fence to keep the rest of us out.

More people file in, mostly couples. A lot of softball chicks and their dudes. Then Tara Thompson shows up single, and it's pretty obvious that something fishy is going on. It's very likely that the main reason Ricky asked me to come along was to hook me up with her. Of course, I like Tara. Tara is great. I'd date her in a second if it wasn't for the Cassidy fiasco. But that's what pisses me off. Ricky knows that. I've told him I can't ever date her. And still he's plotting against me.

Now, not only is the party lame, it's awkward. I'm standing around with a group of guys who are talking about tennis of all things, while Tara sits across the room next to Courtney, shooting glances my way about every fifteen seconds. There's nothing to do but put a heavy, heavy dent in the flask.

Okay, I could go talk to her. After all, she's probably the most fun person here. But then I'd just be leading her on. When we sat together in the botanical gardens that night, everything was cool. I had a girlfriend then. It's like having a force field around you that keeps romantic expectations at bay. Tara and I could talk about anything. We could even hug. But it was just as friends.

I try going into the adjoining suite. It's less awkward, but the lame factor is off the charts. Everyone's sitting around while this girl named Taylor something plays guitar and sings contemporary Christian songs. No one seems to think this is an odd choice for entertainment at a beer bust. And it's fine with me, really. Even Jesus needs to party now and then. It's just boring.

Naturally, I feel the duty to inject a little zip into the proceedings. So, when the song's over, I stand up on a chair and go, "That was fabulous, Taylor." I give her a round of applause. "Now, let me try one. Taylor, see if you can play along with me."

I start in with a Sutter Keely original off the top of my head, something with a Caribbean feel.

Listen to Sutter Keely
Listen to the Sutterman
He's the king of feely-feely
He's the master of romance

"Come on, everybody, dance along with me!" I go into a sultry hip swivel.

Let's do the raunchy rumba
Let's do the nasty dance
Give me the humba-bumba
Down in me underpants
Yes, yes, yes,
Down in me underpants

Now, you'd think everybody would get into the spirit and want to sing along but no. They're like, "Give it up, Sutter. We want to hear Taylor play some real music," and "Aren't you supposed to be in rehab?"

Ricky and Bethany are standing in the doorway between the two rooms. Ricky's grinning, but Bethany has this look on her face like I'm a poodle that just shit on the rug.

"Hey," I say. "I'm only trying to be of service. I didn't mean to break up your funeral or anything."

I hop down from the chair, walk over to Ricky, and go, "When you're ready to leave this mausoleum, I'll be downstairs at the arcade."

Chapter 37

I'm not really a big arcade-game guy, but anything would have to be better than this motel party. At the restaurant downstairs, I get a 7UP to go, and as I'm heading to the atrium, I hear a girl shout, "Yo, Carmine!"

Walking across the foyer with three of her friends is my old girlfriend Shawnie Brown from back in my crazy-for-black-hair-and-brown-eyes phase. Carmine is my name in the Italian mobster routine we do whenever we run into each other. In fact, we're both Carmine, so I yell back, "Oh-ay, Carmine, how ya doin'?"

She says something to her friends, and they head on to the elevators while she comes over to me. She has a very sexy walk. "I'm doin' bravissimo, Carmine. Whatchoo doin' heah?"

"Nuttin'. Just tryin' to put some distance between me and dem stiffs upstairs at dat lame-ass party. You know what I'm talkin' about?"

"Ay-oh, I was just goin' to dat party. No good?"

"Fuggettaboudit."

"No, you fuggettaboudit."

"Aaaay, you're breakin' my balls heah."

"No, you're breakin' my balls."

We could go on and on this way, but we crack each other up too much.

"So, really," she says when she gets done laughing. "The party's lame?"

"Remember that party we went to sophomore year at Heather Simons's house and it turned out her parents were there?"

"That bad?"

"Maybe not that bad, but close."

"What a waste. And I'm just starting to get a good buzz on too. What's in the cup, whisky and Seven?"

"Of course. Want a sip?"

"Sure." She takes a drink and hands the cup back.

I explain the weak beer situation upstairs and suggest I buy her a 7UP of her own so that she can fortify it with some of my Seagram's.

"There's a Ping-Pong table in the atrium. You up for a match?"

She gives me a sly look. "You know I'll kick your ass, just like in the good old days."

"No way," I tell her. "I'm on steroids now. My head's grown six hat sizes."

She laughs. "I'll still kick your ass."

Turns out the only reason Shawnie got sucked into coming to Courtney's party is her friends thought there might be some cute guys. This is news because she's been dating a dude named Dan Odette for about six months. I ask her what happened to him, and she goes, "He got on my nerves. Too possessive."

"That's always the way it is with the dangerous bad boy."

"Why didn't you tell me that before I started dating him?"

"Would it have made a difference?"

"No, probably not."

"I guess we're just a couple of singles out on the town. It's fabulous, huh?"

"So, you don't miss Cassidy?"

"I'm way past that."

"Just keep telling yourself that."

After we score her a 7UP and doctor it thoroughly with whisky, we head to the atrium. She wasn't kidding about the Ping-Pong. Out of three games, I don't win a single one. That girl always could bang out some serious Ping-Pong, no matter how much she's had to drink. It doesn't bother me, though. I'm not one of these macho dudes who thinks it's some kind of disgrace to lose to a girl. It's just a joke when I suggest we head over to the workout room so I can wreak my revenge by beating her at weight lifting, but she's up for it one hundred percent.

She's like, "Spot me ten pounds?"

"Are you kidding? I'll spot you fifty pounds and still beat you." Which, of course, is an exaggeration. Shawnie's no weakling.

The workout facility is pretty nice. Since it's Saturday night, we're the only ones weird enough to be in there, but they don't have weights, just treadmills and exercise bikes. That's okay. I'm never at a loss for ideas.

I saddle up on one of the bikes and go, "How about a race?"

She grins. "You're on."

It's pretty hilarious. There we are, side by side, pedaling away like a couple of Lance Armstrongs. We're both doing the commentary, and, of course, I'm winning in my commentary and she's winning in hers. The thing is, though, that riding a bike—even if it is stationary—can be a challenge after a few stout whiskies. At least it is for me. Just as I'm imagining myself shooting down the homestretch, my foot slips off the pedal and I go crashing to the floor, cracking my head on the left handlebar along the way. This is not a minor tumble either. I mean, it hurts.

Of course, Shawnie can't quit laughing. I'm sitting there checking my forehead for blood, and tears are streaming down her face.

I'm like, "Hey, I'm injured here," and she's like, "I'm sorry, but you should've seen yourself." She's still laughing as she comes over to help me up.

"You know," she says, "that's something I always liked about you. You don't get embarrassed about anything."

I go, "Embarrassment's a waste of time. Now, where's the hot tub? I need a hot tub. I'm an injured man."

Sure enough, they do have a brand-spanking-new shiny hot tub too. It looks like the perfect thing to heal all ailments. Just what I need.

Shawnie's like, "You're not getting in there, are you?"

"Of course I am."

"Bullshit."

"Come on," I tell her. "If I'm going in, so are you."

"No way," she says. "You're not getting me to take my clothes off."

I give her the old eyebrow cock. "Who said anything about taking anyone's clothes off?"

And there I go, fully dressed, easing myself down, the warm, healing waters gathering around my chest.

"You're crazy," Shawnie says.

"Yeah, but that's why you like me so much."

"That's true."

"So, Miss Queen of Ping-Pong, do you choose to test the waters or do you choose to be a loser?"

"You can never outdo me, Sutter. You know that." And sure enough, here she comes, right in next to me. "How's your forehead?"

"Not bad. For a tragic head wound."

She inspects my head for a second. "It's just a red spot. Here, let me apply some of these magic waters to it." She reaches up and dabs my skin with her wet fingertips. It feels good, a whole lot better than the feeling I got from beating up those shrubs with Jeremy Holtz.

"That better?"

"That's perfect."

She leans her shoulder into mine. "You know what, Sutter? You're my favorite ex-boyfriend of all time."

I look into her dark brown eyes and my stomach starts to melt. Shawnie's one of these girls you might not think is that great-looking at first—big nose and all—but once you start talking to her, it's like this humongous, sparkly, fun spirit bursts out of her eyes, and you go, *Wow, this girl is beautiful!* Plus, she has a stellar bod.

"We've sure had a lot of fun together," I say. "You remember that Flaming Lips concert?"

"Are you kidding? That was the most amazing thing ever."

We trade memories of the show—the crowd dressed in crazy outfits, like Santas and Easter Bunnies and Halloween skeletons; the huge flying saucer that landed on the outdoor stage; the light show; the balloons filled with confetti; the crazy-great band with Wayne Coyne walking across the crowd's upraised hands in his giant space-hamster ball. And most of all just the feeling of being there, the enormous wild beauty of it. It was almost like we were the music, soaring across the galaxy.

"It was so funny when you went crowd surfing," Shawnie says. "But then I didn't see you again for about thirty minutes."

"Yeah, but I made up for it when we went parking by the lake afterward. You remember that?"

"Of course. That was pretty incredible too."

"And here we are—single again."

"Yeah. Here we are."

And there we are, all right, staring into each other's eyes, the warm water and the warm memories both hugging us, and I can tell we're thinking the same thing. I lean toward her, and she closes her eyes and opens her mouth just a little, inviting a kiss. It's nice. Her lips taste like strawberry lip gloss. I run my fingers down her neck, and then it happens—she starts to giggle right into my mouth.

I pull back and her giggle turns into a full-out laugh, and then it hits me, and I bust out laughing too. She's right. It's ridiculous. You just can't make out with someone you have a continuing Italian mobster routine with.

She hugs my arm tight. "Carmine, you're da greatest."

I kiss the top of her head. "No, Carmine, *you're* da greatest."

We sit there for a while just enjoying being next to each other. Then I go, "So, do you think this Cassidy-and-Marcus thing's going to last?"

"I thought you said you were over that."

"I am. I'm just wondering how long they'll last, that's all."

"You know what?" she says. "I wouldn't waste any time thinking about that. We both need to find ourselves someone completely new."

"Well, you won't have a problem. Except there aren't any guys out there worthy of you."

"Yeah, sure."

"No, I mean it. You have the fun, you have the bod, you have the deep soul-force. What dude can possibly be good enough for you?"

"You're right." She laughs. "But I might go ahead and give some guy a break anyway."

"So whatever happened to us? I mean, we get along so great. Why didn't we make it as a couple?"

"Oh, you don't want to go over that again, do you?"

"I'm just wondering. I mean, here I am, out on my ass without a girlfriend again. It might be educational to know what happened to us. What changed?"

She mulls it over for a moment. "I don't think it's so much that something changed as that things didn't change. We just kept being the same as we started out, you know?"

"Not really."

"It's like we were always buddies instead of boyfriend and girlfriend. Even when we had sex it was kind of like two buddies just fooling around."

"And that's not good?"

"No, it was good. It was fun. And I know girls always say they want a guy that's like their best friend, but somewhere along the line we really want more than that."

"*More?* See, that's just the thing. It's that *more* part I get stuck on."

"You'll get the hang of it one of these days. You just need to find a girl that brings it out of you. Someone completely different from Cassidy."

"I tried that. I asked out Whitney Stowe."

"No way." She pulls back and looks me in the face. "*You* asked out Whitney Stowe?"

"Seemed like a good idea at the time. She has great legs."

"But she's one of these girls that, like, has a schedule worked out for every second of the day. How could you possibly fit into that? You'd be like a dog on a leash."

"Yeah, I guess it was pretty stupid."

"Just wait. Someone's going to come along, someone you never expected, someone who needs you because you're you."

"You think?"

"Sure. And besides, you need someone you can beat at Ping-Pong every once in a while."

"Carmine, you're breakin' my balls."

"No, you're breakin' my balls."

"Fuggettaboudit."

"No, you fuggettaboudit."

I'm sure some people might get a little worn out with the Italian mobster routine, but not us.

"So," I say. "Carmine, should we head back to da party and astound dem stiffs wit our new drenched-to-da-bone eveningwear?"

She squeezes my knee underwater. "You got it, Carmine."

"Bada bing, bada boom."

Chapter 38

Talk about bad luck. My last class of the day is over, I'm in the middle of the parking lot, only two rows from the safety of my car, and all of a sudden here comes Krystal Krittenbrink, heading straight toward me. What am I going to do, run? That's too weird, even for me.

"Sutter Keely, I want to talk to you." Her little black eyes narrow, and her dime-size mouth twists down to about the size of a screw head. She has this strange fur collar on her blouse, apparently from a moose. "I just want to know who you think you are."

"Um, the king of Mexico?"

She stops about an inch away from me. "Aimee told me about your little party out by the lake."

"Yeah, that was fun."

"And now you're avoiding her."

"I'm not avoiding anybody. I've been laid up in bed with a case of the seventy-two-hour elephantiasis."

"Don't think you're going to joke your way out of this."

"Hey, I'm not trying to joke my way out of anything. I'm not avoiding her. Besides, it's none of your business, so get off my back."

"Ha, I knew it."

"Knew what?"

"I was telling Aimee what she ought to do about you, and she said that same thing—told me to get off her back. I knew she had to get that from you."

"She said that? Good for her." I have to admit it makes me a little proud to hear Aimee took my advice about standing up to people.

But Krystal's like, "No, that's not good. Aimee's not mean like that. She's a sweet girl, and she doesn't need you sniffing around her like a hyena and then skulking off when you don't get what you want."

"A hyena? Sounds like you've been watching too much Animal Planet."

"I don't know what else you'd call it. It's been almost two weeks since that stupid party, but have you called her or taken her to lunch? No. You haven't even talked to her one time."

"So? What do I look like, the Lord of Time or something? I'm not responsible for how much time goes by. The only problem Aimee has is you bossing her around like she's your own personal robot. It sure isn't me."

On that, I wheel around and make a beeline for my car. I'm sure she's still back there comparing me to African wildlife, but I can't hear her now.

Funny thing, though, that evening at work while I'm running the dust mop across the tiles, Krystal's voice comes back loud and clear. Sure, she's probably jealous that Aimee's been getting some male attention, but as much as I hate to admit it, she also has a point. I have let the Aimee project slide. I mean, the whole idea was to bolster her confidence, give her a good shot of independence, but now she probably has to sit around for hours listening to Krystal tell her how stupid she was for going to that party with me in the first place.

And the truth is I miss Aimee. She has a way about her that latches on to you. It's nothing big or audacious. It's small and cool, like the first sip of beer on a hot afternoon. If I was going to follow Shawnie's advice and find someone completely different from Cassidy, I wouldn't have to look any farther than

Aimee Finecky. She's definitely different, all right. But I have to chuckle at the very idea of dating her. If Shawnie thought it was ridiculous that I asked out Whitney Stowe, what would she think of me dating Aimee Finecky?

But, I tell myself, it wouldn't hurt to run by her place after work and pay her a friendly visit, catch her by surprise before she has a chance to slap on any lipstick. We'll just hang out a little bit. It's not like I'll be leading her on or anything. She'll just be another one of my girl buddies. Actually dating her is beyond the call of duty.

That's what I tell myself.

When I get to her house, the Finecky family truck is parked in the driveway and just about every light in the house is on. Still, it takes a while for someone to open the door. It's her little brother, and as soon as he sees me, he cranes his head around and yells for Aimee, then disappears, leaving me standing on the porch.

From somewhere, Aimee hollers back, asking him what he wants, and he goes, "Your boyfriend's at the door!"

So then, she's like, "Who?"

"I don't know his name. That guy who came over a couple of weeks ago."

"Oh God, um, tell him to hold on a second, I'll be right there."

"You tell him," says Shane, and someone else—I assume it's their mother—goes, "Well, don't make him wait on the porch. Ask him to come in."

"Come on in," Shane yells.

Who would've thought Aimee could be related to people who crank the decibels up like that? It's really quite the production. And the scene inside is fabulous. Mom and Randy, her eBay entrepreneur boyfriend, are both splayed out on the couch with their feet propped up on the coffee table. Mom's got an egg body with stick arms and legs and wears her hair in a she-mullet. Randy-the-boyfriend's basically a walrus in sweats that are way too tight. He has a bowl of Cocoa Puffs balanced on his pooch-belly.

"You ever watch *CSI?*" asks Mom, checking me over like there must be something wrong with me for coming to see her daughter. "We have thirteen episodes recorded. This is a good one. Wild and woolly."

"They showed a cut-off head," adds Shane, and I'm like, "Well, I can see you're a man that enjoys a good decapitation. Maybe someone will get vivisected later. That'd really be something."

Randy doesn't say a thing, but lets it be known with a pained squint that all this talk is causing him to concentrate on the show way more than he wants to.

I start to follow up on the grisly maiming topic, but already no one's paying attention to me anymore.

Finally, Aimee pops out of the back room. She's wearing the kind of nice white Wal-Mart sweater that people don't usually lounge around the house in, and her hair is all staticky from a high-speed, sixty-second brushing. Luckily, no lipstick, though.

"Sutter," she says. "I didn't know you were coming over."

"Well, I've been really busy preparing for the big alligator rodeo."

"Really, there's an alligator rodeo?"

"No." The girl really does need some help in the humor department. "The thing is, I've had a lot going on the last few days. But I just got off work a little while ago and thought, 'You know what? I don't care how busy I am. I'm going to see Aimee.'"

"Hey," Randy calls out. "We're trying to watch a show in here."

"We want to talk to your friend," says Mom, "but let's wait for the show to end. It'll just be a few minutes."

Aimee's eyes fill with actual dread. She seems to think the prospect of a motherly cross-examination will be enough to send me scrambling back to my car, never to return. But I'm in this thing now, and I'm going to stay in it.

So there we are, loitering in the shadow of the plastic hanging plant, no one but the *CSI* team uttering a word. A good five minutes pass. Everyone but Aimee seems to have forgotten me. I smile at her. She shrugs. Finally, I'm like, "How about we go get a Coke and some fries or something," and she's, "Uh, okay, let me get my coat."

Picturing the resurrection of the puffy purple monstrosity, I suggest it's way too nice out for a coat. She tells her mom where we're headed, and Mom just nods. I'll bet Aimee could've said we were going on a cross-country murder spree and garnered the same result.

No matter. I'm quite the matador, having dodged Mom's interview, and better yet, the possibility of having to dredge up something to say to Randy-the-Sweat-Suit-Walrus. Freedom awaits in the Mitsubishi, along with the big 7UP.

Chapter 39

Aimee asks where we're headed and I suggest a place called Marvin's Diner. Now, just because Marvin's is no high school hotspot like SONIC, that doesn't mean I'm ashamed to be seen with her. I'm just not in the mood to have somebody like Jason Doyle wise-assing me right now.

Marvin's is way over on the southwest edge of town under the radio towers. You can see the red lights blinking on the towers from miles away. "You know what they remind me of?" I ask Aimee. "They remind me of where my dad works—the Chase building downtown in the city. I'll bet they're about the same height. My dad works on the very top floor. He's a business executive."

"I remember you telling me that before. But, you know, I thought there was, like, a restaurant or a club at the top of that building."

"Oh, well, yeah. There's a hoity-toit club at the *very* top. I'm talking about the highest floor that the offices are on. That's where the big deals go down."

At Marvin's, we grab a booth in the corner. This is one of my favorite places to eat, and believe me, since we almost never have meals together around my house, I've tried just about every restaurant in town. Nobody cares who you are in Marvin's. It'd be a perfect place for adulterers, except it's such a greasy spoon. We order a big plate of chili fries, and two 7UPs, and in Marvin's dim lighting, there's no problem at all spiking our drinks with a little whisky.

Aimee takes a gulp and goes, "Wow, that's strong!" And I'm like, "You want me to order you another drink?"

"No." Her eyes are watering a little. "That's all right. It's fine."

The number one best thing about Marvin's is they have a jukebox with plenty of Dean Martin, so I plug in a few songs and we settle back to talk. Just to get the conversation primed, I start out by making up stories for the other people in there, the waitress, the fat guy sitting behind the front counter where the register is (who may or may not be Marvin), the lonesome traveling sales dude at a table by himself, and best of all, the ugly couple in the booth across the way.

I explain to Aimee how I figure they're worn out with their relationship. Really, they pretty much hate each other but have to stay together because they murdered her ex-husband for his three-hundred-dollar life insurance policy. Now, when she gets mad at him, she whips him across the shoulder blades with a windshield wiper, and he's too big of a wimp to fight back, so he's slowly poisoning her by slipping kitty litter into her morning oatmeal.

Instead of even getting a little chuckle out of that, Aimee's like, "I guess you don't have a very high opinion of marriage, huh?"

"It's not so much the idea of marriage," I tell her, "as the idea of forever. That's a concept I just can't get my mind around."

"Oh, I can."

"Really? I mean, your parents weren't married forever, right?"

She sets her drink down and looks off toward the lonesome salesman. "My dad died."

"I'm sorry."

"No, that's okay. It was a pretty long time ago."

"What happened?" Sometimes my tact takes a vacation. Tonight it must've gone to Kuwait or somewhere.

"My father was really a good guy. He was a big animal person, practically an activist. And smart. Just for fun, he read books on physics and Aristotle and everything. He loved van Gogh. He used to read out loud to me, and I thought it was the greatest thing in the world. But he had this problem."

She pauses, and I'm like, "You can tell me. I'm a very non-judgmental dude."

She starts nervously winding a strand of her hair around her forefinger, but she goes on. "Well, the thing is, he was addicted to inhaling gasoline fumes. He kept big containers full of gas in the shed behind our old house."

I'm thinking, *My God, the dude blew himself up!* I can just see him taking in a snootful of fumes, then lighting a cigarette, and *kablooie!* But that's not it.

What actually happens is that the gas eats away at the blood vessels in his brain until one day, Aimee's big sister, Ambith, comes home and finds him lying in the doorway to the shed, stiff as a rake. Aneurysm.

I'm like, "Jesus. That's a tough way to go. I've seen it on TV. Not the gasoline thing, the aneurysm."

"Yeah." She takes a hefty pull on her drink and this time doesn't even flinch at its stoutness. "But it's going to be different when I get married. I've thought it all out. That's what you have to do. You can't just go into something like that blind."

Now, I know better than to get the subject of marriage cranked up around a girl, but I'm ready to put as much distance as possible between us and the gasoline-huffing, dead-dad story, so I ask her to tell me all about this vision of marriage she has.

"Well, when I get married, we'll live on a horse ranch."

"Right. And you'll work for NASA."

"Right." She smiles at how I remember that.

"Will the guy have to work for NASA too, like maybe as an astronaut or an accountant?"

"Oh God, no. We won't have to have all the same interests. I don't believe in that—the husband and wife having to be just alike. I think it's better if they kind of offset each other. Like if they have these different dimensions they can bring to each other."

"I like that idea. That's cool."

This potential husband dude—I don't know—he seems about like a cross between Peter Parker from *Spider-Man* and Han Solo from *Star Wars*, with a little bit of one of those old, dead romantic poets thrown in for good measure.

The ranch is just as implausible, like some fantastic foreign-planet wonderland. Purple sunsets, bluebells, jonquils, Queen Anne's lace, a crystal-clear stream winding through the valley, a big red silo the size of a rocket ship. And horses. Herds of them, red, black, silver, appaloosas, and paints, galloping everywhere—like horses never get tired.

It all sounds like something a nine-year-old would dream up, but what am I going to do, tell her it's not feasible? Maybe say, "Look, there's no such thing as flying saucers or Martians, or Santa Claus, and there's no chance you'll ever land a ranch or a husband like that"? I'm no dream crusher. The real world already does enough of that without me getting into the business.

Besides, it doesn't matter if it's real. It never does with dreams. They aren't anything anyway but lifesavers to cling to so you don't drown. Life is an ocean, and most everyone's hanging on to some kind of dream to keep afloat. Me, I'm just dog-paddling on my own, but Aimee's lifesaver's a beauty. I love it. Anyone would if they could see the way her face beams as she clutches that thing with all her strength.

Chapter 40

Before we know it, Marvin's is closing down. We score a couple of 7UPs for the road, and when we get to the car, she lets me doctor hers with whisky again. Neither one of us is really ready to head home, but there's nowhere else to go on a weeknight. Plus, there's a curfew for teenagers, if you're the type that pays attention to that kind of thing.

So we end up parked in front of her house, talking and drinking. The lights inside are all off now. I tell the story of my parents' divorce and the advent of Geech and how my sister got a boob job and snared Kevin-pronounced-Keevin. I've never seen anyone listen so hard. It's like I'm pouring out some rare, expensive wine and she doesn't want a drop to miss her cup.

Cassidy was never like that. She always listened with a wispy smile on her face and one eyebrow slightly raised as if she thought a punch line was somewhere right around the corner.

Finally, there's a lull, which can always be dangerous when you're talking to a girl.

"So," Aimee says, a look on her face like she's getting ready to jump off the high dive for the first time in her life. "Did you mean what you said when we were driving home from the party last week?"

Uh-oh.

"I don't know," I say. "We talked about a lot of things, and I was a little drunk. To tell you the truth, I'm not sure I remember everything I said."

"You don't remember?"

"Not everything. But I'm sure I meant whatever I said. I'm very honest when I'm drunk."

She takes a sip of whisky. "Do you remember asking me to the prom?"

"Oh, that. Sure, I remember that. Are you kidding? I wouldn't forget that."

There's a pause and then she's like, "So, do you still want to go? I mean, I know we were drinking and everything, so if you don't, I'll understand."

She can't look at me. Her lifesaver's drifted away, and she's lost at sea on her own.

"No," I say. "What are you talking about? Of course, I still want to. I wouldn't have asked you if I didn't want to."

"Really?" When she looks up with that little smile, I have no regrets.

"Of course. Come here." I cup my hand around the back of her neck and lean in for a kiss. I figure on just a short one—a peck to show her I mean business on this prom deal—but she's ready for more.

I don't know. It's strange the way she feels in my arms. So trusting. Like she's completely sure I have something important in me that she needs.

I take her glasses off and set them on the dashboard and the next thing I know my hands are under her sweater, gliding up her back. She sighs as I kiss her neck, and when I lick inside her ear, her whole body quivers.

She pulls back, and I fully expect her to tell me we're moving too fast, but that isn't it.

"Sutter . . ." She can't look any higher than my chin.

"What's the matter?"

"Nothing. It's just, I'm wondering, does this mean we're, like, boyfriend and girlfriend?"

That one catches me off guard. "What do you think?" I ask

to buy time. After all, this is exactly the kind of thing I'd pledged to avoid.

"I don't know," she says. "I've never had a boyfriend before."

"Well, you do now." The words march right off my tongue, as if I'd been planning to say them for a month, but what else can I do? The girl needs to hear that, and to tell the truth, it feels pretty good to say it.

"Really? You want me to be, like, your *real* girlfriend?"

I could make a joke about fake girlfriends, blow-up dolls with plastic hair and suck-me mouths, but this isn't the time. "You got it. My one hundred percent authentic real girlfriend. If you want to."

"Yes," she says. "I do." And her mouth locks back onto mine.

There's no doubt that I could unsnap her jeans and go all the way with her right here and now, but that wouldn't be right, not with Aimee.

Besides, when I go to change positions, I accidentally honk the horn, and about five seconds later a light flashes on in the house. Ten seconds after that, her mother's standing on the front porch with her hands on her hips.

Aimee brushes back a loose strand of hair. She looks like a girl who just woke up from a beautiful dream. "Lunch tomorrow?" she says.

"I'll be there."

Chapter 41

You know what? I am there the next day. Right on time. And I'm right on time for our date Friday night too. And then for a movie Sunday afternoon. Of course, Ricky's dumbstruck over this development. He's like, "Dude, what are you doing? I told you this girl was going to fall for you. Don't you have a spine? Couldn't you just stand up to her and tell her you're only her friend or benefactor or whatever it is you are?"

"Hey, did it ever cross your mind that I might actually be attracted to her?"

"No."

"Well, you haven't really looked at her. You have to talk to her for a while before you can really see her. She exudes purity of heart, dude. Besides, all I'm doing is providing her with some boyfriend experience. I mean, look, I give it a month tops before she gets tired of me and figures she'll be a lot better off with some dude who plays first trombone in the stage band or something."

"And what if she doesn't get tired of you?"

"Hey, it's me. Have you ever known a girl yet that didn't get tired of dating me?"

He nods. "I have to admit you have a point there. And who knows, maybe she'll be a good influence on you."

"Yeah, right."

I don't know what Ricky's complaining about anyway. It's not like we've done much hanging out since he met Bethany.

Except for the lame motel bash, he hasn't partied with me a single time since then. Of course, I have my other buddies, and over the next couple of weeks I alternate—Fridays with Aimee and Saturdays getting festive with the likes of Cody Dennis and Brody Moore. I even go for another binge with Jeremy Holtz's semi-thug crowd, but I have to exit stage left when they get the idea to burglarize an Episcopal church.

After that, I start to wonder why I didn't just hang out with Aimee instead. I could even see myself hanging out with her both weekend nights on occasion. It's very fun watching her learn how to be spontaneous. The fact is she has a lot more to her than science-fiction novels, NASA, and horse ranches. We actually have some things in common.

For one, we both like old music better than the crap they pass off on the radio today. I'm a huge Dean Martin fan, and Aimee loves the hippie music from the 1960s. She's got the whole soundtrack to the movie *Woodstock* and everything. She sings me this sixties song called "Where Have All the Flowers Gone," and I mean, sure, her voice is a little thin, but still, the girl closes her eyes and siphons it straight up from the left ventricle. You have to appreciate that. For about two and a half minutes, I actually feel like a complete hippie.

She's different from the girls I'm used to dating. She doesn't get tired of my stories and jokes or expect me to start reading her mind. She doesn't want me to dress better or put highlights in my hair or serious up. I'm not a lifestyle accessory to her. I'm a necessity. I'm the guy that's going to crack open her cocoon. She doesn't need to change me—she needs me to change her. At least until her little butterfly wings get strong enough to fly away.

And who would've guessed this five-foot-three-inch, small, bespectacled chick can drink like she can. Turns out whisky isn't really her thing, but she can put away the wine coolers. Then I take the initiative and buy her a bottle of Grey Goose citrus vodka and mix it with cranapple juice, and she's like, "Wow, this is the greatest drink ever!"

It's so funny—we're at the grocery store one afternoon after putting away some pretty serious alcohol, and who do we run into but Krystal Krittenbrink. We're in the junk food aisle, a canyon of Twinkies and coconut snowballs, and Krystal's like, "So, Aimee, didn't you see the sign on the door out front? You're not supposed to bring pets into the store."

Of course, she means me. It's an old joke, and nothing I'm likely to even think twice about, but Aimee steps right up and goes, "Hey, Krystal, didn't anybody ever tell you that if you eat another box of Ding Dongs, your big fat butt's going to explode?"

Okay, so that's not the most original thing in the world either, but still it's pretty awesome considering Aimee's track record with Krystal.

"Are you drunk?" Krystal asks after getting over the surprise of seeing meek little Aimee with a backbone.

"Yes, I am," Aimee says proudly. "I am spectacularly drunk."

Krystal stares me in the eye. "That's just great. I hope you're proud. If you keep at it, maybe you can change her into as big an idiot as you are."

She wheels around and stomps off, and Aimee starts laughing. "Look at that big old butt shake. I'll bet it could hit about a seven-point-eight on the Richter scale. Probably a nine on the modified Mercalli intensity scale."

She grabs my arm and leans into my side and just about folds in two from laughing. I laugh along with her, but the truth is I can't help feeling a touch sorry for Krystal. Nobody likes seeing someone lose a friend. She's wrong about me trying to change Aimee, though. If I was trying to change her, I'd talk her into trading in her glasses for a set of contacts or tell her to stop wearing those T-shirts with the horse faces on front.

For sure, I've never forced her to get drunk. Can I help it if she happens to like it? I mean, what's not to like?

Chapter 42

Now just because I'm doing the dating thing with Aimee doesn't mean I can't hang out with other girls. You can always see me in the hall between classes talking to Angela Diaz or Mandy Stansberry or someone like that. And of course, there's the usual mobster routine and fun and games with Shawnie. Nothing wrong with that. We're buddies.

Aimee's cool with it, but I'm not sure she'd be so cool with me having drinks with Cassidy on Thursday afternoons like we've been doing. There's no fooling around going on, but I have to admit we do have a more complicated connection than I have with those other girls. The old feelings for each other are still right there beneath the surface.

Since all we're doing is sitting around talking, you might think I should go ahead and tell Aimee about it, but I figure her confidence isn't up to that just yet. No use getting things stirred up for nothing. I assume Cassidy hasn't told Marcus either, but I guess with girls you should never rely too much on assuming.

One Friday afternoon after my last class, I'm just escaping out the front door when Derrick Ransom calls my name.

"Sutter. Hey, Sutter, Marcus is looking for you, man."

"Marcus? What for?"

"I'll let him tell you that."

I don't like the look on Derrick's face. He seems a little bit too happy in a malicious kind of way.

"Well," I say as I head toward the parking lot, "he'll probably have a hard time finding me."

"Why's that?"

"I left for Lichtenstein yesterday."

Now, I'm not usually one to dwell on the potential for evil to come swooping down on me with its dark, crooked talons, but later that evening at work, I can't help thinking about what Marcus has in mind. Did he somehow happen to find out about my Thursday afternoon drinks with Cassidy? Or worse, did Cassidy have a brain malfunction and tell him about that time we made out and almost had sex? Neither option bodes well for the Sutterman.

I've seen what happens when jealousy poisons the bloodstream. Denver Quigley comes to mind. All he has to do is see some dude talking to Alisa Norman and he's ready to kick ass. Before Alisa, when we were juniors, he practically murdered Curtis Fields for cruising Twelfth Street with Dawn Wamsley. Quigley hadn't even been dating Dawn for a week. I mean, this girl discarded guys like used tampons. Still, there's Quigley going all silverback gorilla on someone he used to be friends with.

As I fold shirts, I try running a movie through my head starring me as Sutter "Wild Man" Keely, World Kickboxing Champion. There I am dancing and dodging, moving with cheetah-like swiftness, laying Marcus out with one brutal, whirling kick to the chin—*keeeraaaack!*

But it doesn't help much. I've never taken a kickboxing lesson in my life, and anyway, Marcus is so tall I'd probably strain my entire groin trying to kick him anywhere higher than his belt buckle.

It's enough to depress even me, and I used to never get depressed. That was something I was always proud of. I wore it like the Congressional Medal of Honor. But lately—I don't know—it's weird—sometimes there's this black crack running down through my stomach, the same one as that time when Cassidy told me what she wanted me to do for her, and I didn't pay attention. Only now, it's more like I was daydreaming when the Supreme Being told me what I should do with my life, and it's too late to ask what it was.

Occasionally, the bell over the front door jangles, and I can't help but whip my head around to see if it's doom walking in. After about the third time, Bob asks me if I'm expecting someone, so I come clean and explain the situation.

"So am I a bad guy for wanting to hang with my ex-girlfriend?" I ask him. "Is that something I should get a fist in the eye for?"

Bob ponders that for a second. You have to love him. He treats you like your life means something, like you're worth straining the vein in his forehead over.

"No," he says. "You're not a bad guy, Sutter. You're a good guy. You just don't have a real firm grasp on the concept of consequences."

I have to admit he's right. But I've always worn that like the Congressional Medal of Honor too.

After seven-thirty, the bell over the front door pretty much stops jangling—it's another slow night—but a little before closing time, a car pulls into the parking lot. The headlights shut off, but no one gets out. If it's Marcus's Taurus, I can't tell from here.

At eight we lock the doors and shut off most of the lights. The car's still out there. Usually, I go ahead and leave while Bob stays behind to do the paperwork, but tonight I'm in no hurry.

Bob's like, "I'll walk out there with you if you want," but that seems way too grade school. It wouldn't be so bad, though, if maybe he'd just watch from the window so he could break things up before Marcus starts swinging those long arms around.

"All right," he says. "Give me a low wave if you want me out there. Flash me a high one if everything's all right."

Chapter 43

Nothing happens till I'm almost to my car, and then there he is—Marcus unfolding himself from the Taurus. "Hey, Sutter, man, I need to have a word with you."

"Uh, sure, if it doesn't take too long. I'm supposed to be at a big police banquet in about thirty seconds. They'll probably send a car by for me if I'm late."

No smile.

I lean casually against the side of my car, trying to ease some relaxation into the moment. He doesn't follow my example and instead stops right in front of me, an uncomfortable couple of inches inside my personal space.

"What's going on with you and Cassidy?" No beating around the bush for Marcus.

"What do you mean?" I'm thinking, Damn, Cassidy and I didn't even wind up having sex and I'm still in trouble.

"I heard you been seeing her on Thursday afternoons behind my back."

Questioning his source doesn't seem like such a good tactic at the moment, so I'm like, "Yeah, we hang out some. We're friendly, you know?"

"I know. I'm just wondering how friendly."

Bob's still standing in the window, but I haven't read the situation well enough yet to give him a wave, high or low.

I look Marcus in the eyes. "She and I, we're good friends, dude. Tight. Just because we're not dating anymore doesn't change that."

He breaks eye contact, and that's when I see it. He's not here to murder me at all. He's here because he's wounded. Self-doubt has cut the mighty Marcus West to the core. Suddenly, any jealousy I might have left over evaporates, and I realize I'm the one with the power in this situation. Either I can twist the knife deeper into his heart or I can pull it out. Me being me, I go for the second choice.

"Hey, Marcus, buddy, Cassidy and I are always going to be friends. But here's the deal—we may be friends, but I'm dating someone else now."

"Yeah, but everyone knows you'd drop Aimee Finecky in a second if you could get back with Cassidy."

"Maybe people think that," I say, more than a little annoyed. "But that's just because they don't know Aimee. She's my girlfriend now and Cassidy's yours. Case closed."

"I don't know about that." His baritone cracks in mid-sentence. I can't believe it—he's actually bordering on tears.

"That's the way it is," I assure him. How could I stay annoyed with that pitiful expression staring me in the face? "Look, nothing's going on between me and Cassidy except we have some fun, blow off some steam." Obviously, I don't mention anything about the lingering feelings from our dating days.

Marcus looks down at his hands. He's twisting his key chain nervously. "Yeah, well, that's the problem. She shouldn't have to go looking for another guy to have fun with. I want to be that guy. I want to be the one who makes her laugh."

I glance Bob's way and give him the high wave.

"Look, Marcus, You *can* be that guy. I mean, there's no reason she can't have fun with me and you both, just in different ways."

He shakes his head. "Naw, man, I know myself and I'm not that fun. And she needs fun, I can tell by the way she talks about you. But I don't know how to make her laugh or anything like that. I can't come with the funny like you."

This is too weird. Marcus has always seemed so smooth and cool. Now here he is beating himself over the head because he's not funny. That's love for you.

So I'm like, "But, hey, you're Marcus West. You've got the cool, the glide. You're a doer, dude. You don't just dream things, you get them done. If our whole generation was like you, maybe we really would change the world."

"Yeah, but it'd be a boring world."

"You aren't boring, Marcus. You're an interesting guy. You have all these opinions and causes and everything. And I can tell you're crazy about Cassidy, aren't you?"

"I am, man. I really am."

My heart's bleeding for the dude, but I'm also doing this for Cassidy. If she needs another boyfriend right now, she could do a lot worse than Marcus West.

"Look, Marcus." I would give him a pat on the shoulder, but it'd be awkward as tall as he is. "Let me give you some advice. For one thing, she's into you. She told me she is, so you can believe that, one hundred percent."

"She told you that?"

"Absolutely." Okay, so admitting this hurts more than I thought it would, but it's for a higher cause. "And another thing." I'm on a roll now. "She's also into all your causes and everything. The girl used to wear me out with that stuff. But maybe you could back off on saving the world just a fraction. I mean, as fucked up as the world is, with all the war and torture camps and exploding buildings and shit, it can crush you into a powder just thinking about it."

"Hey, that's not what I'm trying to do." I've never seen anyone look so earnest. In fact, I haven't seen many people over the age of nine look any kind of earnest. He's like, "No single person can save the whole world. I'm just trying to do my part. I get that from my mom and my brothers and the church we go to. You know? You just start with the small stuff in your own world and let it spread from there. That's all I'm trying to do."

"Yeah, well, it can be a little much for someone like Cassidy who's a lot more used to talking about doing that stuff than actually doing it."

"I thought she liked doing it, though. But, I mean, she doesn't have to do everything I do. Everyone's different. To tell you the truth, sometimes I get a little stressed myself. I got a lot of pressure on me. Sometimes it's like I got this wire stretched tight inside me, about to break, but I don't figure that's any reason to give up."

"Well, let her know that. Don't go around playing the macho man who won't tell his girlfriend his problems. Sit down and talk to her, get it all out in the open. And, dude, don't plan everything out so much—just let it happen. Plus, it wouldn't hurt you to have a beer every now and then. Maybe even some whisky."

"I'm not into that."

"It was just a thought."

He studies me for a second. "I really appreciate you talking to me like this, Sutter. It's big of you. I guess I was always like some of the other guys—I figured you were kind of a joke, but you're not. A long way from it."

"Wait a minute. Who thinks I'm a joke?"

"I'm just saying—you got a lot more to you than you let on. You got heart, man."

"Oh yeah, I have that, all right. I have a heart the size of a tuba."

"You know what, man? I bet if you put your head to it, you could really be a difference-maker yourself."

"I'll leave that to you, Marcus. You got it all under control." I put out my hand, and he gives it a good, warm shake. He's back to being Marcus West again.

"Why don't you head over to Cassidy's," I tell him. "I'm sure she'd love to see you right about now."

He smiles. "I think I'll do that. Thanks again. You're a good man."

He ambles away and folds himself back into the Taurus. Bob's standing in the window again. What a damn good guy. I shoot him another high wave to let him know everything's all right. Doom has passed me by for now.

But as I drive away, I can't help going over the conversation. There are no two ways about it. I handed him the keys to Cassidy, all right. At least for a couple of months. That's all I give their relationship before it collapses under the weight of Marcus's immense sincerity.

Chapter 44

Aimee's still not tired of me, and I can't say that's a bad thing. I'm really enjoying hanging with her. She's up for just about anything I want to do. The thing is, now that the secret's out about my afternoons with Cassidy, I have to explain it to Aimee before it gets back to her through someone else. Krystal Krittenbrink would love to pass that piece of gossip along.

Lunch seems like a good time to spring the news. It's harder for an argument to get out of control in the middle of McDonald's than if it's just the two of you at home. Of course, Aimee's never given me the least cause to think she's the fit-throwing type, but you never know what might happen.

I turn out to be a genius, though. I start by telling her about me setting Marcus straight on how much Cassidy's into him. Then I casually mention the good things Cassidy has to say about her whenever we get together for drinks on Thursday afternoons. And it's true—Cassidy has told me she thinks Aimee's an absolute sweetheart. Still, the *Thursday afternoons* part doesn't escape Aimee's attention.

"I thought you had to work Thursday afternoons," she says.

"I do but not until later. It never hurts to get a little fortified before work, you know."

She stares at her burger. "So where do you two go to have drinks?"

"Nowhere. We just hang out on the patio mostly."

"At her house?"

"Yeah. In fact, we were just talking about going on a double date—me, you, Cassidy, and Marcus." Maybe that's not exactly the truth, but it is something that could be arranged somewhere down the line, and it gets the subject back on a positive track. "How about that? Think we should do it sometime?"

"Uh, sure, that'd be all right, I guess."

"Great. You want some of my French fries?"

"Okay."

And that's that. No accusations, no tears, no big scene. Everything's cool. For the time being.

Of course, the situation might have become more emotional if we were having sex, but I have wisely steered away from that so things don't get too messy when the end comes. So far, it's just been the same old car-in-the-driveway kiss and rub. I figure we'll never go too far as long as there's the threat of Aimee's mom or Randy-the-Walrus walking up on us at any second.

See, I agree with what Cassidy says—once you have sex you'll always be sewn together with an astral thread. I'm no expert on astral stuff, but she's definitely onto something there, and I sure don't want Aimee getting all tangled up in a sticky thread like that come time for her to say adios to the Sutterman.

It's not easy, though. I've counted to about a million, listed most of the presidents, and played mental reruns of my favorite old movie, *Dumb and Dumber*, just to keep the horniness at bay while making out with her. I know I told Ricky there's no way she could ever be a hottie, but the body doesn't lie. The head does, but not the body. My blue balls testify to that every time I drive home from her house.

But my greatest challenge is yet to come. Only a couple of days after our Cassidy talk at McDonald's, Aimee hits me with the big question—Do I want to sleep over and help with the paper route the next morning while little brother Shane's spending the night with a friend and Mom and Randy are off for an all-night run on the Indian casinos?

Maybe the timing is just a coincidence, but I can't help wondering if Aimee wants to shift our relationship into the bedroom as a way of competing with Cassidy. Of course, just because we're spending the night together doesn't mean we have to have sex, but it's sure going to make it a lot tougher to avoid it. But you know me—I'm always up for a challenge.

When the big night rolls around, I do the usual deal, tell my mom I'm spending the night at Ricky's. Then I load up on videos, pizza, chips, salsa, Twinkies, whisky, 7UP, vodka, and cranapple juice. Of course, when I get to Aimee's, she has the soft sixties music playing and the candles stationed around the living room, so I'm starting out with a ten-degrees-of-difficulty super-challenge already.

We have three movies to choose from, two comedies and one moody sci-fi flick. Nothing too romantic. Definitely nothing with nudity. We start off with the sci-fi, which works out fine since, with Aimee explaining it to me, there's not much time for the conversation to tilt toward relationshippy issues. That's the big fear right there—getting caught up in one of those "Where are we going?" talks.

Strange thing is I actually find the movie and her commentary interesting, especially after she hits a couple of vodkas and really starts cranking. It's one of those movies set in a screwed-up society in the near future. Totalitarianism rules. Half the characters look like refugees from a seventies punk-rock club and the other half look like space Nazis. One of the women is pretty hot for a bald chick.

Aimee says the themes are simple: Goodbye individuality, goodbye uniqueness. The uniform, soulless future is coming and the seeds have already been planted. She's read or watched about a billion similar stories. That's what people fear, she says, because they think it's like death and that death is the ultimate robber of identity.

"Do *you* think that's what death's really like?" I ask.

"No," she says. "I think, when we die, we don't lose our identity, we gain a much, much bigger one. As big as the universe."

"That's the best news I've heard all day," I tell her, and we clink our glasses together to toast our grand universal selves.

There's a little punk-rock girl in the movie with an old, punk-rock father. I think the guy playing him used to be a pretty big star. It's sad, in a way, to watch movie stars grow old beneath their fabulous hair. But this is the only part of the movie that seems fresh to Aimee. When the movie's over, she admits the guy reminds her of her own father because they understood each other when no one else did.

Her father was the one who turned her on to sixties music. He even used to sing the songs to her. He read to her, too, even when she was old enough to read for herself. He loved some writer dude named Kurt Vonnegut and another one named Isaac Asimov. I'm sure they did science-fiction stuff. In the evenings, he'd read her chapters at a time and explain all the philosophy behind it as he went.

"He used to set his little red ashtray on the window sill and blow his cigarette smoke outside so I wouldn't have to breathe it. And he had this old, beat-up St. Louis Cardinals cap that tilted back on his head, and sometimes he'd crack up laughing so hard at what he was reading he could barely go on."

"I like him," I said.

"He was a dreamer."

"That's all right. I like listening to people's dreams. My dad, I don't think he had any dreams. He was like me—every second's a dream for guys like us."

"Well, he must have been ambitious to end up working at the top of the Chase building making all those business deals."

"What?"

"You know, you told me he works in the Chase building downtown?"

"Oh, right, right, right. I guess I kind of drifted off, thinking about how he used to be. Man, he was fun. He's a workaholic now, though."

She nestles in closer and puts her hand on my leg. "Maybe we should go see him sometime. I'd love to meet him. After all, you've already met my whole family, and I haven't met any of yours."

"Yeah, we'll have to do that sometime."

"When?"

"I don't know. Sometime."

"How about tomorrow? I mean, if it's not too short notice."

"I don't think so." I stare off at the TV, even though the movie's ended. "Besides, he'll probably be burning the midnight oil at the office."

"On a Sunday night?"

"Like I told you—he's a workaholic."

"How about this, then—we surprise him at the office. We'll bring him some leftover pizza."

"Not a good idea."

"I've always wanted to see the view from the top of one of those buildings."

"Goddamn." I pull my hand away from hers and look her in the face. "Would you shut up about going to see my dad? It's not going to happen, all right?"

Her face flushes red and she shrinks away. You'd think I slapped her or something. But, really, the girl just did not know when to stop.

"I'm sorry," she says, her voice cracking.

"Well, you just kept going on and on. I don't like to be badgered, you know?"

"I know, I know, that was so stupid. I don't know what's wrong with me."

I swear, she looks like she's about to shrink all the way down into the crack between the sofa cushions.

"Hey." I pat her leg. "It's not that bad. It just got on my nerves a little."

"No, I know. I'm acting just like my mom, and I said I never would. But I guess when your family's screwed up, you're going to be screwed up too." She's actually sniffling now.

"You are not screwed up. Come here." I wrap my arm around her. "I'm just a little touchy about my dad, you know, spending more time working than with me."

"I'm so sorry." She wipes her tears on my shoulder. "I'm so dumb. I should've known that."

The girl cannot stop apologizing, so I do what I have to. I kiss her. And kiss her and kiss her, until finally the sniffles dry up, and by then we're lying clamped together on the couch with our hands under each other's shirts, and she's going, "I'm so glad I met you," and I'm like, "I'm glad I met you too," and then the words get lost in more kissing.

Chapter 45

I kiss her mouth, her eyelids, her eyebrows, her forehead, her ears, her neck, even her breasts through the fabric of her T-shirt. We roll one way, then the other. I'm on top, then she is, then we're both on our sides, and the couch is so small she almost rolls off onto the floor. I squeeze her tight, and go, "Don't worry. I won't let you fall," and she says, very softly, "Can we go back to my room? There's more room on the bed."

"Sure, we can," I tell her, gearing up to imagine the complete expanded edition of *Dumb and Dumber,* count to a billion, and maybe even work in a visual of full-frontal frog dissection. Anything to keep from taking it too far with this girl. I mean, if she's going to start crying just because I told her to shut up, what'll happen when she has to dump someone she's had sex with for the first time?

It's strange being on her bed in the middle of a room full of sci-fi novels and drawings of Commander Amanda Gallico on horseback. You might think it would be the least sexy place in the world, but that's not the case. Instead, it's mega-intimate, like we're alone together in our own little, weird space capsule, hurtling through the universe.

"I like you so much," she says between kisses. And I can tell she wants to say *love* instead of *like,* not because she really does love me but because she just wants to say it. Of course, she can't, though. Not when I haven't said it first.

"I mean, I really, really like you."

"You're spectacular," I tell her. "You really are."

"Can we take off our clothes?" she says.

What am I going to do? Say *no*? I mean, there's no movie funny enough, no number big enough, no dead frog ugly enough to stop things now.

"Sure, we can." My mouth is so close to hers the words seem to drop one by one down into her like pennies into a wishing well.

This is always the awkward part. Am I going to take her clothes off? Is she going to take mine off? Or do we take our own off? I mean, who wants to fool around with someone else's socks? So we do a little bit of both.

I have to withdraw everything I ever said about this girl not being hot. Without her goofy horse-face T-shirts and the off-brand, baggy-butt jeans, her body is absolutely fabulous. I'm not talking about gaudy curves. It's more that her skin is so pristine. Alabaster in the glow of the digital clock.

"Nudity," I tell her, "looks awesome on you."

She's not bashful about where she puts her hands, so neither am I. We're chugging full speed ahead when all of a sudden, she sits up and says, "Wait right here. I'll be back in a second."

I'm like, *Crap!* Did she freak out after getting me to the point of no return? But then she skips back into the room and hops into bed with a condom from her mother's nightstand.

"Just to be on the safe side," she says. The girl's thought of everything.

Cassidy always liked to be on top, and it's splendid that way, but with Aimee, I figure the old-fashioned method will be best. We can get fancy some other time. Right now, I just need to help her through. I figure it's probably even for the best that we're doing it. She can get some experience with a guy that only really has her best interests at heart. No worries. All positives.

In the middle of it, I look down at her face. Her expression is sublime, her eyes closed and her lips moving slightly with the little peeps that squeeze out of her. She looks like a saint at prayer. Suddenly, I feel all the layers that have grown over my own purity stripping away. The faster we go, the more layers burn away, until magic time hits, and there's nothing left but the original me, as pristine as her body, shining and glorious.

Chapter 46

We lie there silently for a long time, and I stroke her hair until finally she's like, "You're incredible. It was like we were just one soul joined together."

I kiss her forehead and go, "Thanks. I guess it's pretty easy to seem incredible to someone on their first time."

She doesn't say anything back to that, and I'm like, "This *was* your first time, right?"

No answer.

"Aimee?"

Finally, she's like, "Not exactly."

"What do you mean? I thought you told me you never had a boyfriend."

Again, she hesitates, her eyes closed, her chin tucked down. It's bizarre—this weird, negative electricity buzzes through my stomach as I wait for her answer. It's like I'm actually afraid of what she's getting ready to say.

"I don't want you to hate me."

I kiss her forehead. "That's never going to happen. You're unhatable."

"You promise?"

"Cross my heart and swear on a stack of Supreme Beings."

"Be serious."

"I am. I promise I won't hate you."

She lets out a hard sigh. "It's just something that happened," she says. "I mean, I didn't plan it."

"Hey, I understand. I hardly plan anything."

"The thing is, I was fourteen, and you know, I didn't know anything about being with boys, and Randy's son was over spending the night."

"Jesus, Randy-the-Walrus's son?"

"Yeah," she says in a small apologetic voice. "Mom made up the couch for him to sleep on, but sometime after everyone else was in bed, he came back to my room and asked if he could sleep with me. He said the couch was too small and it was hurting his back."

"God, what a line of bullshit."

"And I thought it would be okay. I mean, we were practically related in a way. So he gets in under the covers and slides right up against me. And he's like telling me how comfortable my bed is and how warm my body is, and then he starts telling me how he was watching me all through dinner and liked the way I ate."

"He said he liked the way you ate?"

"Yeah. And I was just lying there flat on my back and he put his hand on my stomach and started kind of nuzzling his nose against my hair and telling me how pretty I was. I just shut my eyes and tried to slow down my heart from beating so fast, but I couldn't. I hadn't really had anyone be interested in me before, and he seemed like he really was."

"I'm sure he was."

Her face squinches up. "No, he wasn't. Maybe just for that one thing, but not for me. I should've known better. I mean, what twenty-year-old guy's really going to be interested in a fourteen-year-old?"

"Damn! Are you kidding me? He was twenty? What a perv."

"Well, but the thing was, I felt like here's this older guy and he sees something in me none of the guys at school see. That nobody anywhere sees. He's, like, even telling me he loves me, and I hadn't heard that since my dad, and so I just felt so special. It was like I was Sleeping Beauty waking up from his kisses. But I didn't really know what to do, so I just lay there and let him do it, and I started crying and he put his hand over my mouth. And then, when it was over, he went back to the couch, and later at breakfast, he wouldn't look at me. He's never come back since. I think he lives in Colorado now."

"That dude is the king of the creeps. I can't believe your mother stayed with Randy after that crap."

"I never told her about it."

"What? You should have. That's statutory rape."

"I never told anyone. Till now."

"Not even Krystal Krittenbrink?"

"Just you."

We both lie there quietly. It's hard to think of something to say after that. After a while, I feel her tears on my shoulder.

"Don't cry," I tell her.

"You must think I'm terrible," she says.

"I don't think you're terrible. Why would you say that?"

"You can't even talk to me now."

I pet her hair. "I'm just thinking. There's something I haven't told you about me either, something I've never told anyone else. But you have to promise you won't hate me just like I promised you."

She promises.

"You know how I told you my dad works at the top of the Chase building?"

"Yeah."

"Well, I was lying. I've been lying about that to everybody since I was in grade school. Even to Ricky. The truth is I don't even know where my dad is. After my mom kicked him out, he just disappeared. So I started pretending he was a big-shot executive. I pretended it so hard I almost started believing it myself, so maybe it's only kind of a semi-lie."

"You never heard from him again?"

"I think I got one birthday card from him a long time ago. But basically my mom threw him away, and now she'd like to throw me away. But that's how the world is, you know. Everything's disposable."

She wraps her arm around my waist and lays her head on my chest. "Don't worry," she says. "I'll never throw you away."

Chapter 47

Girls have the wrong idea about how guys are with their buddies. It's like they think all we do is talk about sports and porn, tell dirty jokes, and brag about our sexploits. Or lie about them. And, okay, a certain amount of that does go on, but if you have a best friend, you can go further. You can unlock all the rooms. Well, except one. I can't tell anyone the story of Aimee and Randy-the-Walrus's son.

But believe me, when I tell Ricky about having sex with Aimee, I'm not bragging. Bragging's only for guys who never get it steady anyway. It's disappointing, though, because Ricky doesn't get me the way he usually does. He's all like, "Dude, I thought you said you weren't going there with this girl. I thought you were keeping this deal on the surface level. Now you're boinking her?"

"It's not like that," I tell him. "It's not a *boink*."

"Really? Well, I'll tell you what it sounds like to me. It's like you're one of these con-artist dudes who goes around preying on the feeble. You know, those guys who promise to put a new roof on some 102-year-old blind lady's house, and then they skip off with the money. Same thing with you. You filch a little sugar off this girl and next thing you know, you'll be in the breeze. That's not good, dude."

I tell him that's not how this was. I explain the whole purity deal and how she looked like a saint at prayer, and he's like, "Sure, sure. That's just what you want to believe she looked like. You're just pretending so you can believe it was all pure and innocent."

"So what? Who doesn't need a little purity in their lives? I mean, that's what I'm saying. It was a soul thing."

"That's right," he says. "Reverend Sutter Keely, the man who can save everybody's soul but his own."

"Whatever, dude." I'm starting to wonder if the reason he can't understand is because he still hasn't done the deed with Bethany. I wouldn't put it past him. He's probably still in the hand-holding-on-the-couch stage. Which is pretty lame if you ask me. Look, if you have to go to church with a girl Sunday morning, you sure better be going to bed with her Saturday night.

What really surprises me, though, is Cassidy's take on the whole thing. There we are, having our Thursday drinks on a spectacular afternoon—Marcus and Aimee seem to be cool with us and our friendly get-togethers now, or at least that's what they say—and I try out my purity theory on her. I was afraid she'd fillet me for taking advantage of Aimee, but it's pretty much the opposite. Instead, she's like, "You know, I admire you for going out with Aimee."

"Admire? That's an odd word for it."

"No, what I mean is, at first I thought it was just some kind of strange rebound thing, but now I can see it. I had French with her last year. She's shy and everything, but she's deep. I guess I was just kind of surprised that you saw that in her, but the more I think about it the more sense it makes. I think you're a good fit."

"What do you mean, she's deep but you didn't think I'd see that. You didn't think I could be deep?"

"No, you know that's not it. I just thought maybe you wouldn't see it in a girl that went around in a coat that looks like a big purple Christmas ornament."

"Hey, that coat's in the back of the closet now."

"Well, you know what I mean. A girl who's a little subtle in the looks department."

Now, maybe she doesn't mean anything negative with the "subtle" remark, but for some reason it makes me feel a kind of duty to Aimee, and the next thing I know I'm defending her alabaster-in-the-digital-clock-glow body.

Cassidy looks off across the backyard like all of a sudden the birdbath has become worth studying. "Well, good," she says, though I get the idea she's no more eager to hear about my sex life with Aimee than I am to hear about hers with Marcus. "The thing is, I'm glad you two are together. She'll be good for you."

What's the deal with people thinking I need some kind of good influence in my life?

"Who knows?" She shoots me her sly smile. "Maybe you'll amount to something after all."

"Hey." I slip her a wink. "I'm already something. I'm an absolutely miraculous marvel."

She laughs.

It's weird. Our relationship is doing this surreal metamorphosis right in front of my eyes. The old feelings for each other aren't completely gone, but they seem to be slipping further and further away. That's okay, I tell myself. I'm with Aimee for now. Cassidy's just another ex-girlfriend. All right, maybe she's really more like some kind of new, mutant, never-seen-before type of friend, but she is just a friend.

That's good, I tell myself. It's really, really a good fit. We can talk about anything, and there aren't all the little booby traps to avoid like when you're boyfriend and girlfriend. Yes, I tell myself, this will work out great.

But somehow after leaving her house that afternoon, I'm hit with this big fat urge to get gloriously, panoramically ripped.

Chapter 48

So, the prom's barreling straight my way at full speed, out of control with the high beams on. No worries, though. I have a plan. I envision a perfect replica of a Dean Martin tuxedo and a long white limo. Of course, I'll need someone to chip in on the limo, so I go straight to Ricky.

"Sorry, dude," he says. "No can do. Bethany's already made arrangements for us to split a limo with Tara and Brian Roush."

"Roush? You're splitting a limo with Roush?"

"Yeah, he asked Tara to the prom, and you know how tight Bethany and Tara are. See, that could've been you riding high and tight in our limo if you'd started dating Tara like I told you to."

"Well, still, if we get a stretch limo, I'm sure three couples can fit in there, easy."

He grimaces.

"What?"

"Yeah, um, it's just that you aren't exactly Bethany's favorite guy."

"Me? What's she got against me? I thought you just said I'd be in your limo if I was dating Tara."

"That's right. *If* you were dating Tara. As it is, I think she's afraid you might be a little, um, too wild for her taste."

"Wild? I'm not wild. I'm fun."

"Okay. Then I guess she thinks you're a little too fun for her taste."

That's that. No limo with Ricky. What happened to loyalty in this world? After all, who got Ricky and Bethany together in the first place?

Not being one to give up easily, I hit Cody Dennis with the idea, but of course, he's too scared to even ask a girl to the prom. In fact, he's too scared to have *me* ask a girl to the prom for him.

Then I come up with a truly fabulous solution. Why not finally cash in on the idea of a double date with Cassidy and Marcus? They probably need a little spark of fun in their evening. This requires a delicate touch, though. Sure, Marcus is okay with Cassidy and me hanging out as friends now, but that doesn't mean he'll be so gung ho about me tagging along to the prom with them. No, the way to show them the beauty of the proposition is to first pitch the simple idea of a double date to the movies. Once they see how much fun we are as a foursome, the prom date will be a cinch.

Cassidy thinks it's a stroke of genius, and Marcus goes along with her, but you can tell he's not exactly a tsunami of enthusiasm. So that Saturday, off we go to a restaurant and then to see *Lovestruck Fool* at the cineplex in Bricktown. To me, everything goes super-stupendously, except maybe for after the movie when Aimee accidentally drops the vodka bottle out of her purse and it shatters on the foyer floor. That kind of thing is simply funny to me, but not everybody has the same fully developed sense of humor. Marcus actually looks askance at us. That's right, *askance*.

So, the next day I call Cassidy—she's on her cell while delivering meals to elderly shut-ins with Marcus—and I pitch her the prom scheme, only to find out they already have plans to rent a limo with some of his buddies and their dates.

I'm like, "But we had so much fun at the movies. We're a stellar foursome."

And she's, "I'm sorry but our plans are all set. I mean, what did you expect, Sutter? The prom's this weekend. Everyone already has plans. You probably can't even get a limo by now."

"Well, I guess that means I should probably go order my tux tomorrow."

"What? You haven't even ordered your tux?"

"Hey, I was thinking about waiting till the day of the prom."

"Sutter, you'd better not mess up this prom for Aimee. This is a big deal for a girl."

"Don't worry," I tell her, all nonchalant. "Everything's cool. The stars are in perfect alignment for a fantabulous time. All I have to do is let things fall into place."

Chapter 49

Things do fall into place. Mostly. There's absolutely no problem in finding the perfect Dean Martin tux. The cost of renting a limo by myself is way too steep, but so what if I have to take my own car? Do you think I'd ask Geech to borrow his Cadillac? Not in a million years. No, the Mitsubishi will do just fine.

There's just one thing left—Aimee has to figure out a way to get out of throwing the paper route the morning after the prom. She asks me to be there with her when she confronts her mom, but I'm like, "No way. This is something you have to do on your own. You have to stand up to her. How else do you think you're ever going to break away from her and go to school in St. Louis?"

To tell the truth, I don't know how she's handled the paper route this long. We've partied pretty hard, and still she gets up in the morning to throw that route. I really intended to go with her more often than that one time when I spent the night at her house, but I kept forgetting to set the alarm, which could happen to anybody. You can't blame me for that.

Anyway, finally, just a few days before the prom she comes over to my house after school, all excited. She did it. She laid things on the line with her mom.

"I just told her this was my prom, it was a once-in-a-lifetime experience, and I wasn't going to wreck it by throwing that old paper route."

"I'm proud of you!"

"I'm proud of myself!"

She jumps into my arms, and to celebrate, we take the pitcher of martinis I just made and head straight up to bed. It's not till after the congratulatory sex, when we're lying there with our martini glasses, that she runs through the whole story for me, how she walked right over, turned off the TV, and mapped out the entire plan before her mom or Randy could open their mouths. She didn't raise her voice or even get emotional. She just told it like it was.

When her mom tried to come with this line about how she and Randy might want to hit the casinos that night, Aimee had the facts ready. She'd delivered the route by herself over thirty times in the last year, while never getting a single day off herself. Therefore, she was going to take one off now and she was going to take one off for graduation, and there weren't any two ways about it.

Of course, she didn't exactly tell her mother about how we planned to get a motel room. Instead, she explained that the school was sponsoring all these heavily chaperoned after-prom events that lasted till sunup. Which is true, but only the mortally clueless actually go to those. Not to say I haven't taken a wait-and-see attitude toward the laser tag thing. That would be absolutely hilarious to go to wasted.

"I didn't actually lie," she says. "I just told her the school was sponsoring the events. I never said we were going."

"That's perfect," I tell her. I am really authentically proud of her. "You're my hero. I might have to get you to come over and set my mom straight on a few things sometime."

She's quiet for a second before she comes out with, "Maybe it's time you stood up to your mom too."

"What are you talking about? My mom doesn't care if I stay out all night for the prom. She'd barely notice if I didn't come back for a week."

"That's not what I mean. I mean you should talk to her

about your dad. Have you even asked her what really happened between them?"

"I never had to. She was always way too glad to feed me her phony story about him being a big cheating louse."

"Maybe you should ask *him*."

"How am I going to do that? Take an elevator to the top of the Chase building and ask him? Oh, that's right. He's not really there."

"Then, ask your mom where he is. It's time you talked to him and found out his side of the story. I'd go with you."

Okay, it's great that Aimee's getting more assertive, but she's starting to bug me a little with it now.

"Jesus, Aimee, what's all this interest in my dad?"

"It's just that, you know, I lost my dad before I could say everything I wanted to say to him."

"Look, I'm glad you stood up to your mom. That was great. But that doesn't mean you can fix my parental quagmire for me."

"It might help if we could just talk to him, though."

"No, I know what'll help. A big fat party." I roll over and grab my pants from the back of the chair. "I say, bring on the prom. All solutions will be found in the land of the all-night buzz."

Chapter 50

My bow tie, cummerbund, and red breast-pocket handkerchief are perfectly Dino-rific. Aimee's mom opens the door, her fabulous she-mullet glinting in the TV glow. "Don't you look like the sophisticated gentleman," she says, then turns and yells, "Aimee, your date's here."

Aimee doesn't come out immediately, so there I am, stuck in the living room trading awkward glances with Mom and Randy-the-Walrus.

Then Aimee appears in the hall, and it strikes me that she postponed her grand entrance on purpose for dramatic effect. You have to know she stood in front of the mirror for about a month fixing everything just right, but Aimee's Aimee—fancy really isn't her specialty.

Of course, she has the lipstick again and even some eye shadow this time. On top of that—and I mean on top of that literally—she's done her hair up, and it's tilting just slightly off-kilter—the Leaning Tower of Pisa–style. Her dress is this vague yellow color that doesn't go too well with her skin tone. The faux silkiness of it actually does give her hips a sexy, slinky touch, but the cleavage is pretty nonexistent.

The whole ensemble has this effect on me like I just want to grab her and hold on to her, pet her, and tell her she's the most beautiful sight in the entire galaxy. Don't worry about any wisecracks from the likes of Jason Doyle, I want to tell her. But she wouldn't have the slightest idea why wisecracks would be in order in the first place.

We do the boutonniere and corsage exchange, and Mom takes a couple of photos with one of those little yellow disposable cameras, and then we're on our way. Now, I know everybody else is going to fancy restaurants like The Mantel or Nikz at the Top, but Aimee and I aren't everybody else.

"So," she says. "What's the surprise? Where are we going for dinner?"

"Just wait. You'll see."

About ten minutes later, the radio-tower lights come into view, and she's like, "Wait, are we going to Marvin's Diner?"

"You are correct," I proclaim, all game-show-hosty. "Give the lady a new refrigerator and a ceramic greyhound!"

"Aren't we kind of overdressed?"

"Doesn't matter. It's the sentimental history of the place—the scene of our first date."

"I thought the party at the lake was our first date."

"I mean our first sit-down-and-eat date."

"All we had was chili fries."

"What's the matter? Don't you like the idea?

"No, it's not that."

"I mean, this place is, like, special. It's *our place*."

"Really? Our place?"

"Of course."

"It's perfect, then," she says, smiling.

At Marvin's, I'm sort of expecting the staff to really get a kick out of us coming in all decked out in our prom gear, but the guy behind the front counter—who may or may not be Marvin—gives us this look like we must be crazy.

"We're going to the prom," I tell him, "and we could think of no more splendid establishment than Marvin's for our special occasion."

"Really?" the guy says flatly. He looks at Aimee. "And you went along with this?"

"Sure," she says. "It's our place."

The guy cocks his head to the side. "Okay. Try not to get chili on your dress."

We take our favorite booth and when the waitress comes over, she's a little more into the spirit of things. "Don't you two look sweet," she says. "We'll have to get you something special. How about the chicken-fried steak?"

"Can we get it with chili fries?"

"You can get it with anything you want, sugar."

After we order and the waitress has disappeared into the back, I pull a small package from my pocket. It's wrapped in red and green paper and tied off with a bright red ribbon. Okay, so it's leftover Christmas wrapping, but it still looks nice.

"Here." I hand the package to Aimee. "I just wanted to get you a little something for tonight."

Her eyes light up and she sort of pets the box. "You didn't have to get me anything."

"I know. I just wanted to."

Very gingerly, she chips at the paper as if maybe she doesn't want to tear it so she can save it for a souvenir. Finally, she slides the paper off, removes the lid from the box, and stares inside.

"It's a flask," she says.

"Yes, it is. It's just like mine."

She sets the box down. "I love it."

"And you'll notice it's already full too."

Everything's perfect. We doctor our drinks, Dean Martin croons from the jukebox, and the chicken-fried steaks and chili fries couldn't be better. The waitress even sets a candle on our table for romantic effect. If Aimee had any qualms about Marvin's before, I don't see how she could have any left by the time we leave for the prom.

———

The next stop is Remington Park, where the prom is being held. Yes, it's a horse-racing track, but they also have this really swank facility with a super-cool banquet room. The building itself looks like a palace, all lit up with a golden glow, banners waving from the rooftop. Also, they have this great entryway with a big red awning that makes you feel like you're walking into the Oscars or something. Very upscale.

Inside, the banquet room brims with padded chairs and tables with white tablecloths, row after row of them on five different tiers. Along one side, huge windows—a wall of glass really—face out on the track, which is lit up for our viewing pleasure. Of course, there's no horse racing tonight, but it's a magnificent scene with the way the light shines on the brown track and glitters across the two ponds on the north side of the infield.

I have to hand it to the planning committee—this is a great locale, but the decorations are just what the *Puttin' on the Ritz* theme led me to expect—cheesy cutouts of top hats and canes and tiaras, along with some glittery stars and moon slivers. They're truly awful in the most glorious way. Yes, we're puttin' on the ritz, all right. Here we are, the kings and queens of lame. It's our night!

Aimee and I arrive a little late since I got lost a couple of times on the way over, but luckily Cassidy saved us a seat at her table. It's the least she could do after shooting down my limo idea. Ricky's at a table clear across the room surrounded by Bethany and Tara's friends. What he has to talk about with these people, I couldn't begin to guess. From the look of his awkward, two-sizes-too-tight smile, I'd say he doesn't have much of an idea either.

The punch mixes perfectly with Aimee's Grey Goose but doesn't really cut it with my whisky, so I have to sneak in straight shots whenever I get the chance, which I don't mind, except this is supposed to be our special night. Couldn't they have some 7UP around somewhere?

Also, I thought we should have live music, but they hired a DJ instead. This idiot thinks he's smooth too. Hat on sideways. Wrap-around sunglasses. I mean, dude, we're inside and it's night. What do you need sunglasses for? His patter is a born-and-bred white Okie's version of West Coast hip and his song selection is the same as what the radio projectile-vomits day in and day out. But that's all right. I brought my secret weapon— *The Essential Dean Martin*. I'm just waiting for the right time to slip it into the mix.

Despite the hideous music, the dance floor's packed, and after a while of me entertaining our table with a few of my comic stories, Cassidy and Marcus squeeze their way into the crowd. Now, believe me, Marcus has this completely smooth look— immaculate white tux with black shirt and tie—but he's a little bit of a whooping crane on the dance floor, long stiff legs and a goofy back-and-forth head bob. Cassidy, on the other hand— you might think she'd jiggle too much, but no—she moves like liquid grace.

I know I'm here with Aimee—and I'm glad to be with her—but how can you not stare at Cassidy? She's wearing this gorgeous turquoise gown that hugs every opulent curve. The turquoise sets her eyes off so that they glow like blue diamonds, and her perfect skin gleams like polished milk. Whereas Aimee has to keep tugging at the straps on her dress to keep them on her shoulders, Cassidy's gown has no straps. Her magnificent cleavage does the job all on its own like some awesome miracle of anatomical engineering.

"She's a good dancer," Aimee says.

"What?"

"Cassidy. She's a good dancer."

"Oh yeah, I guess she is. I hadn't noticed."

When the song ends, Cassidy heads back to the table, pulling Marcus along by the hand. "Why aren't you out there dancing?" she asks me.

"You know I hate this kind of music."

"So what? I hate it too. But aren't you the one who always says, 'Embrace the weird'? Just get out there and have some fun."

She has a point. I'm not one of these people who worries about the hipness quotient of my music. I just like what I like. Besides, I'm a great dancer.

"Come on." I grab Aimee's hand as another terrible song cranks up. "I *really* hate this song. We'll have a blast!"

But my hand tug meets with unexpected resistance. "I don't know," she says. "I'm not much of a dancer."

"Hey, with my moves, I can make anyone look good."

"Maybe later." She holds up her cup as if to say, *It'll take a few more drinks to get me out there.*

From the other side, Cassidy grabs my arm. "You don't mind if I borrow him for this dance, then, do you?"

"Uh, sure," Aimee says. "No, that'd be great."

On the dance floor, it's a little awkward at first. Cassidy and I have never danced as just friends. "So." She raises her voice to compete with the music. "Aimee looks nice."

"Yeah."

"You look pretty good yourself."

"You look amazing."

She smiles and glances away.

It feels comfortable now. No use trying to hide the fact that there's still a spark between us.

I spin her, then we pull together, then step apart and pull back again, moving together as smoothly as ever. Only once do I get a little too rambunctious and accidentally collide with Derrick Ransom.

He's like, "Watch where you're going, Sutter," and I'm,

"Hey, it's just this dance floor. It's way too small to contain my fabulous moves."

"Yeah, right."

The song ends and a slow one starts up.

"You want to dance one more?" Cassidy says.

"Sure. One more sounds good."

It's been a while since I held her like this. There's so much to hold on to. The warmth of her is nearly overwhelming. Her perfume smells like she looks—blue and white and golden. This is not the time to raise a stiffy, but the song's only halfway through, and my defenses are weakening.

"I hope Aimee doesn't mind us slow dancing," she says.

"What's there to mind?"

"Oh, I don't know. I might mind if it was me."

"How about Marcus. You think he's all right with it?"

"He'd better be."

"That's easy for you to say."

"So how are you and Aimee doing?" Her lips are right next to my ear now.

"We're good."

"You're treating her all right, aren't you?"

"Sir Galahad has nothing on me in the chivalry department."

She laughs and her breath is warm against my neck. "I noticed her pull out a flask and spice up her punch. You're not turning her into a lush, are you?"

I pull back and look her in the face. "What is this? Did you want to dance or give me a lecture about Aimee?"

She leans her cheek against mine. "Dance," she says.

When the song's over, she pats my cheek and we head back to the table. Seems like Marcus hasn't even been paying attention to us. He's deep in conversation with Darius Carter and Jimmy McManus. Aimee's sitting off to the side with the kind of strained expression on her face that people get when they're trying to look like they don't mind being left alone in the middle of a crowd.

I kiss her on the cheek and ask how her flask is holding out. "I still have a little left."

"A little?" I take a sip of her punch. "Wow. That's one high-octane libation." I take another sip. "But not bad. Not bad at all."

The prom swirls around us. It's a spectacular stage in the life of the buzz, the stage when you feel connected to everybody and everything. The memories I have with these people are too many to count. So many buddies with so many funny stories to go along with them. Sometimes I can just picture their faces and it cracks me up.

And then there are the ex-girlfriends. They look incredible, every one of them. Next to Cassidy, Shawnie is probably the most beautiful, the way her red gown goes with her black hair and deep tan and glittering eyes. It's good to see her so happy. I was a little worried when I found out she'd started dating Jeremy Holtz, but they actually seem good together. I wouldn't have expected Jeremy to even care about coming to the prom, but here he is, and I've never seen him smile so much.

These are my people. We're all dressed up and celebrating our common bond—youth. That's what the prom is—St. Patrick's Day for the young. Only we're not toasting shamrocks or chasing snakes out of Ireland. We're toasting the chlorophyll rising in our bodies, catching the energy from the universe. Nobody's ever been young like we are right at this moment. We're the Faster-than-the-Speed-of-Light Generation.

Finally, another slow song plays, and this time Aimee doesn't resist. She practically melts into my chest as we sway to the music. It's so different having her in my arms compared to

Cassidy. Cassidy brings something beautiful to me from the out-side. Aimee brings something beautiful up from the depths of my insides.

"I can't dance like Cassidy," she says.

"Yeah, but you dance like Aimee. And that's perfect."

Chapter 51

Finally, that part of the prom arrives that I don't have any use for—crowning the king and queen. We're all kings and queens to my way of thinking. Why would you want to wreck the togetherness of the situation by holding two people above the rest?

To avoid the whole creepy deal, I take Aimee for a walk. The building is a cool place to check out, especially for a horse lover like she is. Pictures of racehorses and jockeys' colors decorate the walls, and a really awesome horse statue stands in the foyer. There are also clubs and restaurants and a casino, all closed for now, but you can feel the ghosts of the gamblers haunting the corridors. I've been to the races a couple of times and explain to Aimee how the betting works.

"I'd probably lose all my money," she says.

"That's all right. It's just part of the cost of coming out here. I mean, I don't know a thing about horses myself, but that doesn't matter either. I just pick the ones with the most pathetic-sounding names—like Fat Cat or Snickerdoodle-dandy—and bet on them. I figure they could use the support, you know?"

"What if there was a horse named Cassidy?"

"What do you mean? Cassidy's not a pathetic name."

"But would you bet on it?"

"Why would you ask a question like that?"

"It's just, you know, I saw the way you were slow dancing with her."

"Hey, she asked me to dance, not the other way around. And you said it was all right."

"But you should've known it wouldn't really be all right."

Uh-oh. Here it is—we've finally reached the *you-should-have-read-my-mind* stage.

"How am I supposed to know that?" I ask. "You have to tell me these things. ESP isn't one of my many talents, you know."

We walk outside where the moon and the big lights shine on the precisely landscaped grounds. Neither one of us says anything for a while. Finally, I break the silence. "Look, I'm here with you. Cassidy's with Marcus. She and I are just good friends. What do I have to do to get you to have a little faith in the Sutterman?"

We sit on a stone bench, and she gazes at the perfect garden in front of us and goes, "I was thinking of something you could do."

"What? I'll do anything."

"You know how you keep telling me I need to stand up to my mom and quit the paper route and move to St. Louis with my sister? Well, I think I'm really going to do it. My grades have dropped a little lately, but that's okay. It's too late to apply for fall, so I can just go to the community college there for a year. I've already talked to Ambith and she said she can get me a job at the bookstore where she's the assistant manager."

"A job at a bookstore? That's perfect for you."

"It really is. Next to working at NASA, that's pretty much like my dream job."

"And you'll get to take control of your own money."

"I know!"

It's weird. This is exactly what I set out to get her to do from the very beginning, but now that she's actually talking about leaving, I don't want her to go. I can't tell her that, though. She needs to go.

"That's great," I say, working up a smile. "I can't think of anything better. This situation you're in right now is just, like, smothering. It's unacceptable. St. Louis would be muy fantastico. If you want me to help you move, don't worry. I'm your man."

"That's not exactly what I was thinking about." She takes a deep breath. "I was hoping you'd say you'll move there with me."

"Move there?"

"You could go to the community college, too, and we'd both have jobs and we could get an apartment together."

This isn't what I expected, to say the least. Yes, I've become a lot more attached to Aimee than I ever thought I would, but you know me. I'm committed to absolutely avoiding the topic of future living arrangements. Sure, I've always thought eventually I might move in with a girl someday, maybe even get married, but that was always more like a kid thinking he'd be the captain of a big ship one day. I mean, it never had any concrete reality for me. Now, here's Aimee hitting me right in the face with it like a frozen sea bass.

So I'm like, "Wow. Move in together, huh?"

"My sister said I could move in with her, but I'm sure if you'd come with me, we could get a place in the same apartment complex that she lives in. It's not that expensive at all."

"You've really done some planning."

"I don't even want to spend the summer here. I want to go as soon as school's out."

"That's coming up pretty quick."

She looks down at her fingers. "Don't you want to go? I mean, you're always telling me I should break away from my mom and go up there, but I don't want to go without you."

"Yeah, but moving in together? That's big. Seeing as how my parents were these huge monumental failures at that, I don't know if it's such a good idea."

"But maybe it is." She grabs my hand and finally looks me in the eye. "Maybe it's just what you need to get over what happened with your parents."

"Oh, I'm way over that."

"Are you?" She squeezes my hand more tightly. "Then why does it always bug you so much when I bring up your dad? You always close off whenever I bring up trying to find him. But that's exactly what I think you need to do, find him and talk to him. If you know what really happened, then you can make sure it doesn't happen to us."

"You think?" I have to admit the topic of finding my dad still annoys me, but I can't show that now that she's busted me for it.

"Yes, I do." No more two-syllable *yeses*. Her voice has a whole tankful of certainty now. "I think it's worth trying anything to keep us together."

"But what if we find out something terrible, like that he's a serial killer or a game-show host? Will you still want me to go with you to St. Louis then?"

"I'll want you to go with me no matter what. The question is, do you want to go?"

Of course, I should do like Ricky told me, grow a spine and just tell her no, there's no way I'm going to find my dad and no way I can move to St. Louis with her and no way we can ever work out in the long run. But Ricky's not the one sitting here staring at the pleading in this girl's pale blue eyes.

So I do the kind of thing I do instead—put my arm around her shoulder, pull her to me, and say, "Yes, I do. That could really work. You're exactly right. Moving in together would be spectacular. In fact, that sounds like the greatest idea in the history of the universe."

Chapter 52

Back in the banquet hall, the mood of the prom has changed. Or maybe it's just that I'm sinking into the next stage of the life of the buzz—the lull, the valley that lies between peaks. This is just something that's been happening lately. Used to, it was pretty much all peaks, but I guess you have to expect a valley every now and then when you're in it for the long haul.

I look across the room, and this sorrowful feeling washes over me, almost bittersweet but with a whole lot more bitter. The beauty of the lame decorations has worn thin and now they're just pathetic. The glitter is crumbling. Desperation seeps into the room. People's smiles seem as fake as the cardboard moons.

This idea comes to me that we're all grass blades on the same lawn. We've grown up together, shoulder to shoulder, under the same sun, drinking the same rain. But you know what happens to grass blades—somebody cuts them down just when they reach their prime.

A lot of kids have left for their after-parties. Cassidy and Marcus are nowhere to be seen. Neither is Ricky. But the dance floor's still half-full, and that might be the worst thing of all. What is it about this crappy music that makes anyone even bother to lift a foot? It sounds like it was spit out by the atomic vampire's de-soul-inator machine. Still, there they are, gyrating and grinning, even coming off with the occasional sexy pout they learned from TV. Zach Waldrop goes for a comedy dance to make up for his lack of rhythm. Mandy Stansberry, my old wild-child girlfriend from junior high, gives it the bump and grind like she's the latest cookie-cutter teen pop diva. Or is it teen porn diva? What's the difference?

We're not the Faster-than-the-Speed-of-Light Generation anymore. We're not even the Next-New-Thing Generation. We're the Soon-to-Be-Obsolete Kids, and we've crowded in here to hide from the future and the past. We know what's up—the future looms straight ahead like a black wrought-iron gate and the past is charging after us a like a badass Doberman, only this one doesn't have any letup in him.

That's all right. Never fear. Sutter Keely is a veteran of the life of the buzz. I know the stages as well as I know the months of summer. And the only thing to do now is to power through the valley to the next stage—the I-don't-give-a-damn-just-bring-it-on stage.

When the DJ takes a break, I nudge Aimee and go, "You know what? This prom's turning to dust in its own casket. What it needs is a serious personality makeover, and I'm just the man for the job." Without further explanation, I bounce right up to the DJ booth, ready to inject some essential Dean into the abyss.

But there's a problem—the equipment is a little complicated and I've had a few drinks, so I abort the original mission and go for a new-and-improved one: the Sutterman himself belting out the Dino hits straight from his very own gut.

I tap the mike a couple of times. "Can I have everybody's attention?"

Somewhere in the middle of the room, somebody yells, "Whoo! Sutter!"

"I just want to change the mood a little bit." I give it my best suave-and-low microphone voice. "Add a little class to the evening. A little panache."

I start off with "You're Nobody 'Til Somebody Loves You,"

giving it the full Dino croon. I crinkle my eyes like Dean and sway and wave my cup around like him.

"Ow!" someone yells a few tables away.

Unfortunately, I don't remember all the words, so I have to segue into "Ain't Love a Kick in the Head" after a few lines. But even that is a stroke of genius. The perfect medley. Those two songs pretty much sum up the state of the world. In fact, they're not just songs. They're revelations. Suddenly the prom has lost its cheese factor and a big fat dose of *profound* sweeps the room.

But there's always somebody who doesn't get it. Like Mr. Asterhole.

He's there as part of the prom Gestapo unit, ready to pounce on anyone who veers the least little bit off the highway of bland. I'm just going back for a second helping of the chorus of "You're Nobody 'Til Somebody Loves You" when his grip clamps down on my arm.

"All right, that's enough, Mr. Keely. Time to head back to your table."

"But this is what it's all about," I tell him with perfect sincerity. "This is the gospel according to Dino."

"Sit down!" somebody yells from the crowd, probably the same person who came up with *Puttin' on the Ritz* as a theme.

"Bite me," I intone in my deep microphone voice.

"That'll be enough," says Mr. Asterhole, tugging at my arm.

"But, Mr. Asterhole," I say, still keeping it low and smooth. "This is our last night to be young, or did you forget how that feels?"

I should point out that the whole thing, the "Mr. Asterhole" part and all, booms out through the mike. A couple of whoops go up, along with a couple more "Sit downs," and Mr. Aster's eyes bulge.

"Okay, that's it," he says. "Your prom's over."

I swear he's so hot it looks like his hair might catch fire. But

I'm just like, "That's cool. This carcass is ready for the morgue anyway."

"Out, Mr. Keely. I'm not going to say it again."

Walking back to the table to collect Aimee, I maintain perfect dignity. Okay, so a couple of people call out, "Go home, dumbass," but who cares? The ones who get it are on my side. "Way to go, Sutter," they tell me. "See you at the after-party, dude!"

Leaving early doesn't disappoint Aimee at all. She's already gathered her things by the time I reach the table. As soon as we hit the cool air outside, we both take long swigs of our drinks. Yes, the next stage in the life of the buzz is kicking in.

Chapter 53

There are plenty of after-parties to hit, but most of my friends will be at Cassidy's best friend Kendra's house. The party is likely to last all night, so we have plenty of time to stop at our motel room. The plan is to change clothes, refill our flasks, and take off, but Aimee has something else in mind.

Before I can get my jeans pulled up, she comes out of the bathroom in just her panties, walks over, and kisses me on the chest. "We don't have to go to any more parties," she says.

"But it's prom night."

She runs her finger along my stomach. "We can make it special right here."

The girl is a rookie, see. She doesn't understand the stages of the life of the buzz. I kiss her long and hard, then pull away. "We can make it special here *after* the party. Now, come on, get dressed. We want to be there when they pop the cork on the champagne."

"But do we have to go to a party where Cassidy's going to be?"

"You're not still worried about that, are you? Look, she's my friend. You have to get used to being around her. Come on now. Have a little faith in the Sutterman. The best part of the night is just beginning."

"Really?"

"Really. Now go get dressed."

This stage in the life of the buzz is truly fabulous. It's not even a buzz anymore. It's a roar. The world opens up and everything's yours right here, right now. You've probably heard the expression—All good things must come to an end. Well, this stage in the life of the buzz never heard anything close to that. This stage says, "I will never end. I am indestructible. I will last fabulously forever." And, of course, you believe it. To hell with tomorrow. To hell with all problems and barriers. Nothing matters but the Spectacular Now.

Not everyone can get all the way through to this stage. It takes practice and dedication. It's like learning how to pilot a plane—you have to put in your air miles before you can really fly on your own.

And believe me, by the time we get to Kendra's, I'm soaring. Crowds gather round and I'm making up jokes, doing the Italian mobster routine with Shawnie Brown, chugging glasses of champagne while standing on my head—bringing the crazy fun. A couple of people egg me on to climb up on the coffee table and sing some more Dino, and you can be sure it doesn't take much egging. This is how a party should be. Not an adult anywhere near to shut us down. Kendra's parents are geniuses. They turned the house over to her and said, "We trust you, honey, just don't let anyone get in the pool."

Right. Good luck with that!

The only downside is no Ricky. The dude promised he'd show, but where is he? For all I know, he's actually playing school-sponsored laser tag with Bethany right now. Of course, Cassidy's here with Marcus, and every once in a while I catch her staring at me, flashing her little Mona Lisa smile and shaking her head. I know what she's thinking: "Why did I ever trade in someone that's so awesomely fun for Mr. Stone Cold Sober in the kitchen discussing politics?"

What can I say? Everyone makes mistakes.

At some point, I lose touch with where Aimee is. Last time

I saw her she was sitting on the end of the sofa with her drink in her hand and an awkward smile on her face, so I'm glad she got up and started mingling. I really do mean to check on her just in case she's stuck listening to the blather of someone foul like Courtney Skinner or worse, Jason Doyle, but I end up getting a little sidetracked.

The thing is, just as I start to look for her, Brody Moore grabs me by the arm and whispers a beautiful suggestion in my ear. "The swimming pool is calling," he says. "It only takes one person to dive in first."

Brody knows all too well that I'm willing to do my duty and be that first person. "To the patio door," I say. "Full speed ahead and damn the potatoes."

By the time Brody and I get to the pool, there's a nice crowd following us, and I lift my hands in the air to start a cheer: "Dive, Sutter, dive! Dive, Sutter, dive!"

The diving board is way too low for the kind of drama that the situation requires, so naturally, I have a couple of dudes boost me up to the roof of the little cabana on the deep-end side. It's far enough away from the pool that I have to back up to get a running start, but that just adds to the excitement.

The cheers grow louder. "Dive, Sutter, dive! Dive, Sutter, dive!"

The thought does cross my mind that I could slip and end up cracking my head on the pavement just short of the pool, but if you're always going to worry about minor drawbacks, then you'll never accomplish anything. So, without another thought, I take about three big steps and out I fly—fully clothed—catching some tasty air, rolling and tucking, almost completing an entire flip, but not quite. When I come up for air, everyone's clapping and whooping. A couple of people in the front row got thoroughly splashed, but they don't mind.

"Marco!" I holler.

"Polo!" responds Brody just before cannonballing into the deep end.

After that, it's a free-for-all. There must be twenty kids in the pool, guys and girls both, some still in their formal gear. The water churns, people take turns dunking each other, girls' blouses and gowns cling magnificently to their breasts. Shouts and laughter careen every which way. Watching it from the side of the pool, my shoes, socks, and pants legs dangling in the water, I smile an all-time, big, Guinness-Book-worthy smile, soaking in the vastness of what I've accomplished. I don't even hear Cassidy calling my name until she's right behind me.

Chapter 54

"Sutter, you have to come inside."

I look up, and there Cassidy is, standing above me, the patio lights shining in her hair. She's beautiful.

"I can't come inside. I'm all wet."

"I'll get you a towel."

"What's the emergency?" I get up and start toward the patio door with her.

"It's Aimee. She's sick. Kelsey found her in the bathroom lying on the floor. She threw up in the bathtub."

"God. I guess maybe we shouldn't have had all those chili fries at Marvin's."

"Or maybe all that liquor?"

"Look, here's an idea. Why don't you go in and bring her out here. Maybe if I take her for a swim it'll make her feel better."

"A swim? Sutter, she can't swim. She'd sink like a stone."

"Hey, I'd be right there with her. I wouldn't let her sink."

"Right, like you've been with her all night at this party? You haven't spent a minute with her since you've been here."

"Well, what does that have to do with you? Wasn't it enough for you to tell me how to be a boyfriend when we were together? Now you're going to tell me how to be a boyfriend to someone else?"

"This isn't about me and you." She stops in front of me and grabs my arms like maybe she wants to shake some sense into me. "You know I care for you, and I always will, but this is about—"

She doesn't get a chance to finish. Aimee cuts her off. We're standing by the patio furniture about ten yards from the door, and here she comes, walking at a little bit of a tilt but determined-looking nonetheless.

"He doesn't give a damn if you care for him or not," she says about fifty decibels too loud. "You're not his boyfriend. I mean, he's not your girlfriend. I mean—you know what I mean."

Cassidy's like, "Aimee, I was just trying to get him to come inside and help you."

But Aimee goes, "I know what you were trying to do." Her face is very pale, more than usual. Even the lipstick is gone. There's a little fleck of vomit on her cheek. "You've been trying to do it all night long. You were practically fucking him on the dance floor."

"No, she wasn't," I tell her, completely amazed. I mean, sure, I taught her the value of swearing for certain reasons, but who would've thought the word *fucking* could roll off her tongue so easily?

"It was just a friendly dance," I say and try to take her arm, but she pulls away and goes for Cassidy.

"I don't ever want to see you around him anymore," she says. "You big fat bitch."

Then, the next thing I know, she hauls off and slaps Cassidy right across the cheek. The force of her swing throws her off balance, and she crashes down onto this glass patio end table, shattering it into a jumble of jigsaw pieces.

So, here I have one girl with a big red slap mark on her face and another lying in a pile of patio end table shards. Which one do I go to? I don't know if it says anything about me, but I go to Aimee.

I cup my hand behind her neck. "Can you sit up? Are you cut?"

"Do I look awful?" she says. "I bet I look awful."

"Come on, let's get you up in this chair."

I get her in the chair and look her over for cuts. There's just a scratch on the back of her arm, nothing bad.

"Looks like you're all right," I tell her, and she buries her face in my wet shirt and goes, "No, I'm not. I'm so stupid. I did this thing in the bathroom. Do I have vomit in my hair?"

"No, your hair smells sweet," I tell her, but the truth is the *fragrance de vomit* is a little on the overpowering side.

From behind me, Kendra shrieks, "Sutter Keely! When they told me what happened out here, I should've known you'd be involved. I hope you know you're going to pay for this table, Sutter."

"That's cool," I say, completely calm and dignified. "Just send me the bill."

She's not done, though. "And I want you and your wasted girlfriend out of here. Now!" She's boiling over with all the self-righteous anger of somebody's mom.

"Why should we leave? I said I'd pay for your stupid table."

"Why should you leave?" She surveys the patio and pool as if she's an insurance adjuster showing up after Hurricane Katrina. "Here's a couple of reasons: First, you got everyone in the pool when I said they weren't supposed to, and now little miss binge drinker causes a big stupid scene, slaps my best friend for no reason, and breaks a two-hundred-dollar table."

"Hey, it's a party. Things happen."

"No, Sutter. A party is for fun. You don't know how to have fun like a normal person."

"Me? Are you kidding? Look at everybody in the pool. You think they're not having fun? Which do you think they're going to remember more, playing some little game around the dining room table with you or laughing and swimming with their clothes on?"

Before Kendra can shoot back some lame reply, Cassidy

steps up and takes my arm. "Sutter." She stares me straight in the eye, giving me her best serious expression. I know it all too well. It's not mean or accusatory or anything like that. She's just letting me know there's no room for jokes now. "It's time to take Aimee home. She doesn't want to be here like this."

And she's right, of course. Aimee's sitting there all pale, looking like she could puke again at any second. This isn't how she wants people to know her, and it's not how I want them to know her.

"She's not usually like this," I say. "She's just not used to partying so much. I guess she needs a little more practice, you know?"

Cassidy pats my back. "Take her home."

Aimee's leaning so far forward in the chair now, it looks like she might fall over on her face, but she doesn't. She throws up again instead.

"Jesus," someone says. "Look at the puke machine."

I kneel down by her and pull back her hair. "Come on, baby," I say softly. "It's time to leave. You'll be all right. Everything will be fine."

Chapter 55

So, all in all, I'd say, despite the two-day hangover, the prom was a golden success. For days afterward, I have people coming up and congratulating me on my Dean Martin medley and my near-perfect, fully clothed flip into Kendra's swimming pool.

On the down side, a few idiots have started calling Aimee *Puke-a-reena*. Guys like Chad Lammel pass by in the hall and go, "Hey, Sutter, where's Puke-a-reena," or "Has Puke-a-reena busted up any more lawn furniture lately?" Aimee says that in English, just as she's sitting down, some dude goes, "Hey, Puke-a-reena, don't break the desk."

"That's okay," I tell her. "Screw that guy. We'll see what he has to say someday when you're a hotshot at NASA, and he's working at some poultry plant cutting off chicken heads for a living."

Aimee's not so preoccupied with NASA anymore these days, though. Now she's all about how we're going to locate my dad and move off to St. Louis, like it's a package deal. I'd kind of hoped that was just the vodka talking, but no such luck. She's already told her sister we're coming.

We sit down for lunch at Mickey D's one day and the first thing she says is, "Have you talked to your mom about finding your dad?" Second day in a row she's asked that.

"No, I decided I'd better talk to my sister about it instead. Only I have to approach it just right. My sister and I don't get along so great."

"I can't wait to meet him," she says. "I think this will be a

239

really, really great thing for you. But we don't have a whole bunch of time. Ambith's expecting us to come pretty much right after graduation."

"Don't worry. I told you I'd do it, and you know me—I do what I say I will."

Of course, the truth is that—regardless of how I've come to feel about her—I still expect Aimee to dump me. The signs are piling up. Just like all my other girlfriends, she's starting to look for that certain something *more* in me that I don't quite seem to have—whatever it is.

But time is running out if she's going to break up with me before the day we're supposed to move to St. Louis. In fact, now that the prom's over, it seems like the school year's pretty much finished too. We're all just going through the motions, biding our time till graduation.

Unfortunately, for some of us, graduation might be postponed a tad. I haven't told Aimee, but Mr. Asterhole has it in for me now. Apparently, according to him, it *seems* that I have to get at least a C on the last test to pass his class.

"And if you don't," he says, all stern and self-important, "it seems like I'll be seeing you in summer school, young man."

There he goes with the "young man" business.

I guess I could've had Aimee do more of my homework for me, but I didn't want to run the risk of making her think that's the only reason I was hanging out with her.

Anyway, I really do tell myself that I'm going to call my sister, Holly, and ask her about Dad. Maybe moving off to St. Louis isn't so realistic, but the idea of locating my father has started to grow on me. I'll bet I could really talk to him about things. It would be the Keely men, bonding at last. I can even see us going out to a baseball game together again. This time I'd have a tall, cold beer of my very own.

It's not hard to come up with excuses for not calling Holly, though—especially since she never really forgave me for the suit-burning incident—but today I have a really legitimate one. Bob, my manager at the clothing store, asked me to come to work a couple of hours early. I mean, I can't start some big, long-lost-dad conversation and then say, "Look, Holly, I'll call you back later. I have to go to work."

At Mr. Leon's, I bring up the subject with Bob, but he seems distracted and doesn't come across with his usual wisdom. Later, at the end of the shift, I find out why. He calls me into his office and tells me to have a seat.

"Sutter," he says, tenting his fingers on the desk in front of him. "Do you know why I asked you to come in early today?" He doesn't give me a chance to answer before going on. "Obviously we weren't extra busy. In fact, we're never busy anymore. That's the problem. The front office knows it, and they told me I have to cut hours starting the week after next. So I wanted you to get some extra time in before we have to do that."

"How many hours do you have to cut?" I ask. "I'm only working three days a week as it is, and not even eight-hour shifts. I was hoping to maybe get five days a week this summer."

I guess that shows where my mind is. I'm still thinking in terms of living here and not St. Louis.

Bob looks down and rubs his thumb along the edge of the desk. "And I'd like to give you those five days, Sutter. I really would. But the thing is, the way the front office wants it, I can only keep one clerk on. Now, we both know I like you and the customers like you—most of them anyway—so if I had my way, you'd be the one to keep."

"That's excellent, Bob. You won't regret it."

"Hold on for a second, Sutter. That's not all. I've given this some hard thought, and the only way I can let you stay is if you promise me—one hundred percent—that you won't ever come in with even a light buzz on. And I mean not even once.

Otherwise, I don't have any choice but to give you your two weeks' notice."

Bob looks me right in the eye now. He's got this heavy sadness about him, like whether I lie or tell the truth, he's bound to be disappointed. And of course, I can't lie to him. He's Bob Lewis. He's too good a guy.

"Well, Bob," I say. "You've got me there. You know I can't promise you that. I wish I could, but I can't."

He continues looking me in the eye for a long moment, then nods. "I appreciate your honesty, Sutter. I guess if I was your dad I'd try to give you a lecture or something about what you're doing to yourself, but that's not really my place."

I reach out and shake his hand. "Bob, if you were my dad, you probably wouldn't have to lecture me about that. It's been great working with you."

"We still have two more weeks to work together." I swear he looks like he's about to cry. "And after that, if you ever decide to get things on track, you come back by here, and we'll see if there's an opening."

"You can count on it."

It's pretty awkward around there after that, so I leave early instead of hanging around and talking to Bob while he counts out the till. Sure, I feel bad about getting fired, but I would've felt a lot worse if I'd lied. In fact, I'm pretty proud of myself, and as I walk out of the store, the air actually tastes a little sweet. Until I see Marcus's car parked next to mine.

Chapter 56

My first thought is, Great, what now? I just got my ass canned and somehow Marcus has gone jealous again?

But as I approach the car, he's not the one that steps out. It's Cassidy. I ask her what's up, and she says, "We just want to talk to you for a minute." I'm like, "Who's we?" and she goes, "Marcus and Ricky and I."

She has her serious face working, so I have to wonder what I've done now. Thumbing back through recent memories, I can't come up with anything. In fact, it seems like, except for getting fired, I've been a real upstanding citizen.

I sit next to Ricky in the backseat while Cassidy and Marcus sit up front. Everybody's staring at me, so I'm like, "What's going on? What'd I do now?"

They trade glances, and then Ricky starts off. "It's nothing you did," he says. "It's more like something we want you to consider doing."

I look from face to face. They're all dead serious, so I'm like, "Oh Jesus, this isn't one of those 'We're so worried about your drinking' intervention things, is it?"

"No, dude," says Ricky. "It's more like an Aimee Finecky intervention thing."

That's a little bit of a relief. I'd hate to see a couple of people I've partied with on such a monumental level go all school counselor on me. "Look," I say. "I already said I'd pay for that patio table."

"Dude, it's not the patio table we're worried about. It's Aimee herself."

I look at Cassidy. Her blue eyes nearly swallow me.

"Come on," I say. "Cassidy, you know Aimee didn't mean anything she said to you at the party. She was just a little bit wasted. She feels bad as hell about slapping you."

"I know she does," Cassidy says. "She's already apologized to me. I'm not worried about that."

"Well, then, what's this all about?"

After a long stretch of uncomfortable silence, Ricky goes, "It's just that we don't think it's working out."

"What?"

"You and Aimee, dude. Your relationship's not working out."

"Oh, really? Well, let me ask you this—since when do you have a say in whether my relationships are working out? I mean, look at you all. First, we have Mr. One Girlfriend in His Entire Life, then we have the chick who broke up with me for helping him get that girlfriend, then we have the dude who stole *my* girlfriend. Pardon me if I don't give a rat's ass what you think about my relationships."

"Wait a minute, man," says Marcus. "I didn't steal your girlfriend."

"Right. What, is she just on loan, like a library book?"

"No," says Cassidy. "What he means is I asked *him* out—*after* you and I broke up."

"Great. That's perfect. When was that, about fifteen minutes later? Sure, it's obvious to me now. That gives you the right to, like, break up my relationships with every future girlfriend I might ever have. I guess I should've read the fine print."

"Hold on, dude." Ricky leans forward. "Quit making this about you. It's about Aimee. It's about what's happening to her. I mean, we know better than to try to tell you to lay off drinking, but it's too much for her. I mean, I never used to see her drinking. Now she's like this big lush."

"That's right—you never saw her drinking. You know why? Because she was never at a party. She didn't have any friends, except for one who treated her like a dog."

"And now she's smashing vodka bottles in movie theaters," says Marcus. "That's not the type of person she's cut out to be."

"Yeah? What *type* of person is she? Do you look at her and just see this little nerd that should keep hiding in the corner and never come out? Because I see a lot more than that. I see someone whose dreams are as big as all of yours put together. And I see someone who can stand up for herself now. Before she started going out with me, she let everyone in her life walk over her like she was Sir Walter Raleigh's cloak."

"And you know what I see," says Ricky. "I see someone who people are calling Puke-a-reena at school now. You think you're this girl's savior, dude? Give it a rest. You just go around acting like you're saving other people so you don't have to deal with your own problems."

"Yeah? What problems do I have to deal with? Self-righteous hypocrites like you?"

"Hold on a second," Cassidy says. It's more of a plea than a demand. "Let's not get into a big argument. Guys, how about letting me and Sutter talk alone for a little bit?"

They agree and start to get out of the car, but she thinks it would be better if she and I get out instead. Which I go along with one hundred percent. The atmosphere in the car is more than a little stuffy.

We walk over and lean, side by side, against my car. "It's a nice night," she says, and I'm like, "I've had better."

"This was my idea," she says. "So don't blame the guys. Maybe it was stupid, but I know you really do want the best for Aimee."

"But you don't think I could ever be the best thing for her, right?"

"No, I think you could if you tried. But right now I don't think you are."

"So in your all-seeing wisdom, you proclaim that I should break up with her."

"I don't proclaim it. It's just my advice. That's all."

"Because I'm turning her into a lush like me?"

"Don't put it that way. She's not like you, Sutter. She doesn't have to be outgoing and carouse around with a lot of people. Besides, you know you're not in this thing for the long term."

"What makes you say that?"

"How long did you and I date, eight months? And in all that time, you made it very clear that you didn't have any long-range plans."

"Hey, I don't have any long-range plans about anything."

"I know. That's what I'm talking about. I knew you weren't ever going to really commit to us, and obviously, it's going to be the same way with Aimee. So, all I'm saying is that you'd be doing her a big favor if you just ended it before she gets drawn into something she can't get herself out of."

For a moment, I stand there and watch a burger wrapper blow across the parking lot. There's one big thing that Cassidy and the others don't know, something I can't tell them—the story about what happened with Aimee and Randy-the-Walrus's son. Even if I wanted to, how could I just break up with the girl when I know she has that rotten corpse buried in her past?

So I'm like, "Look, Cassidy, if you have this vast encyclopedic knowledge about me and my relationships, then you know I don't need to break anything off. She'll do that when she gets ready. She'll get tired of me, just like you did."

"You don't get it, do you? This girl loves you. She's not going to break up with you, not until something really bad happens."

"Oh, come on. Sure, she *likes* me, but she's not *in love* with me."

"That's so you. I don't know what happened, but for some reason, you never believe anyone loves you. Your mom, your sister. *Me*. I mean, if you can't believe anyone loves you, how are you ever going to break through that *everything's-oh-so-fabulous* front of yours and really commit to somebody?"

"Hey, it's not a front. And, by the way, it was, like, real apparent that you loved me by how you bounced me to the curb so easily."

"You think it was easy? Do you think I didn't cry about it? Sometimes I still do. But I've got to move on with my life and so do you. So does Aimee. It's just that she can't see it because you've become her whole world. She can't see going anywhere without you. But I can't picture you two moving in the same direction. Can you?"

"Yeah. I can. In fact, we're moving to St. Louis together after graduation." Okay, so this is kind of a knee-jerk response, but I'm not going to stand here and let Cassidy predict my life for me. "Our plan's all set. Her sister lives out there and she's finding us an apartment. We're both gonna get jobs and go to college. I just gave my two weeks' notice to Bob."

She takes my arm. "You can't be serious."

"You just wait and see." I pull away from her and open my car door. "Tell the guys they suck. See you in school."

Chapter 57

It's the middle of the afternoon, and Holly's decked out in a silky gold blouse, black gaucho-type pants, and sandals with straps that twine up past her ankles. You'd think she's going to brunch with some of her upscale girlfriends instead of just entertaining her wayward, black-sheep brother. But I guess since it's so rare that we even get together she wants to make an occasion of it.

Out we go to the deck overlooking the pool. She probably thinks if we stay inside I'll set something on fire. On the table, there's a plate of fruit and a pitcher of iced tea, which, of course, is unnecessary for me since I have my big 7UP.

As we sit at the table, she goes, "How do you like the way we've relandscaped back here?" She doesn't wait for an answer. "At first, we had a terrible time with the people we hired to do it, but, you know, I made it very clear what I wanted and when I wanted it done by, and if they didn't like it, I'd simply hire someone else. Oh, there was some muttering under their breath, but they got the work done. I think it turned out wonderfully."

"It's fantastic," I say in a mock-chipper way. I'm sure she's trying to postpone the dad conversation for as long as possible, but I'm really not in the mood for small talk.

She presses on with it, though. "Kevin wanted an apple tree, but I had to put my foot down and tell him it wasn't practical. Besides, I really don't like the way they look."

"Uh-huh," I say, surveying the yard. "Apple trees are so

yesterday. Anyway, like I said on the phone, I wanted to talk to you about Dad."

As quick as changing a TV channel, she goes from fruit-tray, gaucho-wearing hostess back to being the big sister again. "Oh, Sutter, I don't know why you want to dredge that up."

"Dredge? Come on, Holly, Dad's not something you *dredge*. He was a good guy. Remember how he used to tell us stories out in the tent in the backyard?"

"That was mostly you. I was a little old for backyard stories by the time he got that ratty old tent."

"Well, you remember that vacation we took to Mexico? Dad could speak a little Spanish and he'd have us go up to people and ask them questions like, 'Where can we find the belt buckle museum?' or 'Why is there no artichoke ice cream?' It was hilarious. And we got those cool Mexican puppets."

"Those questions were embarrassing."

"Embarrassing? People thought it was funny. They loved us."

"They loved you because you were little and cute."

"But the men loved you. The men thought you were a hot little muchacha."

She smiles. "You think so?"

"I know so. I saw the way they looked at you when you walked away." I don't bother to mention that the particular guy I remember was a skinny little hombre of about fifty with more acne scars than teeth. But I know Holly has to have some warm memories of Dad. I just need to bring them out of her.

"One of the best things about Dad," I say. "He never met a stranger."

"That's true." She takes a sip of iced tea. "He did know how to make friends with people. They may not have necessarily been the right kind of people, but he did know how to make people feel good about themselves. At least for a while."

A wistful expression flickers on her face. "I remember when

I was little, before you were born, he took me trick-or-treating. It was just the two of us. I was dressed as a princess with this long, silver, spangly gown and silver tiara. Dad told me I was the most beautiful girl he'd ever seen. He said that for the whole evening I was a real princess and I could do whatever I wanted to and that anything I wished would come true."

"That's Dad for you," I say. "He could be magical."

"The way he seemed to know everyone at every house we went to and talked to all the other little kids on the sidewalks, I really did feel special. I thought, I *am* a princess, and my dad's the king of America. For a while, we sat under a tree and ate candy—he loved Almond Joys—and he told me how no Halloween monsters could ever get us because we had a magic aura wrapped around us that turned all evil into dust bunnies upon touch."

"Yes! He told me that too."

"And then I told him what my biggest wish was. I wished that one day we'd all live together in a giant white castle. I had it all pictured—ivy on the walls, gold furniture with red velvet cushions, Russian wolfhounds as guards. Or some kind of big dogs anyway. And do you know what he said?"

"What?"

"He said, 'Well, you're the princess, and the princess's wishes always come true.'"

"That's Dad, all right. Always positive. But surely you didn't expect to get a big white castle, did you?"

"I did at the time, sure." Her wistful smile unravels. "But later I would have settled for just the part about us all living together. I so would've settled for that."

"Yeah, me too." Suddenly, I feel very close to Holly.

"That's why I never really wanted to talk to you about him much, Sutter. Not just because he let us down so badly, but because I don't want you to turn out like him."

"But maybe it's not his fault he couldn't keep that promise. I mean, after all, Mom's the one that yelled and screamed and made him move out."

Her face pinches in with that constipated look she gets when she thinks I've said something stupid. "But you know what? He gave her some real good reasons to yell and scream. You were too young to know what was going on, but she confided in me. It was almost like we were sisters during that time. She told me all about how she walked up to his car—parked right in our own driveway—and found him on top of the neighbor from down the street. That's the kind of man he is, and that's all I need to know."

That fast, the closeness between us evaporates.

I'm like, "How do you know that's even true? Of course, she made him out to be the bad guy. She talks Dad down every chance she gets. You'd think he was Osama bin Laden or somebody the way she goes on. For once, I'd like to hear what he has to say on the subject."

"Why? So he can lie to you like he lied to Mom? Like he lied to us? Remember when he was moving his things out, and he sat us down on the front porch and told us not to worry, that he'd be just across town and we could call him any time we needed him? Well, where is he?"

"That's exactly what I want to know."

"My point is . . ."

"I know what your point is. But here's my point—it's time I found him. I want to talk to him, really talk to him. A guy wants to know his real dad, not some robot stepfather. I've tried to ask Mom about where he is, but she just gives me some bullshit answer. I don't have the same kind of relationship with her that you do. She thinks you're like this big success."

"Are you kidding me? She thinks you're her shining little boy."

"Her shining little boy? She hasn't thought that since I was six. Now it's more like I'm some kind of cracked knickknack or something that she can't wait to pawn off on somebody at a garage sale. That's why I'm here. I need you to talk to her about where Dad is for me. You're the one that's close to her. She'd tell you."

"You could be close to her too, Sutter. You could be closer to me. But you're always going around acting like you don't need us for anything."

"Well, I'm here now, right? I'm telling you I need you to ask Mom this one question for me."

She looks toward the house. "She doesn't want to talk about him, Sutter. And I don't blame her. After the way he acted? I mean, he's, like, the penultimate loser."

"Penultimate means second to last."

"What?"

"Penultimate—it doesn't mean really, really ultimate. It means second to last. Like the penultimate week of the school year is the second-to-last one."

"Whatever. I'm just saying, as far as Mom's concerned, Dad's nothing but a bad memory, and I don't want to be the one that makes her go through all that again."

"Yeah, well, I'm sure you're right. I'm sure everything that happened before we got the bigger house and the swimming pool is a bad memory for Mom. But how about this—can you at least talk to her for *me*? Could you do that? You're always slamming me over the head with what you think I ought to do. Just once, how about helping me out with something I think is important?"

She sits there staring at the fruit tray.

"Come on," I say. "You could call her at work right now. Tell her that Kevin's interested in talking to him about something. That should do it. She loves Kevin."

Holly starts to say something, then bites her lip like she's trying to solve some complex math problem in her head. Finally, she goes, "I don't have to call her."

"Why not?"

She's still looking at the fruit tray. "Because I know where he is."

"What?"

Finally, she looks at me. "I know where he is—Fort Worth, Texas. He calls Mom probably about twice a year, drunk and asking her to get back with him. Like that could ever happen."

"And Mom tells you this and not me?"

"Can you blame her? You always act like the whole divorce was all her fault. She's probably afraid you'd try to run off and live with him or something."

"Yeah, right." I stand and grab my big 7UP off the table. "Or maybe she doesn't want me to find out the truth about what happened. But she can't keep that under control forever. I'm going to find out. I don't care if I have to drive to Fort Worth to do it."

Chapter 58

Fort Worth is only three and a half hours south of here, maybe less as fast as I'm driving. It's a gray, cloudy day, but that's all right. Anytime you're on the highway cruising at eighty miles an hour, far away from school and work and parents, you can't help but feel high and free. Also, I admit I'm excited about finally seeing the old man after all these years. Aimee's probably twice as stoked as I am, even though we're missing graduation.

I didn't exactly lie about having to meet Dad on graduation weekend. He really did suggest it when we talked on the phone, not that he knew the ceremony was set for Friday night. I'm sure if I told him, he would've been glad to change to another date, but what would be the use? It's not like anyone's giving me a diploma. Mr. Asterhole came through with his threat, all right. It's summer school for me.

Apparently, Aimee's mom wasn't too happy about the situation, though. I'm not sure exactly how Aimee explained it to her, but the truth is I don't think her mom's all that happy about me in general. The whole bad influence thing. But that's okay. I wouldn't expect anything else from a woman whose control over her daughter is slipping away. And that's just what's happening. Now that Aimee has some experience in standing up for herself, she's turning into a real pro at it. Of course, a couple of slugs of vodka always help.

As for my mom, I simply told her the grand festivities weren't until next week, and she never bothered to check into it. There will be plenty of time to explain the summer school situation later. I also didn't tell her anything about going to see Dad, and I asked Holly not to mention it to her either. I don't need Mom slamming me with some lecture on his evil ways and how I'm likely to get infected with them just by talking to him.

I do hate it that Aimee's missing her graduation, though. She worked hard for a long time to get that diploma, but, really, what does a ceremony have to do with anything? Does she really need to parade across a stage along with a line of people who never even really knew her? Besides, it would only spoil things more for her if she knew I wasn't graduating.

We have the music cranked and the scenery's flying by— the low-slung clouds, the pastures, the Arbuckle Mountains of southern Oklahoma. Aimee breaks out some snacks and drinks. Nothing alcoholic. Sure, we might have a shot or two right before meeting Dad, but that's all.

"Are you nervous about seeing him?" she asks, and I'm like, "I guess it is going to be weird to see him, but you know my policy on that."

"You embrace the weird?"

"One hundred percent."

"I'll bet this is going to make your dad's year," she says, pointing the open end of a sack of Bugles my way.

I grab a handful and go, "He sounded pretty pumped on the phone. That's the way he always was—gung ho about life. I remember one time going with him to the grocery store and he backed into a car in the parking lot. He didn't get upset in the least. Instead, he treated it like an opportunity to make friends, went into the store, had the owner of the car called up to the front, gave her his insurance info, and next thing you know, they're just gabbing away and laughing. You would've thought he just handed her a check for winning the lottery instead of hitting her car."

"I can't wait to meet him."

"Hey, he can't wait to meet you too."

Okay, maybe I didn't mention her to Dad on the phone, but you have enough on your mind talking to your long-lost dad after ten years—you can't remember every last detail to mention.

Actually, the call went very well. At first, he sounded confused about who I was—kind of like he thought I should still be a little kid instead of an eighteen-year-old, adult-type person—but once he got used to that idea, we had a really good talk, a bit awkward but in a positive way.

He asked about Mom and Holly and never had a bad word to say about either of them. He even remembered that I used to play Little League Baseball and wanted to know if I kept up with it. I had to admit I quit playing in junior high to pursue other interests, but it was great that he remembered what a good fielder I used to be, even when I was really small.

He never said what kind of job he was doing or why he ended up in Fort Worth, but he seemed to be enjoying himself down there. Still liked to go to baseball games. Still hadn't married again. Still told jokes, although now when he laughed, he had a tendency to break into a coughing fit. I didn't ask him for the truth about what happened between him and Mom. There would be plenty of time for that in Fort Worth.

It's close to dinnertime when Aimee and I hit Fort Worth, and after a few wrong turns we finally locate Dad's duplex. It's not ancient or anything—maybe about ten years old—but has a flimsy look, like something that wouldn't stand up all that well against a high Texas wind. The grass could use a good mowing and the shrubs are scraggly, but so what? Dad probably has a lot better things to do than hanging around the front yard landscaping all the time.

"I think I need that shot of vodka now," says Aimee, and I'm like, "Pass me the whisky, Doctor."

We take our shots followed by a couple more, then follow

those with shots of mouthwash. "Okay," I say. "It's now or never."

At the front door, I ring the bell two or three times but no one comes. Figuring it must be broken, I try knocking, and still no one comes until I've knocked maybe five times. The door opens and it's Dad, only a smaller version than I remember. He's not much taller than I am, and his ruffled hair's flecked with gray and in need of a cut. His blue jeans are faded, and he's wearing a kind of Hawaiian shirt, except instead of flowers it has tumbling dice on the front. He's still handsome but in a worn, creased way.

"Well, hello there, my man," he says, full of the old charisma. "What can I do for you?"

At first, I think he's kidding, but he's not. "It's me," I tell him. "Sutter."

He looks like he's waiting for me to finish.

"Your son?"

"Sutter! Of course. Man, it's great to see you. I forgot you were coming this weekend. Well, what do you know?" He shakes my hand with a firm, warm grip. "And who is this striking young lady?" He offers his hand to Aimee.

I introduce her. She ducks her head shyly while he tells her he mistook her for a Hollywood starlet.

"You're just like your old man," he tells me. "You have an immaculate taste in the ladies."

I wonder what ladies he's had immaculate taste in. Surely he can't mean Mom.

As it turns out, he's already set up plans to meet his current lady friend at a place called Larry's, says he thought I was supposed to come next weekend. Usually, I'd write off something like that as my mistake, but I'm sure we agreed on this date. No use arguing about it, though. We're here now, and he's as happy as can be to have us join him and his friend for some barbecue.

He figures it'll be best if we take separate cars, so Aimee and I load up in the Mitsubishi and he gets into his beat-up old Wagoneer. Spirits are high. Except I can't help wondering whether it might be a little difficult—with this girlfriend of his around—to bring up the topic of why he and Mom split up.

"Another shot of whisky, Doctor?" asks Aimee as we start down the street.

"Stat," I say.

Chapter 59

Larry's is a little smokehouse/bar only about ten minutes from the duplex, a dump from the looks of it, but they always say you get the best ribs in the dumpiest places. Dad's obviously a real regular. There are probably fifteen people in there and they all seem to know him. They're amazed and delighted to meet his boy too. Texas women sure do like to pinch you on the cheek.

His lady friend isn't so happy, though. She comes out of the bathroom just as we get finished passing through the smorgasbord of well-wishers, and she launches into how she's already been there for thirty minutes and is sick of how he treats her. This looks like it could turn grim, but I should know better. Dad just clicks on his broadband smile, and tells her he got held up a little by a visitor.

"I'd like you to meet my son, the amazing Sutter Keely." He makes an exaggerated gesture in my direction. "And, Sutter, this is Mrs. Gates."

As quick as that Mrs. Gates goes all radiant. "Your son? Why didn't you tell me he was coming to town?"

She teeters forward, folds a sloppy hug around me, and kisses me on the cheek. Looks like she's a little tanked already. I think I might like her.

She's not the prettiest forty-five-year-old lady in the world by any means, but she is quite the fabulous specimen in her own way—magnificent fake eyelashes, a full kilo of eyeliner, and best of all, the oversize Texas hair, dyed black with a splotch of white in front where her bangs part. She's statuesque in a way, not tall but like maybe at one time she had the body of a Miss Universe. Only now the statue is turning back into its original block of marble. I mean, she's substantial. I'd hate to run into her with the Mitsubishi.

We gather at a round table near the back wall, and Dad orders up barbecue and a couple of pitchers of beer. The food's delicious, big portions with plenty of sauce, hot and sweet like I like it. But best of all, no one seems to mind that Aimee and I are helping ourselves to the brew. It's frosty cold as Christmas morning—beers with the old man at last!

He cocks back in his chair, lights a cigarette, and goes into his jokes and stories, igniting laughter from everybody, including the antique country-and-western hippies at the next table. The story I like most is about the time we went to some little lake back when things were still okay between him and Mom. It had this beach layout with a small pier and a waterslide, a couple of diving boards, and a lifeguard. After trying to teach me how to swim for a while, Dad decided to do a little showing off on the high dive, so he told me to sit right where I was and not to move. Well, of course, me being me, as soon as he turned his back, off I went running around trying to get into any kind of fun I could find.

So Dad did his dive and then came back to find me missing. Immediately, he panicked, thinking his fabulous boy had slid off the pier into the deep water. He rushed to the lifeguard, but all he did was wade around in the shallow water with his whistle poked in his mouth and his stupid-looking pith helmet glinting in the sun.

It's hilarious the way Dad tells it. He does all the voices and faces, even gets up and imitates the faux heroics of the doofus lifeguard, and then me reappearing, tying up the drawstring on my bathing suit after a visit to the Porta Potti, looking all bug-eyed innocent. Everyone's about to explode from laughter, except Mrs. Gates.

She's all sentimental over the whole thing, sitting there with her eyes welling up and one of the fake eyelashes dangling crooked. She has a large blob of barbecue sauce on her chin that no one tells her to wipe off, and she's muttering, "You got bootiful chidren. You sure do, just bootiful." Apparently, she thinks Aimee's my sister.

Me, I feel all glorious and beaming because I remember when the whole deal really happened. Dad doesn't tell the best part, though—the part when he grabbed me and squeezed me and told me not to go running off like that ever again because what if I did drown? What would he do without his amazing, amazing boy? I've carried that memory with me like a lucky coin ever since.

More stories from the past go around, all of them panoramic and warm as the Pacific Ocean. When I remind Dad of how we used to listen to Jimmy Buffett songs in the backyard on summer evenings, his smile takes on a wistful curve. "Those were great, great times, Sutter," he says, and I wonder if there's not just a little regret in his voice. But then his smile goes back into overdrive. "You know what? They have Jimmy on the jukebox right here. We can listen to the whole CD."

After he plugs the jukebox, he shuffles back toward the table with his hands stretched out toward Mrs. Gates. "You got your dancing shoes on?" he says, all sly-eyed, and Mrs. Gates is like, "Hoo-boy, you better believe it."

"Come on, Sutter," Dad tells me. "Let's see if you and Aimee can keep up with us old folks."

Now, to the right music, I'm not a shabby dancer, but Dad and Mrs. Gates are all about Texas swing dancing, which is not my specialty, and doesn't exactly fit the music all that well. That won't stop me for a second, though. I'm up for anything.

And surprisingly enough, so is Aimee. I'm like, Who is this chick? What happened to the girl I practically had to crowbar out of her seat to get her to dance at the prom? Seems like just the fact that I actually took her suggestion to find my dad shot her confidence full of steroids.

So there the four of us are, on the little, patio-size dance floor, Aimee and I bouncing off each other in this spastic display of bad coordination, while Dad and Mrs. Gates, drunk as she is, whirl around like clockwork.

Taking pity on us, they decide to give us some quick lessons. We switch partners for the second song, and the next thing I know, Dad has Aimee twirling like she just graduated from the Grand Ole Opry or something. On the other hand, I nearly throw Mrs. Gates into the lap of a dude with a belt buckle the size of a cheese platter. She doesn't care, though. "You are a fabalus dancer," she tells me. "Just fabalus."

Next thing I know, a slow song is playing and Mrs. Gates squeezes me to her substantial bosom and plants her hands in my back pockets. It would've taken a Molotov cocktail to blow me out of her grasp. Across the way, Dad has Aimee pressed close and scoots her smoothly around the edges of the dance floor. We smile embarrassed smiles at each other, but I can tell she really likes the old man.

You know what? I tell myself. I'm not even going to ask him about what happened with Mom. Better just to ride the smooth breeze and see where that takes us instead. No need to force anything. Tonight's about reconnection, not solving mysteries.

But when we get back to the table to relax with some more brews, Aimee has to go and ask the question that turns our party time completely inside out. You can't blame her for what happens, though. It's a reasonable question. She has no way of knowing that she's setting off a string of firecrackers right in the middle of Larry's Bar and Grill.

Chapter 60

"So, Mr. Keely," Aimee says, still glowing from our dance-floor heroics, "what have you been up to all this time since you left Oklahoma?"

See? It's perfectly innocent and well intentioned.

Dad starts off vague. "A lot of traveling," he says. "Here and there, up and down. I was always restless, I guess." Then the glint sparks in his eye and you know he's conjured a good memory. "One of my favorite places was Key West, Florida. Oh, man, you should see the sunsets. Like a big butterscotch sundae with swirls of strawberry mixed in, melting into the ocean. Time's different down there, slower, more relaxed. I bet if I'd stayed there I'd still be five years younger." He laughs, but I think, in a way, he believes it.

"Why did you leave?" Aimee asks. All evening, she's listened so hard to every word he said, you'd think she expected him to accidentally reveal the meaning of life at any moment.

"Why did I leave?" He takes a pull on his beer. "Man, that's a good question. You know, I guess it boils down to that great old American dilemma—the paycheck. Or the lack thereof. The powers that be expect you to get one if you want to eat, drink, and find lodging. That's the eleventh commandment, man. Thou shalt pay thy debts in a timely manner."

He finishes his beer and pours another. "But I'll bet Sutter's not so interested in why I left Key West as in why I left Oklahoma. Am I right?" He looks at me, one eyebrow raised.

I have to admit the question has crossed my mind.

"And it's a fair question," he says. "No doubt about it. Let me start with this—I did want to be there for you and Holly. Man, did I ever want that. I mean, the two of you were more important to me than anything in the world. But apparently, I wasn't cut out to be a family man, not in the traditional sense anyway. Your mother sure didn't think I was. And things got to be so uncool between her and me that it seemed better if I wasn't around. At least for a while. Problem is sometimes a *while* can turn into an era before you know it."

This answer doesn't sit quite right with me, but I don't get a chance to let it fester. Yet.

"So," Mrs. Gates pipes up. "What happened between you and your wife?" This contribution surprises me. From the way she's been staring at the tabletop, I thought she'd passed out.

"The old story," he says. "Irreconcilable differences. Thing was, she always wanted a future, and I just didn't have one to give her."

"Ha!" exclaims Mrs. Gates. She throws her head back, but she's like a bobblehead doll—her head instantly springs forward again. "In my experience irreconcyclical differences means that the husband and wife have one huge disagreement. She thinks he shouldn't cheat and he thinks he should!"

Keeping it cool, Dad's like, "It's always a mystery to men what women think."

Then, out of nowhere, these words blurt out of my mouth: "Mom told us you cheated." The words feel weird on my tongue, but I'm in it now and have to go on. "She always tried to blame everything on you. I never really believed her, though. I figured she was just using it to get us on her side."

For a moment, Dad rubs his finger along the top of his beer mug, contemplating.

"Well?" says Mrs. Gates. "Did you cheat?"

Without looking up, Dad's like, "Maybe. A little."

I guess it's just one of those things that—when it comes right down to it—he can't lie about. Sure, it sounds ugly, but I'm still trying to tell myself that, with the way Mom treated him, he had to go looking for comfort somewhere.

"Hot damn!" exclaims Mrs. Gates. "Isn't that just like a man to come off with an answer like that? How can you cheat just a little?"

He puts the smile back on but it's not so authentic now. "You know how it is," he explains. "You go out drinking and having a good time and one thing leads to another. The girls don't mean anything. Some of them you don't even remember their faces."

I'm like, "Some of them? How many were there?"

Dad looks like he's actually getting ready to count them, but gives up. "It's not like I kept a running tally," he says.

"That's it. I've heard enough." Mrs. Gates slams her palm onto the table. "I didn't know I was getting involved with a serial rapist!"

"Oh shit." Dad looks at me apologetically. "Here she goes, exaggerating again. I was hoping we could get through tonight without this kind of thing."

Mrs. Gates leans forward. "I am not a *thing*."

"That's not what I said. It's just that you can be like—let's say—way overdramatic?"

"I am not overdram . . . overdram . . . overdramical. How do you expect me to react when I find out you go around having sex a mile a minute with women you don't even love?"

"Hey, I never said I didn't love them. I'm sure I loved them all, even if it was just for forty-five minutes."

"Oh-ho! Forty-five minutes, is it? Tell me this, then—when are *my* forty-five minutes going to be up?"

Dad cocks his head to the side. "How am I supposed to know? I don't even wear a watch."

Even I can tell that's the wrong thing to say.

Mrs. Gates's painted-on eyebrows launch upward so fast you'd think they were getting ready to fly off her head. "Well, now I've heard everything! You cheating dog. Making me think you wanted me to leave my husband and two poor kids for you."

"Your kids? Your kids are twenty-something years old. Besides, I never said I wanted you to leave anybody."

Her face is completely red, right to the roots of her dyed hair. "So now you think you can just throw me away like some old, gnawed-on bone? Well, I'll show you what I think of that." She picks up a plateful of picked-over barbecue rib bones and hurls them straight into Dad's tumbling-dice shirt.

"What the hell?" he says, looking down at the dark sauce stains.

This would be a stellar time for a grand exit, but Mrs. Gates isn't finished. "Let's see how much the ladies like you looking like that." She waves her arm and knocks her full beer mug onto the floor, where it shatters on the brick-colored tiles.

Dad's like, "Jesus Christ, cool it, will you," and a second later, the owner of the place charges over and says, "Dammit, Tommy"—Tommy's my dad's first name—"I've told you not to have this crazy woman in here when she's so drunk. Now get her out before she breaks anything else."

"But my boy's down to see me," Dad says.

"I don't care. People don't come in here for this kind of crapola."

"You couldn't pay me to stay in here," declares Mrs. Gates. She stands up and staggers into the table, sending my dad's mug down to shatter among the ruins of her own.

"Hold on," Dad tells her. He gets up and throws a twenty

onto the table and goes, "Sutter, will you settle up the bill? I better help her out."

I'm like, "Sure," but of course, the twenty isn't enough to pay for all the ribs and beer we've had, so Aimee and I have to chip in to round it out. By the time we get done with that, Dad and Mrs. Gates are already outside.

It's sprinkling now, and under the streetlight at the far side of the parking lot, she's yelling, "Get away from me, you sheep in wolf's clothing."

"Come on, man," he says. "Settle down. You're taking this all the wrong way."

But obviously Mrs. Gates is in the wrong stage of the life of the buzz. Instead of settling down, she slings her bowling-ball-size purse around by the strap and pops Dad right in the face.

"Don't you tell me what to do," she hollers and slings the purse again.

Dad's hunkered over now, holding up his arms in self-defense, but she's a medieval warrior with that purse, slamming him again and again.

"And don't you ever dare ask me for any more loans," she says, and whap—the purse zings into Dad's shoulder. "You're gonna pay me back every last cent of what you already owe me. Don't you think you aren't. You're not gonna use me up and then skip out with my money." Whap, whap, whap.

Finally, Dad gets hold of her arms and pins her against the trunk of her car. She's breathing hard and muttering, "You're a worfless sonvabish. You know that? Worfless."

I suggest that maybe we should pack her into the Mitsubishi and drive her home, but Dad's like, "Thanks, Sutter, but I think I better drive her over there myself. I think I'd better talk to her alone."

"You want us to follow you?"

"No, that's all right. You go on back to my place. I'll meet you there in thirty minutes."

"Are you just going to leave her car here?"

"It'll be all right." He smiles like everything's going great.

"You'll be at your place in thirty minutes?"

"Thirty minutes on the dot."

Chapter 61

Thirty minutes. An hour. An hour and a half. No Dad. The sprinkling turns into a hard rain clattering on the roof of the car. Fat streams cascade down the windshield.

"I don't think he's coming," I say and take a long pull on my whisky and Seven.

"Too bad you don't have his cell phone number."

"Wouldn't help anyway. I don't have a cell phone."

"I thought you got a new one."

"I lost it."

Lightning flashes and thunder cracks so close you'd think the sky's splitting open right above the car.

"It's getting pretty bad out," I say. "We probably better head back home."

"We don't have to. We can wait as long as you want."

"What's the use? Same old Dad. Long gone and no good-byes." I crank the ignition and pull away without bothering to take a last glance at the duplex.

For a while, we're both quiet. I don't even put on any music. It's just the thunder and the windshield wipers sloshing. By now, I've had plenty of time to let the grand, long-awaited meeting with Dad sink in. What a bust. I can take it that he really did cheat on Mom. She could be pretty mean. But the guy doesn't seem to care about anything or anyone but himself. Jesus, he didn't even remember I was coming down to visit. And then there was that lame business about how he wanted to be there so much for me and Holly. But what? He lost track of time? You don't lose track of time if you really love your kids.

Now he's scamming crazy Mrs. Gates. Does he care if he breaks up her marriage and makes her kids hate her? No. He doesn't understand the first thing about family. If he did, he couldn't have left me sitting in my car in the rain outside his crummy duplex after I drove all the way down here to see him. But I guess my forty-five minutes' worth of love was up a long time ago.

All these years, I cut him slack. I made up excuses about how Mom chased him away and it was her fault he never called or visited. He was really a good guy, I told myself. At least there was one parent out there that still cared about me—my great, majestic dad.

Yeah, right.

Nobody had to chase him away. He was all too glad to ditch us. He probably ran up a bunch of debt before he skipped off too, left it for Mom to pay off, or to round up Geech to pay it off for her. No wonder she can't stand having me around. I remind her too much of the old man.

And that's what's really scary. Maybe I am like him. Maybe I'm headed nowhere but to the same Loserville he ended up in.

From behind, a car horn blares. I guess the Mitsubishi must've meandered about six inches into the other lane, and some dude back there thinks he's traffic control. I'm like, "Fuck you, dude." There are a lot more hazardous types on the road than me—cell phone talkers, chicks putting on makeup, guys searching their floorboard for some crappy CD they dropped.

Truth is—if I have any skill at all—it's that I'm a magnificent driver under the influence. My record's completely clean, not counting a couple of parking lot scrapes and a light pole. That thing with the dump truck was in my mom's car and I didn't have a license then. The cops didn't even get involved. I mean, it's not like I'm driving around with a four-year-old lodged in my grill. So that dude can just fuck off with his horn blowing. He has a lot worse things to worry about than me.

Finally, when we're back on the interstate north of the city, Aimee starts trying to make me feel better, going on about how she actually likes the old man and how it's too bad that Mrs. Gates turned out like she did. "I don't understand how she could get so mad about your dad having affairs when she's obviously cheating on her own husband."

I'm just like, "I guess it's because people suck."

I'm not in the mood for feel-good bullshit. This is an abnormally dark stage in the life of the buzz. Darker than dark, like God has forsaken his very own drunken boy.

"Not all people suck," Aimee says. "You don't."

"Are you sure? You saw what kind of guy my dad is—a big fat liar and cheater. The kind of dude that sheds his family like a snake sheds its skin. Are you sure I won't slither down that same rut? They say the apple doesn't fall too far from the tree. Do you really want to move off to St. Louis with a snake-apple bastard like that?"

"You're not a snake or an apple. And you're not your dad. I think it's a good thing you found out the truth. You can learn from what he did wrong. If you don't want to be like that you don't have to. We all have free choice."

"Free to choose what? Some kind of spectacular new future for myself? You heard my dad. Mom wanted a future and he didn't have one to give her. Well, I don't have one to give you either. It's like a birth defect, you know? The boy born without a future."

"That's not true, Sutter. You have so many options."

"No, I don't. I saw it in a dream. The same dream over and over. It's me and Ricky playing this game we used to play in junior high with a neighborhood dog, a big black Doberman.

Only in the dream, we don't make friends with him the way we did in junior high. Not hardly. No, he opens his huge slobbering maw and swallows Ricky in one bite, and then it's just me with the dog growling and snapping, chasing me down the drainage ditch until I run into this concrete wall. There's no escape. And then I wake up. It's too brutal for my subconscious to face. It's the season of the dog, all right, only this time it's a mean season. But that's how life is. Just like that. You're just running and running with a wall in front of you and a big black dog snapping at your ass."

She lays her hand on my thigh. "It just seems that way right now. You have to remember to have hope."

"Hope? Are you kidding? That's one thing I've learned for sure—hope is absolutely unnecessary. What there is instead of it, I haven't found out yet. Until then, this drinking will just have to do."

I take a swallow of whisky and Seven but it goes down stale. Nothing helps. I'm a black spot on the chest X-ray of the universe.

Aimee's like, "You know, your dad probably just got hung up having to do something for Mrs. Gates. She seemed like she had some kind of mental problems. I'm sure he really wanted to come back and hang out with us. If it wasn't for her, we'd probably be spending the night with him."

"Yeah, right. And if he hadn't cheated on my mom and run out on me and Holly, then we'd still be a family, and everything would be cozy, and I'd be president of my Sunday school class, and you and I'd ride silver stallions to Pluto."

She's quiet for a moment. Maybe I should feel bad for going all sarcastic on her, but there's no room inside for feeling any worse.

Finally, she's like, "I know it looks bad right now, but parents are just people. They don't always know what to do. That doesn't mean they don't love you."

"I don't need any psychoanalysis from you, Dr. Freud, Jr."

That doesn't faze her. "And even if they didn't, that doesn't mean you just give up. You know? It's like you have to make love work where you can. Like with me, because I do love you. You don't even have to question that. I do."

"Come on, Aimee, you sound like a soap opera. You don't love me. You may want to tell yourself that, but this isn't love. It's more like you're all drunk and feeling grateful. You're just happy someone came along and showed some interest in you as more than a sex doll for a night."

She leans away and crosses her arms. "Don't say that, Sutter. Don't try to mess us up by saying mean things."

But I'm on a roll. "Haven't you figured it out yet? There aren't any Commander Amanda Gallicos. There aren't any Bright Planets out there. No one's coming with the inner prosperity. All we have is the great Holy Trinity of the atomic vampires—the sex god, the money god, and the power god. The god of the beautiful soul starved to death a long time ago."

She uncrosses her arms. "But we can change that."

I shake my head. "It's too big to change. It's too heavy and all sharp-cornered and shit."

"No, it's not. It just seems that way right now because you're afraid, but everyone's afraid."

I stare at her, hard. "Afraid? Afraid of what? I'm not afraid of a damn thing. I'm the guy that jumped off a thousand-foot-tall bridge."

"You know what I mean. You're—hey, watch out!"

"Huh?"

"You're swerving into the other lane!"

Chapter 62

Again, a horn blares over my shoulder, only this time it's the pissed-off blast from a tractor-trailer rig. I crank the wheel back to the right, but the road's slick from all the rain, and we hydroplane hard. The Mitsubishi fishtails crazily down the highway, first one way, then the other. The truck rumbles next to us—a gas tanker—so close that it looks like for sure we'll lurch back and slide right under the belly of it. With no seat belt on, Aimee's busy struggling to squeeze into the floorboard, and a newspaper headline flashes through my mind: DUMBASS KILLS SELF IN FIERY AUTO CRASH; ROBS GIRLFRIEND OF SHINING FUTURE.

The tank looks like it's about two inches away. We're just about to slam into its ribs when the car fishtails back the other way. Now it's only concrete abutments we have to worry about. There's one just ahead to the right, but we only scrape it before I finally regain control and wrestle us to a stop in the high soggy grass.

Aimee peers up from the floorboard, her eyes wide, her bottom lip quivering.

All I can get out is, "Jesus Christ!"

"It's okay," she says. "Are you all right?"

I can't believe it. The girl should be slapping me in the face. "No, I'm not all right," I tell her. "Can't you see that? I'm far from all right. I'm a one hundred percent flaming screwup!"

She crawls up from the floorboard and throws her arms around me. "I'm just so glad no one was hurt."

"Are you kidding?" I peel her arms away. "I nearly killed you and you want to hug me? You need to get as far away from me as you can."

"No, I don't," she says, crying. "I just want to hold onto you and make sure you're okay."

"Well, holy crap, then, I'll get away from you." I sling the door open and stomp down the shoulder of the highway, rain pelting me like nails. "Drive the car back yourself," I yell over my shoulder. "You'll be safer that way."

But, of course, she doesn't do that. Instead, she stumbles onto the shoulder of the road and hollers for me to come back. I just keep walking as fast as I can. It's like if I move fast enough I can even get away from myself.

"Sutter," she yells. "Stop. I'm sorry!"

Unbelievable. She's sorry? For what? I turn to tell her to just get back in the car and let me go, but I don't get the chance. A pair of headlights zoom in right behind her. All I can get out is, "Aimee!" before she staggers left onto the highway. For a second the lights blind me, then there's an awful thump, and the next thing I know she's rolling across the shoulder into the high grass.

My skin feels like it's on fire as I run to her. The rain nearly blinds me. My stomach feels like a crazed animal that's trying to scramble up through my chest and out of my mouth. I'm like, "What have I done? What have I done?" I don't even know if I'm saying it out loud or not. She's lying in the grass, her hair soaked, mud slashed across her cheek. Or is it blood? I kneel beside her. "Aimee, God, Aimee, I'm such a fucking idiot, Aimee."

"Sutter." She doesn't open her eyes. "I think I got hit by a car."

"I know, sweetheart, I know." Somewhere I heard that you're not supposed to move a person who's been in a car accident, something about not damaging the spine, so I just kneel there next to her, afraid to even touch her face.

"Don't worry, I'll get some help," I tell her, but I'm such an idiot I've lost my cell phone and don't have any way to call for an ambulance.

She opens her eyes and tries to sit up.

"Hold on," I say, "I don't think you should move."

"It's okay." She leans her head into my chest. "I think I'm all right. It just clipped my arm."

Looking closer, I can see that it is only mud on her cheek, and I gently smudge it away.

"Can you help me get back to the car?" she says. "We're getting soaked out here."

"Sure, I can, baby, sure I can." I cradle my hand beneath her arm to help her up, but she winces and tells me to stop.

"What is it?"

"It's my arm. I think it might be broken."

"Does it hurt bad?"

From behind us, a voice calls, "My God, is she all right?"

It's a guy and a girl, a couple of years older than us, college students from the look of them.

The guy goes, "She just kind of like stumbled out in front of us. There wasn't anything I could do."

"It was only the side mirror that hit her," says the girl. She's holding an open magazine over her head to keep her hair dry, but it's not helping much. "The whole mirror's ruined. I mean, she was just walking in the road."

"I'm sorry," Aimee says.

The guy's like, "No, don't worry about it. I just hope you're all right."

"I'm fine," she says, but I'm like, "I think her arm's broken."

"She's lucky it's not worse," says the girl. "What were y'all doing out here?"

I start to tell her it's none of her business, but Aimee goes, "We were looking for something. Something fell off our car."

The guy wants to know if we need them to drive us to the hospital, but I tell him that we're all right, we'll handle it ourselves. He seems relieved, and his girlfriend's like, "Y'all really need to be more careful."

I help Aimee up and everything seems to be in working order except for her left arm, but there's no bone sticking out or anything. The guy follows us to the car and opens the passenger-side door for Aimee. His girlfriend's already heading back to their car.

"You sure you're going to be all right to drive?" he says, once we have Aimee tucked safely inside.

"We'll be all right," I tell him. "I don't care if I have to drive ten miles an hour. I'm not going to let anything else happen to her."

As I slide in behind the steering wheel, I tell Aimee I'm driving her to the emergency room, but she refuses. She's afraid they'll call the police on me and her parents on her. "I can wait till tomorrow and go to the doctor then. I'll make up something to tell my mom."

"But doesn't it hurt?"

"Kind of."

"That's it. I'm taking you to the emergency room."

"No, Sutter, you're not." She's sitting there holding her arm, but there's determination in her eyes instead of pain. "I told you. I'll go tomorrow. I don't want anything to get in the way of us going to St. Louis."

"You're sure?"

"I'm sure."

She's drenched and bedraggled, but I've never loved anyone as much as I love her right now. That's how I know I'll have to give her up.

Chapter 63

Ricky's stuffing T-shirts into a backpack, getting ready to go on vacation to Galveston with Bethany and her folks. He's planning on trying out some surfing and, of course, the obligatory girlfriend boat ride around the Gulf of Mexico.

"So," he says, folding another shirt. "Sounds like your dad's hooked up with a semi-crazy woman."

"I don't think there's any *semi* about it."

"Well, I guess that's about what you can expect when you're still out there looking for a girlfriend at forty-something years old."

I figure that comment is aimed at me and my track record with girls, but that's all right—I deserve it.

He stuffs the T-shirt into the backpack. "But what I can't believe is that you had me swallowing that whole my-dad's-a-hotshot-executive-in-the-Chase-building story. I mean, you kept that thing going for years."

"It's not my fault you're gullible. I mean, didn't you even wonder why you never saw him?"

"Hey, I don't know any hotshot executives. I just figured he was always wheeling and dealing."

"Yeah. It was a stupid story. But once you get started with something like that, you're stuck with it."

"I guess."

I can tell he's pretty disappointed in me, and I don't blame him. But when you're a guy you don't come right out and apologize. You think of some other way to make up for it, so I'm like,

"You know, this whole situation with my dad, and with what happened with Aimee and all, has me thinking—you might be right."

"Dude, I'm always right. You know that."

"I mean, about the cutting back on drinking thing. It might be more fun if I just do it on the weekends."

"If you can."

"What's that supposed to mean?"

"Nothing. I just wonder who has more control over the situation, you or the whisky."

"Dude, I'm always in control. You know me, I'm the virtuoso musician. Whisky's just my million-dollar violin."

"Right." He zips up the backpack. "Look, I have to head over to Bethany's. If I don't see you before we head out, look for a postcard from me. Or maybe I'll e-mail you a picture of me riding some wild waves."

And that's it—he goes his way, and I go mine. Used to, we would've broken down that whole story about my dad until we found the very truth of the truth of it, but now it's just, "So long, I'll see you later."

That's all right, though. I have to get over to Aimee's pretty soon anyway. We're going to Marvin's for dinner this evening. I've been postponing it, but there's no more waiting. Time for the Big Talk.

As it is right now, I've been transformed from a semi-villain into a real hero around the Finecky household. Seems Aimee told her mom we had a flat tire on the highway in the rain, and while she was helping me change it, a car swerved off the road and would've killed her if I hadn't risked my life to pull her out of the way. It was just the passenger-side mirror that clipped her, she explained, and she didn't even think her arm was broken until she woke up in so much pain the next morning.

So it's weird going over to her house and having everyone,

even Randy-the-Walrus, beaming at me like I'm James Bond or somebody. In actuality, I feel like a double agent infiltrating their ranks under false pretenses. Not only because of the hero thing, but because of what I have to tell Aimee.

At Marvin's nothing has changed—the lights are still dim, the clientele still sparse, and Dean Martin still available on the jukebox. I guess the only thing that's different is no whisky in the 7UP. Maybe Ricky doesn't have much faith, but I haven't had a drink since the trip to Fort Worth, five whole days.

Aimee's having a great time, even with her arm in this elaborate cast that makes you wonder how she's even able to put a shirt on. Luckily, she's right-handed, so at least wielding a fork isn't too difficult. She just has to make sure not to order anything that requires using a knife.

The first time I saw that cast, I wondered if she'd even be able to move to St. Louis, but she said nothing was going to get in her way now. I asked her if she could still start work at the bookstore, and she said of course she could. All she'd have to do is run the cash register and help customers find what they're looking for. "Think about it," she said. "It'll be a lot easier doing that than trying to fold newspapers."

"I guess you're right about that," I said.

"You bet I am." She grinned. "I'm spectacularly right."

Anyway, for Aimee, our trip to Marvin's makes a nice little ceremony, a good way to say goodbye to our lives in Oklahoma. And it is a ceremony, all right, but for a different kind of goodbye.

That's not something you jump right into, though. You have to go slow, so I start out with the answer to the question Aimee's too tactful to ask—has my father called yet to explain what happened?

"He hasn't called as far as I know. But if he did and got my mom, then I'm sure she wouldn't even tell me."

"Maybe he's embarrassed or feels guilty or something. You could call him."

"I don't think so."

"Did you ever tell your mom or your sister that you went down there?"

"No. Mom would probably shit a Cadillac if she found out I went down there. Holly called me about it, but I told her I had to postpone the trip. I don't want to hear them say *I told you so*. It's bad enough the old man turned out like that. I don't need to see them gloat about it. I'm sure they already think I've got the screwed-up Keely male gene. I just don't want them to know *I* know it. Anyway, that's enough about my so-called family. They're too depressing."

"That's okay." She reaches over with her good hand and squeezes my fingers. "I'll be your family."

Chapter 64

Being on the wagon doesn't seem to bother Aimee a bit. She actually appears a little relieved about it. It's great to see her so confident, though. She even takes the initiative and starts in on some of her own stories. Used to, you had to get about four drinks in her before she'd bust loose with anything very personal, but now she's completely comfortable with it.

This evening, she has another paper route story, a good one too, about the time she met up with the tough girls. I recognize her tactic—telling me a story to make me forget I don't have a real family.

She was fourteen—still had to walk her part of the route at that age—when she ran across these two fifteen-year-olds all dressed in baggy black with silver chains looping down from their belt loops. More mascara than Cleopatra. They'd been up all night and were obviously high on something—drain cleaner, for all Aimee knew.

At first, they're like, "Look, it's Little Red Riding Hood. Whattaya got in the bag, something for your granny?" It was looking bad. Aimee pictured them ripping her bag from her shoulder and scattering her newspapers down the street, which is probably exactly what would've happened if she hadn't somehow come up with the perfect thing to say.

"Did you see that UFO that came through here a while ago?"

They're all, "UFO? What UFO? Are you high or just insane," but Aimee goes on with this detailed description of what it looked like—blinking purple lights, a big banana-shaped hull, a mysterious sound like a music box playing a song previously unknown to humans.

All of a sudden, the girls completely changed. They looked at the sky, and expressions of wonder drove the hardness from their faces. Aimee kept on making stuff up. This wasn't the first time anyone had spotted this UFO, she said. There were stories about it in the news. People had reported positive effects from having witnessed it. "It's the music," Aimee told them. "It leaves people feeling smart and happy and good-looking."

Suddenly, the girls became her best friends. They helped her throw her route, hoping to see the UFO, to hear the music, to transform into new, beautiful beings.

"That is a splendid lie," I tell her.

She's smiling at the memory. "And it didn't even seem like a lie when I was telling it. Then I saw them about a week later at Little Caesar's. They didn't even say anything to me. It was weird—they didn't seem tough anymore. They just seemed kind of pathetic and small and lost."

"I guess they needed some UFOs to believe in."

"Yeah. Luckily, my UFO did come for me."

"It did?"

"Of course. You're it."

"Oh, yeah?"

"I mean, look at how much I've changed in just these last couple of months."

"Yeah, you've changed, all right." I can't help but glance at the mammoth cast on her arm. I mean, this thing is so elaborate she has a hard time walking through doorways.

"And now we're heading to St. Louis. We're really going to do it. No way would I have had the nerve to tell my mom I was going there before I met you."

"Well, I have the feeling that St. Louis is really going to be your own special Bright Planet, you know it? And you're going to be the Commander Amanda Gallico of the whole thing."

"I thought you said there weren't any Bright Planets."

"Oh, that? I was just in a bad mood. I'm over all that." I take a hit off my 7UP. It tastes weird, whiskyless and all. "But the thing is, I've kind of like been wanting to talk to you about this St. Louis deal."

"I know, you're still worried about staying with my sister in her little apartment, but that's only for a couple of weeks. She's got that job all lined up for me, and I'm sure you'll get one too. We'll have our own place and rent furniture and everything. Don't mention that to my mom, though. She still doesn't know you're going to live up there too. She just thinks you're helping me move."

"Yeah, no, that's not what's been worrying me." My hand moves back toward the 7UP glass, but it's just instinct. Plain soda won't change anything right now. "See, there's, like, something I haven't told you. It's kind of embarrassing."

She's still smiling her little smile, and it strikes me that, actually, she is drunk, not on alcohol, but on her St. Louis hopes and dreams. I wouldn't sober her up for anything, but she doesn't need me anymore. She can hang on to her dreams by herself now.

"What happened was, you know how I wasn't doing so hot in algebra? Well, Mr. Asterhole wouldn't cut me a break. I tried to tell him I'd take more algebra in college, but I guess he thought he'd teach me a lesson for thinking he was so boring."

Her smile flatlines. "So, does that mean you didn't graduate?"

"Kind of." I take a drink, but of course it doesn't help. "Looks like, if I want my diploma, I'll have to go to summer school."

284

"Summer school," she repeats, the disappointment seeping into her pale blue eyes.

"Yeah. It doesn't start for a couple more weeks."

"Don't worry," she says, forcing herself to be positive. "I'm sure you can take algebra over in St. Louis somehow."

"No, I checked into that. I have to take it at the school I'm getting my diploma from." Okay, so I didn't actually check, but it makes pretty good sense.

She's not giving up, though. "Well, that just means I'll stay down here with you and help you study. We can go to St. Louis at the end of the summer. That way we'll have more time to plan and get ready."

"No, that's no good. Your sister's all set to come down this weekend to help you move, and she already has that job lined up for you and everything. The only thing that makes sense is for you to go ahead, and I'll stay here and go to summer school and work on the loading dock for Geech and save up some money."

She grabs my hand. "I don't want to go without you. I'd be lost."

I stare into her eyes, shooting confidence beams into her. "You won't be lost. Are you kidding me? You'll be great. You're going to do what you always wanted to do."

Of course, I'm also thinking that she'll find the perfect guy, too, a splendiferous equestrian scientist who'll see her as a fantastic new planet, full of miraculous wonders. But I know she can't accept that right now.

She's like, "I want to do all that with you," and I go, "I know you do, but look at it this way—how great of an organizer am I? Not too great, right? If you go up there first, you can get everything squared away, make all the plans. I'd appreciate it to no end if you'd do that for me."

Once she gets her mind around that notion, it begins to restoke her enthusiasm. Now she has a mission, something she can do for somebody else. She has no shortage of ideas either. She'll learn where everything is in St. Louis and how to get around and where the men's clothing stores are so that I can get a job in one when I come up. And she's like, "As soon as I get some money saved, I'll go ahead and rent our apartment and start buying things for it. And I'll do the artwork for the walls and everything."

"That all sounds great," I say. "But maybe you should hold off on renting the apartment. I mean, I need you to do the planning, but I have to do something too. I'd look at it as a big favor if you'd wait till I send you some money before you go renting an apartment and buying stuff for it. You have to let me feel like I'm making my contribution, okay?"

She smiles and squeezes my hand. "Okay. I guess I can do you that favor."

If I'm a rat for doing things this way, then, all right, I'm a rat. But sometimes you have to choose between honesty and kindness, and I've always been a sucker for the kind side. Besides, I figure she has to get out of town before I can tell her the whole truth or she'll never go. I'll wait till she's been in St. Louis for a month and has her job and her new life. Then I'll drop her a long e-mail. I don't know exactly what it's going to say yet, except for the part about how I won't be coming.

See, I do have a future to give her after all, just not one that includes me.

When I take her home, I have a hard time letting her go. Sure, it's awkward trying to hug her with that huge cast in the way, but I really can't kiss her enough. We've never had sex in the car sober before—or with her arm in a cast—but I'm ready to now, not just because I'm horny, but because I want to be as close to her as I can one last time.

She slows me down, though. She kisses my nose and my forehead and tells me we have plenty of time to make love later. "My mom might walk out on us," she says. "And just think when we're in St. Louis, we'll make love in every room of our new apartment."

I kiss her one more long one. And then we say goodbye.

Chapter 65

What was that one thing that Cassidy wanted me to do for her? To think about someone else's feelings instead of my own for once? I wonder what she'd think about that if she could've seen me with Aimee tonight. I always had the idea she thought I didn't know how to love someone. Well, she'd have to admit I sure do now.

And then there was that other thing she said, something about how I never believe anyone loves me. "You never believed I did," she said. That still bugs me. Of course, I'd believe someone loved me—if they did. It just seems like that's pretty impossible to know for sure.

Right there, cruising down Twelfth Street, I decide to call her on my brand-new, soon-to-be-lost-again cell phone and see exactly what she meant. She'll also probably be interested in what happened with Aimee, not to mention my new only-on-the-weekend drinking policy.

It takes a while before she picks up. Seems she's on the highway with Marcus. They're in New Mexico, heading to Albuquerque, where Marcus is going to play basketball and major in public administration or something weird like that.

"Oh, Sutter," she gushes. "It's so beautiful out here. Twilight is coming on, and there's, like, these mesas and these gorgeous colors I've never seen before. I mean, as soon as we got into New Mexico, I was like, 'Wow, I can see why they call it the Land of Enchantment.' The landscape is, like, so spiritual."

"Well, I guess it'll be a good place for you to visit every once in a while."

She's like, "I'm going to do more than that. I've made up my mind. I'm moving out here to go to school. Marcus wants me to, but I wasn't sure I wanted to till now. We're going to look over the campus tomorrow, but I've already seen pictures of it, and, you know, I've just fallen in love with the whole place."

"But you've been all set to go to OU for months."

"I was, but I have the right to change my mind if I want to."

"But surely it's too late to get enrolled somewhere else now."

"No, it's not. The application deadline isn't until June 15. I checked."

"What about your parents?"

"They're the ones who encouraged me to come out here and look it over. You know how they always thought I should go to school out of state and get a chance to see more of the world and everything. Besides, they absolutely love Marcus."

No big surprise. I'm sure her parents figure Marcus is an enormous step up from me. I don't mention that, though.

"How about the cost?" I ask. "Won't it be a lot more expensive, out-of-state tuition and everything?"

"I'll get a job. Anything's worth working for if you want it enough."

"So I've heard."

"It's like a whole new era in my life is unfolding, Sutter."

"Well, that's great," I say. "That's very cool."

What's the point of arguing? I should be happy for her. We're just friends, after all.

"So, what were you calling about?"

For a second, I completely forget why I called. "Nothing," I say. "It's just been a while since we talked."

There's not much to say after that. She tells me she'll e-mail me some stuff about the college, pictures and all. She'll fill me in about the whole excursion when she gets back.

I'm like, "That's great. That's great." Somehow just about my whole vocabulary has frozen up, except for the word *great*.

A second later, she's gone, vanished into the enchanted New Mexican night. She's gone, Aimee's soon to be gone, and me, all of a sudden, I'm hit with this absolutely incredible thirst.

Chapter 66

Sure, I've pledged to only drink on the weekends, but this is summer. I mean, what's the difference between a weekday and a weekend when school's out? As long as I keep the drinking down to once or twice a week, everything should be hunky-dory. Unfortunately, in a less rational moment, I emptied the faithful flask into the gutter down the street from home, but that's no problem. My favorite liquor store is but minutes away, and then it's just around the corner for the big 7UP, only this time I go for the giant size instead.

Yes, the hometown streets already look friendlier. Cars honk at me left and right. The night is warm and girls flow past with their windows rolled down, their beautiful hair cascading back in the breeze. Wouldn't it be lovely if one flashed her tits at me? I might even chase her down this time. "The summer belongs to the Sutterman," I'd tell her. "You want to come with?"

Talk about enchantment. Forget about working for something just to have it fall apart on you. Let the magic come. That's what I say. Let the magic come and fill in every inch of that little black crack behind your breastbone. Commander Amanda Gallico has her spaceship, and I have my bottle of whisky. We're both on our way to the same planet.

Who knows how long I've been on the cruise when I come across this bar called the Hawaiian Breeze. It's a small baby-blue cube of chipped cinderblock with palm trees painted on the side. A gravel parking lot with four cars. I've always wanted to go in there just to see what it's like. It couldn't be much worse than Larry's place down in Fort Worth. Except for not owning a pistol or a switchblade, I'm bound to fit right in.

Of course, I'm not old enough to buy drinks in there, but I figure what do I have to lose? Inside, there's one rumpled drunk at the bar and two gigantic escaped convicts playing pool. The bartender looks like a junkie version of Buffalo Bill in a Hawaiian shirt.

The rumpled drunk doesn't do anything but continue staring into the top of the bar, but everybody else glares at me like *Who is this twerp and what's he doing in our sanctuary?* Junkie Buffalo Bill is getting ready to tell me to get the hell out, but I cut in first. "Sir," I say, flashing my famous gap-toothed smile. "My name is Sutter Keely, I am eighteen years old and sore at heart, for my romances have all collapsed out from under me. I am in great need of a whisky and Seven."

Just that fast, Junkie Buffalo Bill's scowl turns into a broad, snarly-toothed yellow grin. "Ha! That's the best one I ever heard." He looks at the escaped convicts. "What do you think, boys? The kid's sore at heart. Should I slide him a cocktail?"

The slightly more enormous of the convicts goes, "Hell, yeah. Give old Sutter a drink. I've been sore at heart myself."

The rumpled drunk doesn't comment, except to raise his pasty-white face and howl, "Whooo-weee!"

"One whisky and Seven coming up," says Junkie Buffalo Bill.

The next thing you know I'm buying whisky shots all around. To break the dank silence, I crank up every Jimmy Buffett song on the jukebox and go into the tale of Cassidy and Aimee and my long-lost dad. Everyone's enthralled. They've been there, a long time ago.

"Am I wrong for letting Aimee go like I did?" I ask the boys, and the slightly less enormous escaped convict, the one with the bandanna tied on his head, goes, "No, you're not wrong, Sutter. You're a hero."

"That's right," says Junkie Buffalo Bill, and the rumpled drunk goes, "Whooo-weee!"

The boys of the Hawaiian Breeze love me. I'm their mascot. You should see their eyes light up when I tell the story of the dinner party fiasco and how I burned up Kevin-pronounced-Keevin's thousand-dollar suit.

"Damn," says the more enormous escaped convict. "Kevin. You gotta hate him."

"Suther," sprays the rumpled drunk, his first attempt at words yet. "You are the king. You really are. Are you religious, Suther? You look religious."

It's an odd question considering the circumstances but I go with it. "Of course I'm religious. I'm God's own drunk."

He cranes back his head. "Whooo-weee!" And then in the next second he's clutching my arm and staring at me bleary-eyed and mournful. "You got your whole life ahead of you," he says.

"So do you," I say, holding my arm steady in his grip. It's the only thing keeping him from toppling to the floor.

"No," he says. "All my friends are dead and my life is over."

"Your friends aren't dead," I tell him. "We're your friends."

"Whooo-weee!"

By the time the last Jimmy Buffett song plays, everyone's having a blast. The gloom of the Hawaiian Breeze has lifted. When I announce that it's time to go, no one wants me to leave. "Sorry, boys," I say. "The night awaits. More adventures are in store."

Outside, the streetlight shines on the gravel parking lot. I feel like I'm on the surface of the moon. With painted palm trees in the background. The night is glorious. I'm overflowing with the thrill of having saved the souls of the boys of the Hawaiian Breeze. Maybe Marcus was wrong. Maybe a single person can save the world. I'll bet I could. I could save the whole world—for a night.

And what does Cassidy know about the way I feel? Of course I can feel loved. I open my arms wide and let the wind flow over me. I love the universe and the universe loves me. That's the one-two punch right there, wanting to love and wanting to be loved. Everything else is pure idiocy—shiny fancy outfits, Geech-green Cadillacs, sixty-dollar haircuts, schlock radio, celebrity-rehab idiots, and most of all, the atomic vampires with their de-soul-inators, and flag-draped coffins.

Goodbye to all that, I say. And goodbye to Mr. Asterhole and the Red Death of algebra and to the likes of Geech and Keeeevin. Goodbye to Mom's rented tan and my sister's charge-card boobs. Goodbye to Dad for the second and last time. Goodbye to black spells and jagged hangovers, divorces, and Fort Worth nightmares. To high school and Bob Lewis and once-upon-a-time Ricky. Goodbye to the future and the past and, most of all, to Aimee and Cassidy and all the other girls who came and went and came and went.

Goodbye. Goodbye. I can't feel you anymore. The night is almost too beautifully pure for my soul to contain. I walk with my arms spread open under the big fat moon. Heroic weeds rise up from the cracks in the sidewalk, and the colored lights of the Hawaiian Breeze ignite the broken glass in the gutter. Goodbye, I say, goodbye, as I disappear little by little into the middle of the middle of my own spectacular now.

Tim Tharp lives in Oklahoma, where he writes novels and teaches in the Humanities Department at Rose State College. In addition to earning a master's degree in creative writing from Brown University, he has also spent time as a factory hand, construction laborer, psychiatric aide, record store clerk, and long-distance hitchhiker. Tharp is the author of *Falling Dark*, for which he won the Milkweed National Fiction Prize, and his first novel for young adults, *Knights of the Hill Country*, was an ALA-YALSA Best Book for Young Adults in 2007.